The Days of Noah
Book 1
Conspiracy

Mark Goodwin

Technical information in the book is included to convey realism. The author shall not have liability nor responsibility to any person or entity with respect to any loss or damage caused, or allegedly caused, directly or indirectly by the information contained in this book.

All of the characters, places and incidents are products of the author's imagination or are used fictitiously. Any resemblance to actual people, places or events are entirely coincidental.

Copyright © 2014 Goodwin America Corp.

Unless otherwise noted, all Scripture quotations are taken from the Holy Bible, New International Version®, NIV®. Copyright © 1973, 1978, 1984 by Biblica, Inc™. Used by permission of Zondervan. All rights reserved worldwide. www.zondervan.com.

ISBN: 1500725587
ISBN-13: 978-1500725587

DEDICATION

This book is dedicated to the King Eternal, Jesus Christ.

"I, Jesus, have sent my angel to give you this testimony for the churches. I am the Root and the Offspring of David, and the bright Morning Star." The Spirit and the bride say, "Come!" And let him who hears say, "Come!" Whoever is thirsty, let him come; and whoever wishes, let him take the free gift of the water of life."

Revelation 22:16–17

i

ACKNOWLEDGMENTS

A special thanks to my loving wife for her unyielding support, and to the late Pastor Chuck Smith for faithfully preaching the Word of God, especially the books of Prophecy, which has greatly influenced this book.

I would like to express a special note of gratitude to my fantastic editing team, Catherine Goodwin, Madeleine Swart, and Stacey Kopp.

Thank you to *299 Days* author Glen Tate for consultation on accuracy regarding the courtroom scene.

CHAPTER 1

As it was in the days of Noah, so it will be at the coming of the Son of Man. For in the days before the flood, people were eating and drinking, marrying and giving in marriage, up to the day Noah entered the ark; and they knew nothing about what would happen until the flood came and took them all away. That is how it will be at the coming of the Son of Man.

Matthew 24:37–39

Noah Parker finished his second cup of coffee as he watched the first few minutes of *Fox and Friends*. It was part of his workday routine. If any big news events had occurred overnight, he would be sure to catch them at the beginning of the program. Otherwise, the show rarely reported anything substantive.

Noah set his gym bag near the door, filled up his water bottle, and brushed his teeth. The people on *Fox and Friends* were talking about fall-flavored coffee drinks. Noah didn't think anything of it. As far as the news went, he ate whatever was put on his plate and didn't complain. He turned off the television, grabbed his things, and quietly closed the door behind him.

It was still dark, so Noah was careful not to wake his wife and daughter. His wife, Cassandra, or Cassie as her friends called her, homeschooled their seven-year-old daughter, Lacy. Noah worked as a high school teacher for Sevier County public schools and didn't think they were all that bad. Cassie, however, was adamant about not letting Lacy be poisoned by the new Community Core Standards, which had been designed to replace Common Core. It was touted as a way for parents and teachers to be involved in developing the curriculum, but, in reality, it was just the same old garbage repackaged.

What was worse, states were forced to implement Community Core or be denied all federal funding. Since the second housing bubble had popped, property values, and therefore property taxes, had plummeted to lows not imagined after the first housing bubble. Without funding from the federal government, many public schools would have to close their doors. All states except South Carolina and Alaska had caved in and signed on to the national standards.

Noah had a twenty-minute drive from his house in Kodak, Tennessee, to Sevier County High School, where he taught biology. Like most mornings, he arrived at 6:30 so he could sneak in a forty-minute run at the school track before classes started. Noah was in good physical shape, mostly due to running and Cassie's ability to cook delicious meals that were also quite healthy.

He breathed in the cool mountain air of late September. It was fifty-three degrees that morning, but Noah still wore his running shorts. He would warm up quickly enough. He had run track in college at the University of Tennessee and, before that, in high school.

He had met Cassie at UT his senior year. She had been a new freshman when they had first seen each other at a Chi Alpha Christian Fellowship. Noah had been heavily involved with the group, which offered an alternative to the typical fraternity/sorority, drunken college experience. Noah had been one of the organizers for the Chi Alpha Fall Mixer, held at the beginning of each school year to try to reach incoming freshmen. When he had first seen her getting a sandwich and some chips from the refreshments table, his heart had skipped a beat. Cassie had been stunning. She had had auburn hair, full lips, and an athletic build. The rest of the night had been spent filling Cassie in on the ins and outs of campus life. While she had soaked up the tips and had been very grateful for the advice, Cassie had been more focused on school than getting to know Noah, at least for the first few months. She had finally come around and had fallen in love with him, and they had married two years later.

Noah didn't bother setting his stopwatch anymore. These days, running was just a good way to clear his head and keep his heart healthy. He stretched his calves, hamstrings, quads, and back before he started his first lap. He didn't listen to music or talk radio while he ran. It was his time to be quiet, think through issues, pray, or just sort of meditate. On this morning, Noah thought about how blessed he was to have his wife and daughter. He was thankful for his home, his job, and the fresh air.

Sure, things hadn't really turned out the way he and Cassie had planned, but it was a good life. Straight out of college, Noah had taken a great job teaching his favorite subject, math, in his home town of Knoxville. Cassie was from a near-by town, Cookeville. After they had gotten married, they had rented a nice apartment in downtown Knoxville, near the UT campus. Cassie had graduated two years later, and she had taken an internship at the local NBC affiliate, Channel 10. They had planned to start saving up for a down payment on a house after Cassie had finally been offered a paid position at Channel 10, but Noah had been laid off that same year. The bursting of the first housing bubble had sent shock waves throughout the economy, and Knox County Public Schools were no exception.

James Mitchel, his friend and coworker from the Knoxville school where Noah had been laid off, had left two years earlier to take a position as the principal at Sevier County High School. James had offered Noah a position at SCHS, which he accepted, but it was a forty-five minute commute each way, with no traffic. In the fall, Sevierville became a tourist hot spot for folks wanting to see the majesty of God's handiwork expressed in the brilliant golds and reds of the changing leaves. It was a terrific source of income for the small community, but traffic from tourism had stretched Noah's evening commute to over an hour.

Noah and Cassie had found a foreclosure home in Kodak, Tennessee, about halfway between Sevierville and Knoxville. Not only had they been able to buy a home they never could have afforded in Knoxville, but it also allowed Cassie to keep her job at Channel 10 and had reduced Noah's daily drive time by half. It had taken a few years to renovate the run-down 1900-era farmhouse into their style. When it was finished, they had a beautiful two bedroom, two bath with a finished attic they used for an office and guest room. The home sat on two acres that included a small orchard.

The next event in their lives was pregnancy, during which Cassie was sick most of the time and had been forced to quit her job. After Lacy was born, Cassie had taken a part-time position writing from home and working a few evenings at the local Sevierville newspaper, but she never returned to Channel 10.

Lacy was a healthy, happy little girl—the joy of her father's life. Noah devoted his evenings to being with his daughter.

On nights that Cassie worked, Noah and Lacy assembled puzzles, ate dinner for two at Lacy's plastic play table, or had fun dressing up the cat and the dog. Buster, the mixed-breed farm dog, was much more cooperative than Sox, the cat, when playing dress-up.

Noah slowed his pace for his cool-down lap, and then headed for the shower. He felt relaxed after the run and blessed to be alive. After the shower, he took his gym bag back to the car. James Mitchel was just arriving in the parking lot.

"Good run this morning?" Mitchell asked.

Noah nodded. "Yeah, it was."

"How's biology going?"

"The material is easy enough to get through." Noah tried to be positive.

"How long does it take you to get through the day's assignment?"

"About twenty minutes," Noah replied.

Mitchel shook his head. "What a waste. I guess Communist Core had to be calibrated to the lowest common denominator. I'm sorry we had to cancel the Family Consumer Sciences class you were teaching last year. I know how much you enjoyed it."

Noah sighed. "I feel bad for you. I know how hard you fought to put together a curriculum that actually taught kids things they need to know to get through life. Community Core did away with your agriculture and forestry classes, your vocational classes, and most of your computer literacy courses."

James shrugged. "Yeah, well, I guess we're all just doing time now."

"That's exactly how the kids look at their education," Noah added. "I try to engage them in substantive conversation after we finish the material for the day, but they don't seem to care. It's like the new standards are sucking the life out of them. You should start a private school. You have the management skills to run it."

James Mitchell studied the ground and sighed. "It wouldn't matter. Community Core is mandated across all educational establishments, including private schools."

"I know. Cassie has to use their garbage to home school, but she fills out the standardized tests herself and teaches Lacy what she wants," Noah replied.

James smirked. "You might get away with that if you're home schooling, but not in a private school. The Department of Education sends in what they call mystery shoppers to make sure standards are being adhered to."

"Sounds more like the East German Stasi than mystery shoppers," Noah said.

James chuckled. "Why would Lacy already be taking standardized tests? She's only seven. She should be in first grade."

Noah tilted his head, hoping not to look like he was bragging. "Cassie has her doing fourth grade now. She's trying to get her all the way through before home schooling is banned completely."

"You don't think the government will go that far, do you?" James asked.

"Cassie thinks they will," Noah said.

James patted Noah on the back as they reached the front door. "You have a good day."

"I will." Noah smiled and marched off to class. He did the best he could to maintain a good attitude and teach the kids something, despite the constraints of what James Mitchel had so accurately tagged as "Communist Core."

In sixth period, Noah finished the lesson prescribed by the national standards with thirty minutes still on the clock. He wanted to sneak in a little bit of the material from the class he had taught the year before, so he directed the conversation by asking the kids to go around the class and state what career path they were thinking of taking.

Arron Matheson gave the most curious answer. "I want to work in demolition."

"Like what? Buildings, bridges? What do you want to demolish?" Noah asked.

"Buildings," Arron stated.

Noah nodded. "Well, I guess that is a career. Any particular reason?"

Arron shrugged. "Seems like an easy job. Throw some explosives into a building and watch it blow up."

Noah laughed. "You need an advanced engineering degree to plan the demolition of buildings."

"Why?" Arron Matheson looked sincerely puzzled.

"When demolition teams blow up a building, they have to know exactly where to place the charges so the building doesn't fall over on the building next to it. All the explosions have to be timed with precision. The least amount of error could cause catastrophic damage to neighboring buildings."

Arron shook his head. "That's baloney, Mr. Parker. We just watched the 9/11 footage on Remembrance Day, and the Twin Towers fell straight down, with no planning at all."

Noah was stumped and unsure how to respond. As any good teacher would, he attempted to explain it away. "I'm sure that was some structural anomaly that occurred due to the architectural design of the building." Noah thought, *what does that even mean? Oh well, I just have to snowball some tenth graders. A few big words will usually shut them up.*

Allen Kramer entered the conversation. "What about Building Seven? It fell straight down, too. It was built eleven years after the Twin Towers were finished. Was that an architectural anomaly or whatever you called it?"

Kramer was a smart kid. Not the one you wanted challenging you. Noah had heard a little bit about World Trade Center Building Seven from Cassie. She had a passion for investigative journalism, even if she worked only part-time at the local newspaper. Additionally, Noah suspected that she had a few conspiracy theorists in her Thursday night Bible study group that fed into her eccentric notions. Noah had always steered the conversation to another subject whenever she brought up these undesirable topics. This afternoon, however, he wasn't going to be so fortunate.

Katie Snyder perked up. "Building Seven? What the heck is that? They didn't talk about that in the 9/11 movie."

Allen Kramer was quick to fill in the details. "Building Seven was a forty-seven-story building that also pancaked into its own footprint on September 11, 2001. It was diagonally across the street from the World Trade Center. The official story is that it fell because of an office fire. It was never hit by a plane. It was built to rigid building codes to withstand fire; yet, like the Towers, it dropped straight down, at freefall speed. As Mr. Parker would say, that requires an advanced engineering degree, precise placement of the charges, and highly accurate timing."

"Or a structural anomaly," Arron said.

The class laughed, and Noah knew he shouldn't have tried to speak to something he knew nothing about.

"Is that true, Mr. Parker? Did another building collapse that day?" Katie Snyder asked.

Noah didn't know where to go with this. "There was a third building that fell that day. It was supposedly caused by a fire that weakened the supporting beams."

Allen Kramer jumped up from his seat. Noah had never seen him so engaged in a conversation. "There are lots of facts around the events of 9/11 that don't fit with the official reports. For starters, the WTC maintenance worker, William Rodriguez, worked at WTC for nineteen years prior to the attacks. He claims to have heard an explosion from the sublevels of the North Tower seconds prior to the first plane hitting.

"Next, these buildings were specifically designed to endure the impact of a 707, which was the largest commercial jet at the time they were built. The 767s that hit the buildings weren't much bigger.

"When the planes impacted, most of the fuel burned up in the fireball. The jet fuel that was left burning in the buildings emitted thick black smoke, which suggests the fire was starved for oxygen and was burning at a temperature of around 500 degrees Fahrenheit. The maximum temperature that can be reached by jet fuel burning under ideal conditions is 1,800 degrees. Depending on the alloy metals contained in steel, its melting point is typically around 2,800 degrees. The beams used in the World Trade Center were rated by Underwriters Laboratory to withstand temperatures of up to

2,000 degrees for at least two to three hours before they would begin to weaken. The North Tower fell perfectly into its own footprint one hour and forty-two minutes after it was hit, as if it was a precision-planned demolition. The South Tower did the same thing only fifty-six minutes after the impact.

"Even if you want to believe the official story on the Twin Towers, how can you explain Building Seven collapsing from a small fire? It was never hit by a plane and never exposed to jet fuel, yet it fell, as if it was a planned demolition.

"In fact, several pictures of support beams in the sublevels show perfectly cut beams with molten metal dripping down the front of the beams. It looks exactly like what you would see when thermite shape charges are used in demolition."

"You've certainly memorized a lot of facts and figures," Noah responded.

"Mr. Parker, the implications of what these facts and figures mean makes them the most important set of data in recent history," Kramer replied.

"We have some big problems with the plane that hit the Pentagon as well. For one thing, no pictures of the impact have ever been released. The government should release the videos or pictures that prove the type of plane that crashed. Surveillance cameras are all over the area where the plane hit.

"Another major issue is the size of the hole made by the impact of the plane in the pictures of the Pentagon after the attack and before the wall collapsed. The hole is only seventeen feet wide, and the wingspan of the plane that hit it was one 125 feet. There was no debris that would be consistent with a plane crash of that size. No tail section and no wings that didn't damage the walls. Where did the wings go?"

The class stared at Noah Parker like they were expecting him to debunk Allen Kramer's theory, but he sat silently. He breathed a sigh of relief at the sound of the bell.

Allen Kramer made one last comment. "A few well-made documentaries on YouTube cover a lot of the facts. *Loose Change* is a good one; also check out *Ripple Effect*. If you really want to know what the professionals think, check out the YouTube channel AE911truth. It represents a coalition of over 1,500 architects and engineers, including some very prominent ones, that disagree with the official story we've been told."

Noah gathered his things and kept his head down. He'd had enough of all this. As the last student left, Noah locked the classroom door and headed home.

CHAPTER 2

I live in the Managerial Age, in a world of "Admin." The greatest evil is not now done in those sordid "dens of crime" that Dickens loved to paint. It is not done even in concentration camps and labour camps. In those we see its final result. But it is conceived and ordered (moved, seconded, carried, and minuted) in clean, carpeted, warmed and well-lighted offices, by quiet men with white collars and cut fingernails and smooth-shaven cheeks who do not need to raise their voices. Hence, naturally enough, my symbol for Hell is something like the bureaucracy of a police state or the office of a thoroughly nasty business concern.

C.S. Lewis, *The Screwtape Letters*

Twenty-six-year-old Everett Carroll was recruited straight out of grad school at George Washington University into the CIA. His position as a Directorate of Intelligence Officer was a fancy way of saying analyst, but he knew it was an opportunity he couldn't turn down.

The job started at $88,000. It was understood that part of the pay was considered compensation for keeping your mouth shut, not asking questions, and doing exactly as you were told.

Even with the rapid pace of inflation in recent years, Everett Carroll enjoyed a comfortable lifestyle afforded by the generous starting salary. He drove a new BMW, dressed fashionably, and ate out most evenings. Everett cared about his looks and his health. He hit the gym every morning before work and played tennis on Saturdays, when the weather permitted.

He had been with the Company, what insiders called the CIA, for two years. So far his tasks were menial and narrow in scope. He had never been given the big picture of what the overall mission was. He wasn't allowed to discuss his task list with other coworkers, not that he had enough details to discuss anyway.

Everett didn't work at CIA headquarters in Langley, Virginia; rather, he worked in a sprawling office park west of Leesburg, Virginia. The offices were leased to the CIA by International Technologies but bore no CIA insignia anywhere. Everett was expected to say he worked for International Tech. His keycard and access badge showed the International Tech logo, which was simply IT. Everett suspected other companies that worked for the intelligence community leased space in the office park, but he was not allowed to talk to any of them, so he would never know.

The cafeteria was a sterile room in the basement. Too-bright florescent lights reflected off the stark white walls. It felt like a good space for doing experiments on rats. The food wasn't anything to speak of either, but no restaurants were nearby, and he had only a forty-five-minute lunch break.

"I'll take the chicken parmesan, please." Everett smiled and wondered if the lady serving his food knew she worked in a CIA facility.

Everett took his plastic plate, grabbed a Styrofoam bowl of salad, and proceeded to the cashier.

"Everett!" Twenty-eight-year-old Ken Gordon waved his hand.

Everett joined Ken at his table.

Ken pointed to Everett's plate. "What's that supposed to be?"

"Chicken parm."

Ken nodded and unwrapped a beautiful ham and Swiss on pumpernickel rye.

"Did your girlfriend make that?" Everett asked.

"Yeah. You need to settle down and find a woman who will make you lunch so you don't have to eat that stuff."

Everett cut into his lunch. "Dating is tough when you can't talk about your job. Not that I would know what to say about it anyway. I guess I don't even know what I'm doing."

Ken smiled. "Lisa doesn't ask about my work, but I know what you mean. I don't know the purpose of anything I do."

Ken and Everett had mastered the art of talking about work without talking about work.

"It's not what I had in mind when I was recruited," Everett said.

Ken opened his bag of jalapeno, kettle-cooked potato chips. "Yeah, you would've made a good Jason Bourne."

Everett laughed. "I have to try to catch Jones after lunch."

"That guy creeps me out," Ken said. "Rumor has it that he used to work in the field. His limp is supposedly from a gunshot wound he got in China. It landed him the supervisor position at this facility. And John Jones? There's no way that's his real name. Why on earth would you initiate a conversation with him?"

Everett finished chewing and took a drink from his Evian bottle. "Some credit cards I'm monitoring—oh, I probably shouldn't say anything."

"Don't tell me. I don't want to know. I've learned to suppress my curiosity."

The two finished eating and managed to avoid further work-related subjects. After lunch, Everett stopped by Jones's office. He was still out, so Everett returned to his desk and his work. It was difficult to have a sense of purpose without knowing why he was doing what he was doing.

Two hours later, Agent John Jones stopped by Everett's cubicle. "Everett, you wanted to see me?"

"Yes sir, uh . . . how did you know?" Everett tilted his head.

"Come on back whenever you're ready." Jones walked away without answering.

Everett grabbed his file and followed Agent Jones back to his large glass-walled office. "May I close the door?"

Jones pushed his horn-rimmed glasses into a more secure

position and raised his open hand.

Everett looked in suspense, waiting for an answer. After he sensed he wasn't getting one, he slowly closed the door, giving Agent Jones ample opportunity to stop him if he didn't want the door closed.

Jones pushed a button on the side of his desk, and the blinds lowered to cover the glass walls. "How can I help you, Everett?"

Everett was creeped out. He understood what Ken meant. "I noticed a pattern in some of the credit cards I'm monitoring. A large portion of the ones in a specific file are being used to purchase cryptocurrencies. All of the purchases are being reported as fraudulent charges. The only thing I can see that they have in common is that they are all coming from one specific file. It leads me to believe that it could be someone inside the Company that is siphoning off funds. Once the cryptocurrencies are purchased, the funds are completely anonymous and untraceable."

"Is monitoring fraudulent charges on your task specification dossier?" Jones asked.

"Well, no," Everett replied. "I'm watching for unusual purchases: firearms, ammunition, long-term storage food, tactical equipment, gold bullion, silver coins, components that can be used to manufacture explosives. I'm to cross check those transactions against the NSA database and make sure the purchasers are already flagged by Homeland. If the purchases are of a sufficient dollar amount or quantity, I'm to integrate all of their data to a second-tier watch list. I then aggregate the purchaser's social media posts, e-mails, phone calls, and movements, logged by the GPS in their cell phones, to a level three protocol and forward the analysis to a tier-two watch-list specialist.

"Originally, I thought it could be a group of domestic terrorists diverting the funds to cryptocurrency accounts so they could use them for making untraceable purchases of guns or explosives. After looking closely at the individuals, the only commonality I could find was that they are in the same CIA file. Political views, websites visited, religious affiliations, and geographical locations are as diverse as you can imagine. They look like a random cross section of America—other than the usual things that got them on the list in the first place, of course."

Jones crossed his hands and rocked in his executive chair. "Good work, Everett. I don't think you have anything to worry about, though. No cryptocurrency is untraceable. The NSA just hasn't integrated our systems with the Utah data center yet. Once that's online, you'll be able to trace cryptocurrencies as easily as credit cards and RFID-tagged US paper currency. Out of curiosity, which cryptocurrencies were purchased?"

"Litecoin, Ripple, Darkcoin, Nxt. What was obviously missing from the currencies purchased was bitcoin."

Jones nodded and smiled. "Let me know if you need anything else. I'll see you tomorrow."

Everett knew that was his cue to leave. "Thank you, Agent Jones."

As he returned to his cubicle, Everett glanced at his watch. "Ten till five." He logged out, shut down his computer, and headed toward the door. He cleared security and was soon on his way home.

Everett spoke aloud as he drove. "That guy knew something. I wasn't giving him any new information. If anything, I was only confirming what he was already aware of."

CHAPTER 3

Wisdom is supreme; therefore get wisdom. Though it cost all you have, get understanding.

Proverbs 4:7

"Daddy!" Lacy met her father at the door each day after work.

"Hi, sweetheart." Noah grabbed the little girl and squeezed her in his arms.

"Supper will be ready in twenty minutes," Cassie said. "How was your day?"

"Good. Yours?" Noah put Lacy back down and hugged his wife from behind as she continued preparing the meal.

Cassie smiled. "Well, let me tell you what a smart daughter you have. We learned all about the Revolutionary War today."

"Is that still in the Community Core curriculum you got from the Tennessee Department of Education?" Noah

19

inquired.

"Ha." Cassie shot Noah a look. "You're not serious are you?"

Noah shrugged. "What's for dinner?"

"Pork chops, turnip greens, and fried apples. That's probably that last of the greens we'll get from the garden this year."

"But you froze a lot," Noah said.

"We have a freezer full of vegetables. The garden produced well this year. Hurry up and take your shower. Dinner will be ready in fifteen minutes." Cassie stirred the apples.

Lacy followed Noah as he tossed his running clothes in the wash. He had to do it as soon as he arrived home so he wouldn't forget. If left to cure overnight, his exercise attire would be especially rank.

"I helped Mom pick the apples for dinner," Lacy said.

"That is fantastic! I am very blessed to have two wonderful ladies to take care of the garden and the fruit trees while I'm at work. Daddy's going to get a shower. I'll be right out." Noah kissed Lacy on the head as he closed the bathroom door.

"Okay." Lacy trotted off.

***

At dinner, Noah was quiet.

"So what happened at school today? Something has you

thinking," Cassie probed.

Noah didn't want to have this conversation, but there was no real way around it. "Every year the school has a 9/11 Remembrance Day. It's part of Community Core. It ignited some conspiracy theory debate in sixth period today."

"The 9/11 anniversary was almost two weeks ago. Why are you still talking about it?" Cassie asked.

Noah shook his head. "We were talking about choosing a career, and one kid thought being a demolitions expert wouldn't require much training because of the way the Towers fell. The next thing you know, it was a full-blown conspiracy conversation."

"And you're still sticking with the official story?"

"I don't know, Cass." Noah sighed. "What good does it do to speculate? It's not like we could do anything about it. If it is some government conspiracy, there is absolutely nothing we can do to change what happened. How could anyone possibly know for sure? If the evidence is there, it would be all over the news."

Cassie patted his hand. "Plenty of reputable people have investigated the evidence. It's there if you want to listen to it. As for being able to change the past, you're right. There's nothing we can do. However, we can certainly do our best to figure out what it all means for our future. If the conspiracy theory is true, we can ask ourselves why it was done or why it was allowed to happen."

Noah looked at Lacy to be sure she wasn't getting upset by the conversation. She clearly was listening but didn't look troubled. "What possible reason could the government have in helping to plan or allowing the attacks to happen?"

Cassie cut into her pork chop. "If that's the case, it could have been to get Americans to give up their rights in the name of keeping them safe. It could have been to get public support for military intervention in the Middle East. It could have been to advance the agenda of the globalists, or any combination of those things."

Noah shook his head. "That's hard to believe."

"Have you ever heard of Operation Northwoods?" Cassie replied.

Noah shook his head as he took a forkful of turnip greens.

"It was a top-secret document put together by the Pentagon to use a false-flag operation to get political support for invading Cuba in the sixties. The plan was to switch an American jetliner with a military jet, shoot it down, and blame it on Cuba. The document was declassified, so you can download the whole thing from the Internet," Cassie explained.

Noah furrowed his brow. "Why didn't the news report on that?"

"ABC reported on it decades ago. People don't pay attention to those types of stories. People either trust the government or stick their heads in the sand because they think there's nothing they can do."

"I'm not sticking my head in the sand. I try to be politically informed. I vote. What else can I do?" Noah asked.

"Watching Fox News doesn't make you politically informed. It might be better than the other mainstream-media outlets, but it's a corporate-controlled channel that pours out propaganda, just like the others. Anytime someone gets on there and starts heading for the deep side of the pool, they get cut. To name a few who were cut from Fox, you have John Stossel and Judge Napolitano. I'm no fan of Glenn Beck, but he covered more truth than all the other shows on Fox put together. Huckabee had fantastic ratings, and they cut him," Cassie said.

"I'll look up Operation Northwoods after dinner," Noah said.

"Look into the sinking of the *Lusitania* also," Cassie added. "The Germans sinking that ship filled with American passengers was the reason the US got involved in World War I. The Germans posted warnings in American newspapers not to sail in the area because it was a war zone, yet the *Lusitania* sailed right into a place known to be filled with German subs. If the government was looking for public support to get into the war, that event gave them what they wanted."

Noah considered everything he'd heard as he finished his dinner. That night as he lay in bed, he tried to put it out of his mind so he could sleep. He couldn't deny that Cassie and the rest of the conspiracy people had some valid points in their arguments.

CHAPTER 4

The absence of a police state is that people are free, and if you don't commit crimes you can do what you want. But today, you can't open up a business, you can't develop land, you can't go to the bank, you can't go to the doctor without the government knowing what you're doing. They talk about medical privacy, that's gone. Financial privacy, that's gone. The right to own property, that's essentially gone. So you have to get permission from the government for almost everything. And if that is the definition of a police state, that you can't do anything unless the government gives you permission, we're well on our way.

Ron Paul

Thursday morning Everett Carroll left for work early, so he could stop by his storage unit and retrieve his tablet computer. He paid for the storage unit every month in cash, so it couldn't be tracked through credit-card transactions. He had also purchased the tablet with cash. He kept the camera eye covered with a small piece of electrical tape. That prevented the camera from being remotely activated to run a facial recognition scan on his face while he was using the tablet. Doing this to other people on a daily basis was part of his job.

Everett was well aware of the high level of surveillance maintained on all CIA employees. Since the Snowden leaks, even a low-level analyst like himself was scrutinized as much as high-value domestic terrorist targets. Everett had no Internet-based bad habits, nor a malicious agenda against the nation or the Company, but unlike his friend Ken, he had not learned the art of suppressing his curiosity. Especially after Agent Jones had told him not to worry about the fraudulent credit-card charges, Everett felt compelled to do some digging around.

He parked his car by the Starbucks where he had coffee every morning before work. He left his phone in the car so it would ping his usual location. He fed the meter and walked half a mile down the street to Dunkin' Donuts. Once there, he placed the battery in the tablet and connected to the Internet. He was careful never to check e-mail or log onto any social-media sites from this device. He maintained the tablet strictly for digging around for things he didn't want the CIA to find out about.

Everett scanned the different cryptocurrencies purchased through the unauthorized credit-card transactions he had discovered. While earning his Master's degree in Computer Sciences he had developed a great ability to notice patterns.

While only a small percentage of the total funds were allocated to cryptocurrencies, regular purchases were going to Darkcoin; however, it was a larger percentage of the entire market cap of Darkcoin than the others combined. It was like someone was steadily trying to acquire a significant percentage of all Darkcoins without pushing the price up by purchasing too much at once.

"I wish I could get into that NSA database and find out where all of this money is going," Everett whispered to himself.

He closed down his computer, grabbed his coffee, and headed back to his car. He stopped by Starbucks for a second coffee to keep his observable routine intact. Everett dropped his tablet back at the storage locker and headed to work.

Once there, he cleared security, went to his desk, and started sifting through the piles of transaction data in his computer task box. Everett worked relentlessly to finish scanning the files well before lunch. This would allow him to use the CIA system to do a little more digging. While he did not have access to the Utah data center, he could research financial records of companies who accepted cryptocurrency payments.

"Done!" Everett finished the morning's files just before eleven o'clock. "I've got over an hour to dig around. I'll start by looking for firearms and ammunition distributors who take cryptocurrencies."

Nothing of interest came up, so he shifted his search to chemical and fertilizer companies that could be selling components for explosives. Still, he found nothing out of the ordinary.

"This could be something," Everett muttered. He found several gold and silver dealers who accepted bitcoin for physical delivery of gold and silver coins. What was more, they shipped to post office boxes.

"This is a wide-open method for people to anonymously convert cash into tangible assets. Sure, the NSA could eventually track them down, but for now, no one seems to be watching. A person could purchase Bitcoin with cash then anonymously buy precious metals."

Everett kept digging. *My only problem is that the unauthorized credit-card purchases included almost every cryptocurrency except bitcoin.*

Everett found a few dealers selling coins and bullion for Ripple and Litecoin, but a much smaller percentage than bitcoin. *I'm on to something, but I need access to the NSA system.*

As Everett headed to lunch, he pondered his findings. He floated through the cafeteria line on autopilot. He spotted Ken across the room and headed his way.

"You look like you have something on your mind," Ken said. "You had the hundred-yard stare when you walked into the cafeteria. I waved, but you didn't even see me. Is it a chick?"

Everett blinked. "A chick?"

"Yeah. Are you havin' girl trouble, bro?" Ken asked.

"No, it's work."

"Don't get too deep, man. Punch in, do what you're told, punch out. Nothing more, nothing less."

"What are you eating?" Everett was often impressed with Ken's lunch.

"Chicken Cordon Bleu sandwich," Ken answered.

Everett opened his eyes wide. "Lisa made that for your lunch?"

"It's leftovers from dinner last night," Ken said. "Like I said, you need a woman who can cook."

Everett couldn't quit staring at Ken's lunch. "Yeah, maybe I do."

Ken didn't hesitate. "Lisa has a friend, Courtney. We should all go out this weekend."

"Is that why I need a girl? Because Lisa has been hounding you to find a date for her friend?" Everett shot back.

"Bro! I'm shocked you would even think that. What do you say?"

"What is she like? If she's a bimbo, I'll kill you."

Ken looked offended. "She works in cyber-security."

Everett perked up. "What company?"

"H and M," Ken replied.

"Sounds like an intelligence community cutout or government contractor."

Ken laughed. "I'd put the odds at roughly ninety percent for anyone with that type of job who works within twenty-five miles of Langley, Virginia."

"Not this weekend. Maybe next." Everett had some homework this weekend.

"Great! We'll make it for next Saturday night at eight. I'll let you know where." Ken gathered his things to return to work.

Everett shook his head. "And in Ken's world, 'maybe' means next Saturday at eight."

Ken winked. With a broad smile and a nod, he walked

away.

Everett stopped by Jones's office on the way back to his cube. As usual, he wasn't there. "This guy has it good. He's never in the office." Everett tried to locate the surveillance camera that Jones used to monitor his office. It was nowhere to be seen.

Everett went back to his desk, where he would have a full task box of new transactions to sift through to protect America from the new breed of domestic terrorist. According to the watch list, their numbers would soon include nearly half of the country.

Just past three o'clock, Everett's office phone buzzed. He grabbed the receiver. "Hello?"

"Everett, it's Mr. Jones. I'm back in the office. You can come on in here."

"Right away, sir." Everett hung up and walked through the maze of cubicles.

"You can close the door if you like," Jones said when Everett arrived.

Everett smelled the stench of cigarettes as he closed the door and sat down. *Judging from the smell, he must spend the whole day smoking in the parking lot*, Everett thought.

"I guess you've got more news for me," John Jones stated.

Everett couldn't tell if he really wanted to know or if Jones was annoyed at having to listen to him. "Yes, sir. It would appear that cryptocurrencies are being used to purchase large amounts of gold and silver, which is one thing I am tasked with observing. Without access to the Utah data center, I can't tell if any of the transactions from my task files are involved. To completely do my job, I would need to get into the NSA system."

Jones drummed his fingers on the desk. He looked up at the ceiling then back down at Everett, clearly contemplating his response.

Finally, Agent Jones said, "Everett, that's good work, but you know how tight the Company is about access to secure files since the Snowden leaks. We're all under the microscope. I'll pass the information along, and I'll let you know if anything comes of it."

"Thank you." Everett was disappointed. He let himself out of the office and headed back to his cube.

It's one thing to lock you in a cubicle all day doing monotonous work, but it's quite another to deny people the tools they need to do their work. Ken's right. Clock in, clock out, and go home. It's a good paycheck, nothing more, nothing less.

Everett finished the day and went home. The next day, like a hamster on a wheel, he repeated the cycle. The difference was he didn't bother to stop by the storage shed. What was the point? On the way to lunch, Everett contemplated telling Ken that he would be available this weekend. *Better not. I probably wouldn't be very good company.*

Heading for his car at the end of the day, he stopped short. "Oh great, some clown has a to-go menu on the windshield of my sixty-thousand-dollar BMW."

Everett hated restaurants that canvassed parking lots, littering his car with unwanted ads. It was a common occurrence in his apartment complex. Menus would be placed on his windshield, and then it would rain and make a terrible mess for him to clean.

Then the thought struck him. *If a restaurant is delivering out here, that means I don't have to eat cafeteria food. Hmm. Maybe this one time a to-go menu on the windshield is not so bad.*

Everett snatched the menu with more enthusiasm than he'd had all day. "La Casita? This is in Sterling. There's no way they deliver out here."

Everett looked at the other cars in the lot. No one else had a menu on their windshields. He looked back down at the menu. He flipped it over. "Happy Hour, Monday thru Friday, 5:00 to 7:00."

The 7:00 was highlighted with a yellow highlighter. It was hard to notice, as if the highlighter pen used had seen better days.

"This has to be Ken's work. Okay, I'll play along." Everett headed home to freshen up. His apartment was in Ashburn, so he had to pass by there to get to Sterling anyway.

CHAPTER 5

For our struggle is not against flesh and blood, but against
the rulers, against the authorities, against the powers of this
dark world and against the spiritual forces of evil in the
heavenly realms.

Ephesians 6:12

As usual, Noah's loving daughter met him at the door
when he returned home from his teaching job.

"Lynette Ray is going to be at Mom's Bible study tonight,
and we're going too," Lacy announced.

"Is that so?" Noah picked her up and hugged her tight.

"Hi, honey," Cassie greeted.

Noah smiled. "We're all invited to Bible study tonight?"

"You're always invited. It's just if David and Becky don't
bring Lynette, no one's there for Lacy to play with. Dinner

will be ready in five." Cassie returned to the kitchen.

"What do I smell?" Noah asked.

"Spaghetti," she replied.

"I smell something else."

"Lemon bars."

"Oh, I want one of those now!" Noah loved lemon bars.

"They're for Bible study; you'll have to wait." Cassie rushed to finish cooking.

Over dinner, the conversation covered the routines of work and homeschooling.

"I started a new article for the paper today," Cassie said.

Noah cut Lacy's pasta into bite-sized pieces. "What's it about?"

Cassie topped off her pasta with a healthy portion of Parmesan cheese. "Crime spillover from Knoxville into Sevierville during tourist season. Last year, there was a string of hotel-room burglaries between October and November. I'm interviewing the head of security of the new Hickory Creek Lodge."

"Wow," Noah replied. "I hear that place is swanky."

"Well, we've been invited to come out Saturday night and have dinner on the house. I guess they want to make sure the article presents the lodge in the best light possible," Cassie said.

"That will be great. They're not afraid we'll take up table

space on a weekend?"

"The restaurant gets quite a few locals for dinner on the weekends, but it won't be super busy until the leaves start to turn. When we see Becky tonight, I'll ask if she can watch Lacy for us Saturday," Cassie said.

The Parkers quickly finished dinner and headed out the door. Cassie's Hyundai Santa Fe was newer and got much better mileage than Noah's F-150, so they drove the Hyundai. With gasoline quickly approaching nine dollars per gallon, Noah drove the Santa Fe to work on days when Cassie didn't anticipate having to go anywhere.

"Look, Daddy! That car has a rainbow sticker. My Sunday school teacher said that God gave us a rainbow to promise He would never flood the earth again. Can we get a rainbow sticker on our car?"

Cassie and Noah exchanged looks. Cassie asked, "Do you want to take that one?"

Noah took a deep breath. "That's right; God sent the rainbow to promise He would never destroy the earth again by water. Do you know why He sent the flood?"

"Because the earth was full of mean people," Lacy answered.

"That pretty much sums it up. But just because God won't destroy the earth again by water, that doesn't mean He won't destroy it at all. Second Peter says that God will destroy this earth with fire and make a new earth for us. But we won't be here when He destroys it. We'll be in heaven with Him."

"Because there are more mean people?" Lacy asked.

Noah chuckled. "Yes, the Bible says when God destroys

the earth next time, it will be just like it was when He destroyed it last time, full of mean people."

"Why were the people mean?" Lacy asked.

"I'm not sure why. The Bible says the earth was full of corruption and violence," Noah said.

"What's corruption?" Lacy inquired.

Noah paused to consider his answer. "Well, corruption is being disobedient. The people in those days didn't want to do things God's way. They wanted to do things their own way. It would be like if Mom asked you to pick up your toys or brush your teeth. If you decided not to obey her because you didn't feel like it, that would be corrupt behavior. Does that make sense?"

"But I would never do that! Mom would get the wooden spoon if I did."

Noah laughed. "That's right. You would never do that because you respect Mom. The people in those days didn't respect God."

"Do people respect God now?"

Noah thought for a moment. "Some do. Most don't."

"So is God going to destroy the earth and make a new one soon?" Lacy asked.

"That's a good question. In Matthew twenty-four, Jesus said even He didn't know when the end would be. He said only the Father knew," Noah replied.

"I thought Jesus knew everything," Lacy said.

"He might know now," Noah said. "But at that time, God had not shared that specific piece of knowledge with Him."

"So can we get a rainbow sticker?" Lacy asked.

Cassie reached over and patted Noah on the leg. "You gave it your best shot. It was good; it worked on me. I completely forgot about the rainbow sticker."

She turned to face Lacy in the backseat. "Honey, we already have a fish sticker on the car. We'll look like a bunch of hippies if we start putting stickers all over the car. How about if we get some rainbow stickers for your bike?"

"Okay." Lacy went back to watching the passing scenes through the car window.

Noah looked at Cassie in amazement. "Really? It was that easy?"

They soon arrived at Isaiah Brown's large, two-story home. He bought and meticulously restored the old 1860 Victorian house after retiring from his position as a physics professor at the University of Tennessee. The large formal parlor made the perfect meeting place for the growing Bible study group.

Isaiah met the Parkers at the door. As was his curious fashion, he greeted Lacy and Cassie with a kiss on the hand. He gave Noah a firm, two-handed grip. "Noah, it is so good to see you. We miss you when you're not here."

"I'm glad to be here. Thanks for hosting the get-together." Despite not going to Thursday-night studies, Noah was well acquainted with the regular attendees from Faith Church, where they all attended Sunday service.

"And, Lacy, what a treat to see you, my dear." Isaiah held

out his hand, with a coin in his palm, to the little girl.

Lacy took the coin. "Is it a quarter?"

"No," Isaiah said. "It's a Morgan Silver Dollar. It's very old."

"As old as you?" Lacy inspected the shiny object.

"Lacy!" Cassie exclaimed.

Isaiah laughed. "It's quite all right. I am old. There's nothing wrong with being old. It sure beats the alternative."

Noah laughed along. He thought that Isaiah must get that a lot from kids. Isaiah's white hair and full white beard made him look like a lean version of Santa Claus.

As they entered the house, the Parkers greeted the rest of the guests, who had arrived earlier. David and Becky Ray were there. "Where's Lynette?" Lacy asked.

"In the kitchen, waiting for you." David Ray pointed at the kitchen door. Lacy scurried off to find her playmate. David Ray had served as a combat-medic in Afghanistan and now worked for Sevierville EMS. His wife, Becky, homeschooled their eight-year-old daughter, Lynette.

Henry Whitaker, a single, middle-aged man who worked for Sevier County Code Enforcement, was new to the group but knew most everyone through church. Henry always brought a tasty snack tray. On this particular evening, it included an assortment of crisp vegetables, dips, crackers, and cheese.

Sharon Beck was another regular attendee. She was a mature woman and took very good care of herself. Few folks ever guessed her true age. She owned the Country Kettle, an upscale restaurant in Sevierville that served home-style food. It was popular with the locals in the off-season and regularly had lines out the door during the fall tourist season.

Sharon had struggled to raise two kids by herself on a waitress's salary. She scrimped and saved until she managed to scrape together enough money to open her restaurant ten years ago. With its success, Sharon was able to enjoy life and treat her four grandkids the way she had always wanted to provide for her own children.

Benny Loomis, a longtime attendee of the weekly study, worked as the janitor and maintenance man at Faith Church. Noah knew little about him, because Benny didn't talk much. Noah often saw Benny with Isaiah. Noah figured he opened up to Isaiah when it was just the two of them.

Everyone had just gathered around to open the meeting in prayer, when Jim and Sandy Taylor arrived.

"Sorry. We were running a little late," Sandy said. "Jim had a closing that ran longer than expected."

The Taylors owned a modest real-estate brokerage in the Sevierville area. Like many brokers, they also invested in real estate. Jim and Sandy were nearly wiped out in the first housing bubble, but they rebounded quickly and were well hedged when the second bubble popped.

Isaiah opened the meeting with prayer, and everyone helped themselves to the snacks in the kitchen.

Noah made a planned attack on the lemon bars. He had already scoped out the two largest bars. He stacked them in a napkin so not to look like a pig.

"Straight to dessert?" David Ray asked.

"Yeah, we had a big dinner before we came," Noah answered.

"Are you still running every day?" David made a small plate of celery sticks, cheese, crackers, and sausage balls.

Noah laughed. "I have to if I want to eat lemon bars."

Everyone took their plates into the parlor and sat on the furniture, which was arranged in a large circle.

Isaiah began. "Enjoy your snacks. I'll start and you can find your place in the Bible when you've finished eating.

"We left off in Daniel chapter two last week. To recap for those of you who weren't here, we read about the statue that King Nebuchadnezzar dreamed of. We pick back up with Daniel giving him the interpretation of the dream. Starting in chapter two and verse thirty-one, we read,

"'You looked, O king, and there before you stood a large statue—an enormous, dazzling statue, awesome in appearance. The head of the statue was made of pure gold, its chest and arms of silver, its belly and thighs of bronze, its legs of iron, its feet partly of iron and partly of baked clay. While you were watching, a rock was cut out, but not by human hands. It struck the statue on its feet of iron and clay and smashed them. Then the iron, the clay, the bronze, the silver and the gold were broken to pieces at the same time and became like chaff on a threshing floor in the summer. The wind swept them away without leaving a trace. But the rock that struck the statue became a huge mountain and filled the whole earth. This was the dream, and now we will interpret it to the king. You, O king, are the king of kings. The God of heaven has given you dominion and power and might and glory; in your hands he has placed mankind and the beasts of the field and the birds of the air. Wherever they live, he has made you ruler over them all. You are that head of gold.

"'After you, another kingdom will rise, inferior to yours. Next, a third kingdom, one of bronze, will rule over the whole earth. Finally, there will be a fourth kingdom, strong as iron—for iron breaks and smashes everything—and as iron breaks things to pieces, so it will crush and break all the others. Just as you saw that the feet and toes were partly of baked clay and partly of iron, so this will be a divided kingdom; yet it will have some of the strength of iron in it, even as you saw iron mixed with clay. As the toes were partly iron and partly clay, so this kingdom will be partly strong and partly brittle. And just as you saw the iron mixed with baked clay, so the people will be a mixture and will not remain united, any more than iron mixes with clay.

"'In the time of those kings, the God of heaven will set up a kingdom that will never be destroyed, nor will it be left to another people. It will crush all those kingdoms and bring them to an end, but it will itself endure forever.

"Later on in the text, we learn that initially, the king accepts Daniel's interpretation of the dream and declares that Daniel's God is the true God. Afterward, however, he builds a statue of gold that seems to defy the prophecy of the dream and deny that his kingdom will ever come to an end. Of course, God's prophecies aren't contingent on whether or not we believe them.

"So we have this grand statue in the dream with the head of gold. Daniel explains that King Nebuchadnezzar's Babylon is the head of gold. Next, the statue has a chest made of silver, which Daniel says will be another world empire to come. The book of Daniel tells us that the Medo-Persian Empire conquered the Babylonians on the very night King

Belshazzar misused the articles of God's temple in a drunken festival. The Medo-Persian Empire, like the Babylonian, encompassed all of the civilized world at the time. It extended from modern-day Greece down through Libya and Egypt, covered all of the Middle East, and reached through parts of what is now India and China.

"The statue's waist was made of bronze. The Medo-Persian Empire fell to the Greeks in 331 BC, when Alexander the Great defeated King Darius III at the battle of Issus. You students of history will recall that the Greeks used bronze to make weapons, statues, and water vessels. The Greek playwright Aristophanes alluded to the use of bronze to devalue Greek currency in his comedy *The Frogs*, written in 405 BC. The Athenians may have been the first to debase their currency with bronze to finance the Peloponnesian Wars. Essentially, they were 'printing' money to pay for armies abroad. Does that sound familiar to anyone? Don't let it leave this room," Isaiah said and winked. "I'm sure the folks at the Pentagon and the Treasury think they were the first to think of such a scheme.

"The statue's legs of iron represent the Roman Empire, as I'm sure you all guessed. The Battle of Corinth in 146 BC marked the end of the Greek Empire and the beginning of the Roman Empire. The Romans mastered the art of making weapons with iron and even used it to debase their currency. As empires go, the Romans had to debase their currency to finance their overextended armies, the popular welfare entitlement program known as the grain dole, and foreign aid.

"A quote attributed to the Roman statesman Cicero from the first century BC says, 'The budget should be balanced, the Treasury should be refilled, public debt should be reduced, the arrogance of officialdom should be tempered and controlled, and the assistance to foreign lands should be curtailed lest Rome become bankrupt. People must again learn to work, instead of living on public assistance.'

"With all of these examples from history, one would think that the central bankers would know what is to come of our current monetary system and then correct their course to avoid another catastrophic failure . . . unless that's the plan.

"But I digress. Back to the Bible study. The final empire spoken of in Daniel chapter two is represented by the feet, which are made of iron mixed with clay. Since there has been no world empire since the fall of the Roman Empire, we can deduce that this must be speaking of an empire yet to come."

Henry Whitaker interrupted. "Could we say that America is a global empire?"

Isaiah tilted his head from side to side. "America certainly uses bribes in the form of foreign aid and the global presence of our military to exert a very powerful intimidation campaign, but I would classify this influence more as hegemony than an empire. Besides, I suspect America's influence and global superiority are coming to an end."

"Do you think the United Nations could evolve into this global empire?" Jim Taylor asked.

"Traditional thought has always been that the symbolism of the clay mixed with iron implies that this empire will be some type of global government made up of the pieces of the Roman Empire. That would make it an offshoot of the European Union," Isaiah said.

David Ray added, "The driving forces behind the UN are the EU and the US. At least those are the big players in the World Bank and International Monetary Fund. Now that the UN has finally gained taxing authority over offshore mineral rights, the IMF is facilitating the payment system for the global tax; they're all sort of the same thing, wouldn't you say?"

Isaiah nodded. "You have a point, David."

"Who owns the IMF?" Sharon Beck inquired.

Isaiah looked at Cassandra. "Cassie, I think you probably know as much about that as anyone. Would you care to enlighten us?"

"The IMF was established under the Bretton Woods agreement after World War II. The Agreement established the gold-backed dollar as the global reserve currency. Since the dollar is no longer backed by gold, technically, no member countries are bound by the reserve currency agreement, but that's a different subject. The IMF is owned by the member countries. The ownership interest in the IMF is primarily controlled by the central banks of the member nations. Trying to figure out who controls the central banks is the real challenge—"

"Wait a minute," Becky Ray said. "The dollar isn't backed by gold?"

Cassie shook her head. "It hasn't been since 1971."

"Then what is it backed by?" Becky crossed her arms.

"Nothing," Cassie said. "Well, that's not entirely true. Shortly after Nixon took us off the gold standard, Secretary of State Henry Kissinger went to Saudi Arabia and brokered an arrangement affectionately called the petrodollar system. Essentially, the US agreed to back Saudi Arabia militarily in exchange for the Saudis using their influence to get OPEC to sell oil only in dollars. This creates artificial demand for dollars, which allows the Federal Reserve to print more currency without it being devalued as fast. So I guess you could say the dollar is backed by oil . . . and lead."

Noah smiled. He'd heard all of this before, but he always enjoyed Cassie's snarky comments.

"You're saying America is propping up a Muslim nation that won't let their women drive, that doesn't allow Bibles in the country, and that imprisons or executes any of their citizens who convert to Christianity?" Becky exclaimed.

"And you're paying for it with your tax dollars," Cassie said.

Sharon shook her head. "This is a lot to take in. Back to what you were saying about the central banks. Who owns and controls the Federal Reserve?"

"That is two different questions." Cassie replied. "The Fed is owned by the members who own shares in it."

"So it is a private corporation?" Sandy Taylor asked.

"Yes and no," Cassie answered. "The member banks own the Fed, but they can't sell their shares. Perhaps the more important part of the question is, who controls the Fed. Officially, it's directed by the Board of Governors, a panel of seven people appointed by the President of the United States who serve for fourteen years each. The Federal Open Market Committee, or FOMC, makes the monetary policies for the country. The Board of Governors, plus five presidents of the twelve regional Federal Reserve banks, comprise the FOMC. One of the five is always the New York Fed president, and the other four rotate from the remaining eleven Fed banks. All of these people, the governors and the presidents, are hand selected and placed there by the Illuminati, which is made up of a handful of the most powerful people on the planet."

Cassie looked at Isaiah as if to ask if she'd gone too far.

"Proceed," Isaiah simply said.

Sharon held up her hand as if to stop traffic. "Hold up. Cassie, I've always known you to be a levelheaded person, but if I'd heard this from anyone else, I'd say she was a kook. You said the governors were selected by the president; then you said they were placed there by the Illuminati."

"The president is also hand selected," Cassie said.

Sharon shook her head. "By the Illuminati? I'm sorry; I just can't believe that. We have open and fair elections. I don't believe some secret society is pulling the strings of the entire government and rigging the elections."

"If both of your choices are selected by the Illuminati, the elections wouldn't have to be rigged. In the 2004 presidential elections, you had two candidates who both professed to belong to the secret order of the Skull and Bones. That order is at the top of the food chain for global governance," Cassie said.

Again Sharon protested. "John Kerry and George W. Bush were both members of the same secret society? I just don't buy it. Isaiah, can you help me out here?"

Isaiah shrugged his shoulders. "John Kerry admitted it on MSNBC, so did George Bush. George W. wrote about it in his autobiography. Whether you call it the Illuminati or some other name, it is clear in Bible prophecy that a world leader is going to arise from some type of Luciferean-cult society. From what I know about the cult rituals of the Skull and Bones, it would fit like a glove into Bible prophecy."

Sharon rolled her eyes toward the ceiling. "Cassie, honey, I'm sure you believe what you're telling us, but I don't. I'm sorry."

Benny Loomis spoke for the first time. "I believe you."

Noah was surprised to hear him speak. His simple tone was quiet, but it seemed to Noah as if Benny knew something the others didn't.

"I don't want to disrupt the study. Isaiah, can we get back to the dream?" Cassie said.

Isaiah smiled. "I wouldn't say the conversation is off track. I think it is very relevant. Thank you for sharing your insights with us.

"The statue had ten toes, which many believe represent ten rulers or ten countries that will be running the final global kingdom. Daniel specified that it will be a mix of different peoples. That leaves the door open to the possibility of the UN being the meeting place of the final kingdom.

"The last event in the king's dream was the rock that crushed all of the kingdoms of the earth and established an everlasting kingdom. The rock is Christ, and that kingdom is the final kingdom of Heaven.

"I think it is important to stay focused on the end game. Our citizenship in heaven is secure, no matter what happens on this earth."

"It sounds like you expect things to get bad for us. Don't you believe in a pretribulation rapture?" Jim Taylor asked.

Isaiah snickered. "I think one could believe in a pretribulation rapture and still expect things to get very bad for us in the short run. We could take a break from our study of Daniel to get into a little bit of that if you like."

"I think that is a fantastic idea. Let's take a vote. All in favor?" Sandy said.

All except Sharon raised their hands right away. As she looked around, she slowly put her hand up to join the others.

"I think we've covered enough tonight. I'll have a good study put together for next week," Isaiah said.

Becky stood. "Good timing. We have to get Lynette home. It's past her bedtime." She left the room to find her daughter.

David stood as well. "Cassie, thanks for the information. I'll definitely look into all of that."

Noah went into the TV room to retrieve Lacy. "Time to go, sweetie."

"Okay." Lacy turned off the cartoon they'd been watching and followed Noah.

Becky agreed to watch Lacy on Saturday night so Noah and Cassie could go out for dinner. Everyone collected their coats and the dishes they had brought and said their good-byes as they headed for the door.

CHAPTER 6

For we are opposed around the world by a monolithic and ruthless conspiracy that relies primarily on covert means for expanding its sphere of influence—on infiltration instead of invasion, on subversion instead of elections, on intimidation instead of free choice, on guerrillas by night instead of armies by day. It is a system which has conscripted vast human and material resources into the building of a tightly knit, highly efficient machine that combines military, diplomatic, intelligence, economic, scientific, and political operations.

Its preparations are concealed, not published. Its mistakes are buried, not headlined. Its dissenters are silenced, not praised. No expenditure is questioned, no rumor is printed, no secret is revealed.

John F. Kennedy, Waldorf Astoria, April 1961

Everett strode into the upscale Cuban restaurant. He glanced around at the crisp white tablecloths. "I wonder why I've never checked this place out." Sterling was only about three miles from his apartment.

He scanned the room for Ken, but didn't see him. Everett had met Lisa once before, but he wasn't sure he'd recognize her in a crowd. He did a quick perusal for anyone who could possibly be Lisa. "Maybe I'm the first one here."

Everett took a seat at the bar where he could keep an eye on the door and see them when they walked in.

"What can I get you?" the bartender asked.

"What are your specials?" Everett asked.

"Two for one mojitos, but happy hour is over in five minutes," the man replied.

"Then I'll have two mojitos." Everett wasn't much of a drinker. He figured the second drink would be for Lisa's friend Courtney when she arrived.

Everett watched the television over the bar for several minutes. The financial channel was showing yet another all-time high in the stock market. "Someone made a killing after the last market crash," he said under his breath.

Like the first housing bubble, the second, now called Housing 2.0, had created a massive panic and market sell-off across all indices. The Dow tumbled through the 2009 lows and briefly dipped below 3,000. The Federal Reserve had pulled out all the stops with massive money printing used for federal spending on defense, welfare, bank bailouts, and huge direct stimulus payments to American consumers.

The result was that inflation was now threatening double digits, even by the Bureau of Economic Activity's fabricated numbers. Alternative economic news sources placed inflation well above twenty percent annually.

Everett didn't think much of it. He had been taught by the mainstream media that this was the normal cycle, and it could go on indefinitely. He looked at his watch. *Where are these people?*

When he had first sat down, the three seats on either side of him had been empty. Now someone had taken the seat next to Everett. He glanced over at the man but avoided eye contact. Everett covertly eyed what the man was drinking. *Cuba libre, fancy way of saying rum and coke with lime.*

He noticed the man's ring, a large gold ring with a builder's square, compass, and capital G in the center. *Looks like Agent Jones's ring,* he thought. *For a secret society, the Masons sure like to show it off.* Then he smelled the familiar stench of cigarettes. He looked again, but unlike Agent Jones, the man had a full beard. His ball cap and jacket also looked different from anything he'd seen Jones wearing.

"Double fisting the mojitos, Everett?"

The familiar voice confirmed Everett's suspicions. He tried to stay cool. "I was expecting some friends to join me. The other drink was intended for one of them."

Jones smiled. "I see."

"I didn't recognize you," Everett said.

"I guess that means I've still got it," Jones said. "Would you mind pulling the battery out of your phone?"

Everett pulled his phone out of his pocket, removed the back cover, and took out the battery. He figured the menu must have been placed on his car by Jones. Now the only question was why? *Am I being invited to join the Freemasons? Maybe I'm in trouble.*

"You must be wondering why you're here." Jones sipped his drink.

Everett had to fight back his initial response of *that's very insightful of you*. Not wanting to sound overly sarcastic, he simply said, "Yes, sir."

"The short answer is that we're here to talk about your curiosity. It is something of a conundrum for the Company. They recruit the best and the brightest and then ask them to stifle their intuition and skills."

Everett poked the mint sprig to the bottom of his glass with his straw as he listened.

Jones kept his gaze straight ahead as he spoke. "You haven't popped up on anyone's radar just yet, but you're on your way. If that happens, they'll call me, and I'll give you an official warning to cease and desist. If that's ignored, you'll find yourself unemployed with no official work history. Your files will be scrubbed, and no one at the Company will ever acknowledge that you worked there."

"I suspect you wouldn't organize a covert meeting just to give me a heads up."

"I don't know. I might. The years have made me appear a bit rigid, but I'm not without emotions. When I look at you, Mr. Carroll, I see a bit of the fire I once had." Jones paused before continuing. "But you're right. That's not why we're here. We're here for you because I don't want to see that ingenuity go to waste, and we're here for me because I'm not ready to retire just yet.

"I don't mean to bore you with the details, but I'll have to give you some background, so you can fully appreciate my present predicament."

Everett was impressed that Jones thought so much of him. He was intrigued to hear about Jones's past as well. The office rumor mill spit out just enough information about the man to make him something of a legend. "On the contrary, Agent Jones, I'd enjoy hearing your story."

"I was tapped for the Company while in the Army in the late eighties. I was trained as a field operative and served in the Persian Gulf region for over a decade. I learned the languages and the culture and worked for US interests in the region. In 2003, I was involved in a covert finance operation on the Tajikistan-Chinese border. Someone tipped off the Chinese, so they were waiting for us. I was injured in the operation. I lost my right leg from just above the knee. After that they put me on desk duty."

Everett listened in amazement. It was the type of life he'd envisioned when he had accepted the job. "Sounds pretty dangerous for a finance operation."

Jones nodded. "One of the primary revenue sources for the Taliban was heroin. Our operation was to act as US government contractors who had clearance to transport drugs into the States. We earned their confidence, got to know their trade routes and manufacturing facilities, and then we started robbing them. The best way to unload the product was to sell it to the Chinese drug lords. The Tajikistan-Chinese border is nothing but sand and rocks. No one ever guarded it—until that day. We'd ripped off the Taliban and gotten away with crossing the border for over two years. I guess someone got the same idea to rip us off. While it lasted, we made a ton of money for the Company."

"You were stealing and selling drugs?" Everett had never heard of such a thing.

Jones laughed. "Most of the covert operations performed

by the Company are self-funded. In other words, you can't ask Congress to give you money for operations that 'don't exist.' After I lost my leg, I went to the Emerald City."

"You mean headquarters in Langley?"

"That's right. I got a crash course in computer systems and was assigned as a consultant for Project Prophecy. Prophecy was developed in the years following 9/11 to alert us to the insider trading that always occurs prior to terrorist attacks."

"So the conspiracy theories about the US government's involvement in the attacks are all false?" Everett asked.

"Compartmentalization within the intelligence community is a high priority. I was in Kuwait at the time and heavily invested in relationships with ranking members of Al Qaida. If the government wasn't involved, something should have leaked out and found its way to my ears.

"A CIA covert cell could theoretically be assigned a mission to recruit, organize, and fund an operation like 9/11 without anyone else in the agency knowing anything about it. Everything is on a need-to-know basis. The information flows are heavily guarded, and everyone keeps their mouths shut. Those who don't, eventually become depressed or have delusions that they can fly off buildings. Once a mission comes from the top, you don't question it or discuss it; you just do it."

"So Project Prophecy was developed to catch inside traders who had advanced knowledge of terrorist attacks?" Everett wanted to know more.

"Yes. With the intent of deciphering exactly the nature of the threat. In the week prior to 9/11, there were massive short positions in American Airlines stock, as well as United Airlines.

"As a side effect, the program was soon able to predict market trends with a higher degree of accuracy than any other trading program to date. This lead to Project Markint. The name comes from market intelligence. It was designed to do everything Prophecy could do and more. The capabilities to predict a sovereign country's intentions to financially attack another country are just the beginning of what this technology can do. The next generation of Markint uses the quantum computing capabilities at the Utah data center."

"Utah has a quantum computer?" Everett asked.

"Seven. Six of the quantum computers handle specific tasks, and one acts as the soul that links them all together. The seven computers working in unison form Dragon."

"I thought Utah was just a data storage facility." Everett sat up straight with his eyes wide open.

"DARPA has a thumb drive that holds four terabytes of information. The NSA data center in Utah is over one million square feet. Can you imagine a thumb drive that size? There isn't enough information in the world to fill that. We would never need that much space for storage.

"The intelligence community has learned that the best cover-up is to provide a narrative that is close to the truth. That way, when the inevitable whistle-blower comes out with information, it isn't far enough away from the official story to get any play from the news."

Everett was staring down the rabbit hole. "So the news is independent? You know, we hear all sorts of things around the water cooler. Mostly speculation, I'm sure."

"Yes and no. One of the first initiatives when the CIA began was Operation Mockingbird. The objective was to control public opinion through media, both overseas and in the US. Officially, Mockingbird shut down, but Director of Central Intelligence, William Colby, admitted to the House Intelligence Committee in 1975, that the Company was still engaged in manipulating the media. The only difference between then and now is that we've perfected the art. And it's not just the mainstream news media. We've got our hands in foreign media, Hollywood movies, the music industry, education . . . you name it."

Everett struggled to take in all that Agent Jones was revealing. "The Company is controlling all of that?"

"I didn't say we're controlling any of it. We just have an influential hand in it," Jones said.

"And Director Colby admitted to manipulating the press in a congressional hearing?"

Jones nodded and smirked. "Right before he was replaced as CIA Director by Skull and Bones member George H. W. Bush. We're getting into more detail than I intended. Do you have somewhere you need to be?"

"No. I have all night. If you don't mind my asking, why would you risk telling me all of this? It must be against protocol."

Jones silently studied the wood grain of the bar. After a moment he downed his drink. "Why don't you pay for the drinks and get a table. I'll buy dinner. I'm going to step out for a few minutes for a cigarette. I'll find you and then explain why we're here."

Everett found the hostess, who took him to a table in a quiet corner of the restaurant. He perused the menu while he waited for Agent Jones. "Ropa vieja, shredded beef in a tomato broth with onions over white rice. Served with caramelized sweet plantains. Sounds good."

Jones arrived at the table and sat down. "Anything good on the menu?"

Everett nodded. "I can't believe I've never heard of this place. The menu is spectacular."

The waiter placed a basket of toasted Cuban bread on their table and filled their water glasses. The two men ordered their meals and returned to the conversation.

Jones picked up where he had left off. "I'd been working with a think tank to research the best ways to exploit the unique abilities of the Markint quantum computer linked to Dragon. I could spend weeks telling you the capabilities of Dragon to predict not only terrorist attacks through market analysis but also its ability to predict the trajectory and anticipate volume on any given trading day. Dragon can also change the direction of markets through complex algorithmic trading programs, which it has the ability to develop itself."

"When you say it can steer markets, what are you talking about? Do you mean indices like the S&P and Dow, interest rate markets, or currency markets?" Everett asked.

"Everything."

"And is this absolute control?"

Jones sipped his water. "Almost. Think of the markets as a car. Dragon has the potential to override common market forces, sort of like controlling a car: the steering wheel, brakes, accelerator, and such things. As the driver, Dragon has no absolute control over road conditions or what might equate as liquidity and credit crisis. What it can do is predict those problems well before the 'car' approaches the road hazard. It can make corrections to avoid those hazards to the extent that they can be avoided."

"Sounds like that much power has a high potential for misuse," Everett commented.

Jones laughed. "That's an understatement."

"Working on Dragon must have been more exciting than being an analyst supervisor for some low-level Company outpost."

"And that, Mr. Carroll, is why we're here." Jones took a bite of the bread, chewed, and swallowed, clearly collecting his thoughts. "I was diagnosed with lung cancer last year. Dragon is a delicate program, and the Company can't have people working on it who might not be around six months from now. I was offered a generous retirement package, which I considered."

Everett gasped. "I'm so sorry."

"Don't be. I've lived a full life. I've lived through adventures most people never dream about. Besides, I knew I should have quit smoking years ago but didn't."

"Why didn't you take the retirement package?" Everett asked.

"I don't have any family. My only interests and hobbies are tradecraft." Jones spoke solemnly. "It might sound sick, but I want to live out my days working for the Company."

The food arrived, but neither of the two men seemed interested in it at the moment.

"Working in my capacity, Mr. Carroll, one is asked to do things that seem counterintuitive to the morality of the psyche. One does those things both because he believes that it truly is for the greater good and because of the consequences of rejecting the order.

"Working as an operative in foreign states, I was constantly aware of my mortality, though I was very busy and had little time to contemplate it. I had to focus on the task at hand or risk facing my mortality sooner rather than later. There was also the distraction of the mission and the feeling of being right because of the greater good. As I grew older and saw operation after operation focused on convincing people of things that weren't true, I began to question whether I also may have been deceived by the Company.

"Now, that my hour is fast approaching, I find myself thinking of things I have never considered. With no grand mission to distract me, I commit a large portion of my day pondering these things." Agent Jones studied Everett. "Are you a religious man, Mr. Carroll?"

"No."

Jones smiled and looked down. "I guess I wasn't at your age either. I have, however, started to contemplate these things lately. I do believe there is a God, as well as absolute right and wrong. I wonder how I'll be judged for the things I've done."

The subjects of right and wrong, God, and judgment always made Everett uncomfortable.

Jones must have sensed Everett's uneasiness. "But I'm not here to convert you, Mr. Carroll. I'm here to offer you a mission. Should you choose to accept it, you'll be provided with something to satisfy your curiosity, something with meaning, something I suspect you greatly desire."

"And what will you get out of the deal?" Everett asked.

Jones took a deep breath. "A chance to right a few wrongs. An opportunity to leave a legacy and pass on my tradecraft skills to the next generation. I can't explain how important that is to me.

"I'm not ready to put up my cloak and dagger, Everett. I don't want to be put on the shelf and forgotten. You'll understand these things more when you're older."

"That makes sense," Everett said.

The heaviness of the conversation had passed, and the men began eating.

"We almost let it get cold," Agent Jones remarked. "Still, it tastes great. How is yours?"

"Fantastic," Everett replied.

Jones dipped his bread into the sauce on his plate. "Let's enjoy dinner and resume our discussion at a later date. Of course, we'll avoid the subject at work."

"I assume you'll contact me when it's time to meet again," Everett said.

Jones nodded and winked.

CHAPTER 7

The only thing necessary for the triumph of evil is for good men to do nothing.

Edmund Burke

Sunday afternoon Noah mingled at the back of the church. Faith Church offered bagels, doughnuts, and coffee to encourage congregants to fellowship with one another after the service.

Noah spotted David Ray at the table getting coffee. He walked over. "Looks like all the chocolate glazed doughnuts are gone."

"That'll save you a couple of laps tomorrow morning," David said and chuckled.

Noah laughed. "Thanks again for keeping Lacy last night."

"No problem at all. She keeps Lynette occupied. It's actually almost like a date night for me and Becky. How was

Hickory Creek Lodge?"

"A little too swanky for my taste," Noah replied. "I didn't know if I was using the right silverware or putting my glass in the right place. Cassie enjoyed it, though. The food was really good. Not necessarily better than what you'd get at the Country Kettle, but different."

David helped himself to a spinach bagel. "Prices about the same as the Country Kettle?"

Noah was drinking his coffee and had to fight to keep from laughing and spitting coffee all over himself. "Yeah, *about* the same."

David cocked an eyebrow and grinned, indicating he knew better. "Is Cassie getting Lacy from the children's ministry?"

"Yeah," Noah said. "Probably won't see her for another half hour. I'm sure she has to tell everyone about the lodge."

"I'm looking forward to Thursday night's study. I guess we'll bring Lynette so Becky and I can both go. Are you coming?" David asked.

Noah nodded. "I think so. Especially if Lynette is going to be there. With the girls both being homeschooled, it's good for them to be around each other and have some social interaction. Isaiah doesn't seem to mind having them in the house. Maybe we should try to make it a weekly commitment."

"All right," David said. "Speak of the devil, there's Isaiah."

"Great, I'll let him know you just called him the devil." Noah winked.

"You wouldn't!" David said.

Isaiah joined the two men. "You fellas coming Thursday night?"

"As long as you don't mind having the children around," Noah said.

"They're an absolute joy. The girls are always welcome in my home," Isaiah said.

"You didn't exactly answer Jim's question last Thursday," Noah said.

"About what?" Isaiah asked.

"About the pretribulation rapture. The way you answered left a little room to wonder what you believe," Noah explained.

"Oh, that." Isaiah stroked his beard as he often did when in thought. "As an official facilitator of a small group for Faith Church, I believe in the possibility of a pretribulation rapture. Pretrib is Pastor Mike's position, and as someone teaching under his authority, that is what I teach."

"But . . . ?" David asked.

Isaiah smiled. "There are plenty of verses in the Bible that I genuinely believe support a pretribulation rapture. For one thing, the apostle Paul seemed to be in the pretribulation school. I happen to be a great admirer of Paul and tend to agree with his doctrine. When describing the rapture to the church of Thessalonica, he said, 'For the Lord himself will come down from heaven, with a loud command, with the voice of the archangel and with the trumpet call of God, and the dead in Christ will rise first. After that, we who are still alive and are left will be caught up together with them in the clouds to meet the Lord in the air. And so we will be with the Lord forever.'

"Paul puts himself in the category of those who will be caught up, which, by the way, is where we get the term *rapture*. This tells me that he saw the return of Christ as an imminent event.

"The following chapter, first Thessalonians five, verse nine, says that we are not appointed for wrath. It is not in God's nature to allow His people to go through judgment. He rescued Lot before destroying Sodom, and He rescued Noah before the flood. The flood is the example that Christ used when describing the end times.

"We also have Jesus telling us in Matthew to be ready and always watching. That also makes the rapture sound imminent. If that's the case, it would have to be pretrib."

Noah saw that he was going to have to coax it out of Isaiah. "And folks, not you of course, but other folks who believe in a midtribulation rapture, what verses or passages might they find to support their view?"

Isaiah smiled. "They might look at the book of Revelation and say that they don't see anything that resembles a rapture until chapter fourteen, where the angel is told to harvest the earth. This occurs after the cataclysmic events in chapter six, known as the seal judgments and after the trumpet judgments, which also precede chapter fourteen.

"They might also look to Matthew twenty-four where the Messiah says that He will come on the clouds and send His angels to gather His elect. This occurs in verse thirty-one, after He gave an abbreviated description of the tribulation period."

"How does the pretrib school of thought reconcile those passages?" Noah asked.

"For the Olivet Discourse, they say that God's elect refers

to those who will be saved after the first rapture," Isaiah said.

"The Olivet discourse refers to Matthew twenty-four?" David asked.

"Yes. That conversation occurs on the Mount of Olives, so the Olivet Discourse is the tag for the passage in Matthew, as well as Luke twenty-one and Mark thirteen."

"What about Revelation fourteen? How do they explain that?" David asked.

Isaiah shrugged. "They will tell you that Revelation is not written chronologically. There are events described in the heavenly realm in Revelation that are obviously not chronologically flowing with the tribulation, but the events occurring on the earth seem to follow a continuous timeline."

Lacy and Lynette appeared through the door and ran to their respective fathers.

"I guess this means it's time to go," Noah said. "It's certainly going to be a good study."

"I'm really looking forward to it," David said.

The girls gave Isaiah a big hug and chatted for a short time before leaving for their homes.

***

The next morning, Noah started his routine just after five o'clock. He brewed his coffee, made a quick breakfast, and got his things ready for work. He set his gym bag by the door and flipped on *Fox and Friends* at six o'clock.

The celebrity talk-show reporters had slightly somber tones this morning. One of them was covering the global markets.

"Asian shares are significantly down this morning. European markets are just opening, and it is a blood bath. This will certainly cast a shadow of dread across the trading floors in America today. We don't know of any events that are triggering the global sell-off, but some analysts are suggesting that the run started in Western sovereign debt markets. They say this could be because the BRICS bank will be announcing a new gold-backed currency. For those of you who don't know, the BRICS bank was established several years ago in Shanghai as a way for member countries to settle international trade. The member nations include Brazil, Russia, India, China, and South Africa. We'll keep you updated throughout the day.

"After the break, nutritional author Lucy Gilbert will be showing us some delicious ways to cut calories, and we'll have footage of our own Brooke Tanner competing in last weekend's Lululemon Rollerblade competition. Stay tuned; you won't want to miss that."

Noah switched the TV to CNBC and whispered, "I'll take my chances. We've had four market meltdowns this decade, but it's still more exciting than counting calories and Rollerblading."

The financial-network reporter was standing outside of the NYSE.

"The iconic charging bull statue is the only bull on the street this morning. Rumors of a collapse in US treasuries have Wall Street buzzing with anxiety. Traders are coming in early, and I've never felt such a sense of doom. Indices are down across the board in early morning trading. We'll see what happens when the markets open, but it doesn't look pretty.

"An announcement from the BRICS bank to introduce a new global reserve currency could be the final blow for the dollar, which has lost over fifty percent of its value in recent years. Speculators and those who follow the monetary policy of the member nations of the BRICS bank, especially China and Russia, believe the new currency could be fully, or at the very least fractionally, backed by gold. This would introduce a stable currency not seen since the golden days of the dollar.

"The only green showing on any of the early morning trading boards has come from the precious metals and a handful of commodities. Gold is up a stunning fifteen percent to $3,200 per ounce, while silver is up nearly twenty percent, taking it well past its previous resistance level of $100 per ounce."

Noah glanced at his watch. He was late. He would have to cut his run short today. He switched off the television and headed out the door.

Once at the school, Noah pushed himself on the track to get in more laps in less time. He rushed to the shower and arrived to class just before the bell rang.

Halfway through first period, Assistant Principal Katie Votler interrupted the class. "Noah, James needs to see you in his office right away. I'll watch your class while you're gone."

"Did he say what it is about? What's so urgent?" Noah asked.

"He didn't say, but you should probably take your things," she said.

Noah felt his heart rate pick up. He grabbed his jacket and attaché case and headed toward the office. On the way, his mind raced. *Something has happened to Lacy. Dear God, please let my little girl be all right. Or maybe something happened to Cassie. Please God, let them be safe.*

When he arrived, he saw two Sevier County Sherriff's deputies through the glass window of Principal Mitchel's office. He spoke softly. "Jesus, let it be anything but Cassie and Lacy; please just let them be alive."

He walked in the office.

James Mitchel greeted him. "Thanks for coming down, Noah."

"What's going on?" Noah asked.

"These deputies have a warrant for your arrest," Principal Mitchel replied.

"For what?" Noah was confused.

"One of the parents claims that you are teaching creationism in biology. It's a violation of Community Core," James explained.

Noah was shocked. "I'm not teaching creationism. And even if I was, how can I be arrested for it?"

"Don't say anything else. Wait until you get a lawyer. The union will get you a lawyer. I'll let Cassie know that you were taken in, and I'll help her arrange bail. Just go on in, and we'll get all of this sorted out," James said.

Noah's fear bubbled into anger. "I'm not going anywhere until someone tells me why I'm being arrested!"

Deputy Rodgers said, "The parent is claiming that by teaching creationism, you're abusing her child. By giving the child false information, you are hindering the child's ability to learn, which will have detrimental effects on the child's future.

"In addition to the felony charge of child abuse, you are also being charged under the new bullying law. Part of the Community Core legislation made bullying a criminal offense."

"I never bullied anyone!" Noah shouted.

Rodgers continued. "Since the Bible was used to bully transgender and homosexual children, any reference to the Bible is considered bullying under Community Core."

Noah clinched his fists. "At most, I told the students that there were people who disagreed with evolution and believed the Bible's account of creation. I never told the kids what to think."

Mitchel grabbed Noah's arm. "Noah, shut up. You are digging your hole deeper!"

"All teachers were given a copy of the new criminal codes included in the Community Core legislation. It was part of your new contract. It was the only way Tennessee could get federal education funding. You signed an agreement form as part of your new contract," Deputy Rodgers said.

"That thing was two hundred pages long. No one read that. It was written so that no one could understand it anyway," Noah said.

"I don't make the rules, Mr. Parker. I just enforce them. Turn around and put your hands on your head. The sooner you get booked, the sooner you can bond out and get this all straightened out," Rodgers said.

Noah didn't turn around. "You don't make the rules, but by enforcing them, you're personally responsible for violating my freedom of speech. Do you think this is right? Do you think you should be arresting someone who did nothing but speak his opinion? That is a complete violation of the First Amendment. If you lock me up, you are the criminal. You are the one violating the Constitution. An unconstitutional law has no merit, and it is your duty to disregard it."

"That's not up to me to decide," Rodgers said.

"Yes, it is!" Noah yelled. "You took an oath to defend the Constitution. You are the first line of defense."

Rodgers remained calm, though his tone sharpened. "Mr. Parker, I'm sure you don't want to add resisting arrest to your list of charges. That's only going to increase your bail."

Noah ignored the warning. "Answer me! Did you take an oath to protect the Constitution, and do you think arresting me is fulfilling your oath?"

Rodgers clinched his jaw. "It doesn't matter what I believe. I have a family to feed. If I don't do it, someone else will. I'll be the one in the unemployment line, and you'll still be in jail."

"Do you think that defense would have held up in Nuremburg?" Noah shot back.

"You calling me a Nazi?" Rodgers drew his Taser.

Noah felt the Taser spikes lodge firmly in his torso just before the voltage from the weapon made the world go black.

CHAPTER 8

This is the verdict: Light has come into the world, but men loved darkness instead of light because their deeds were evil. Everyone who does evil hates the light, and will not come into the light for fear that his deeds will be exposed. But whoever lives by the truth comes into the light, so that it may be seen plainly that what he has done has been done through God.

John 3:19–21

Everett Carroll received a text from the office Monday morning asking him to come in as soon as possible. He skipped the gym and had a granola bar, as opposed to his normal bowl of cereal. He went through the drive-thru at Dunkin' Donuts rather than stopping at Starbucks on the way to work. He made it to the office parking lot at 7:15 AM.

I'm almost two hours early; that should be good enough, he thought as he locked the door of his car.

"Everett," a familiar voice called from behind.

He looked to see Ken Gordon sprinting his way. "Hey."

Ken caught up with him, and they proceeded to the security checkpoint together. "Did you get a text to rush in?"

"Yes, I guess you did too. I wonder what this is about."

"Did you watch any news this morning?"

Everett slowed his pace to listen. "No, what happened?"

"Global markets are in a full meltdown."

"Wonder what that has to do with the Company?"

Ken straightened his tie. "I'd say we're about to find out."

Once the two cleared security, the processing agent said, "Everyone in your department is asked to report to briefing room B."

"Thanks," Ken said.

They both went straight to the briefing room.

Agent Jones was in the front of the room, standing near a projector screen. "Take a seat. We'll give the other folks another fifteen minutes before I start the briefing. In the meantime, I'll stream Fox Business News so you can get the gist of what the meeting is about."

Jones clicked on the projector. A Fox Business reporter, Stuart Redman, was interviewing the Chair of the SEC.

"Chairman Douglas, do you anticipate closing the markets early today, or do you intend to allow them to open at all?"

The SEC Chairman's eyes and mouth were downcast, showing his concern. "We're going to be keeping a close watch on markets. As of this moment, we do plan to allow markets to open at their normal time. We've seen these types of heavy losses in early trading before; markets often rebound once the opening bell sounds. The panic is amplified by the low volume in early-morning trading."

Redman raised his eyebrows. "That sounds very optimistic, especially considering the ruinous losses in the European markets."

The SEC Chairman attempted to hide his concern by pursing his lip. "There have been dramatic drops in other markets, but American markets often lead recoveries."

The reporter said, "I know you have a long day ahead of you Chairman Douglas, I'll let you get back to your job. Thank you for taking time to let us know that the SEC is going to be watching out for us today."

Douglas gave the obligatory smile. "Thank you, Stuart."

The ticker scrolling across the bottom of the screen showed the global indices, all followed by downward-pointing red indicators. The only green symbols followed platinum, gold, silver, and oil.

Back in the studio, Heather Smith addressed the viewers.

"Fox Business will be with you throughout the day to bring you the latest developments in real time. The only safe havens seem to be Russian and Chinese bonds. Investors are also rushing into gold and oil, but we've seen both of those get taken out when liquidity starts to vanish from the markets.

"The BRICS Bank has announced that they will be issuing a statement at 1:00 PM Eastern time. If this is indeed the long anticipated declaration of a gold-backed currency, currency markets around the world will be reeling for weeks to come.

"It is unclear how a new currency will affect the independent currencies of the member nations of the BRICS Bank. However, it is certain that it would be detrimental, if not an absolute death sentence, for the dollar, the euro, and the yen."

Jones clicked off the live feed, and a graphic animation of a spinning globe appeared on the screen. "Agents, I'm going to cut to the chase. The president of the BRICS Bank intends to announce a new gold-backed currency this afternoon. It would mean the end of the world as we know it. Safeguards have been put in place to try to circumvent this threat to our national interest.

"It is likely that China and Russia will see these measures as a hostile action against them.

"We are anticipating electronic retaliation against stock exchanges, banking systems, and possibly even defense systems. We have done everything we can to limit access to strategic hardware and disable known threats, but there is always the one attack that slips through the cracks.

"Our facility has been asked to back up the NSA until the threat subsides. Some of you will be monitoring computer logs and communication activities of individuals on lists of known intelligence operatives from China, Russia, and other potentially hostile countries. Others of you will be monitoring electronic infrastructure and watching for potential attacks.

"Today is a big day, people. We'll be bringing in lunch so you can eat at your workstations. We'll most likely be asking everyone to work late tonight and come back early tomorrow. We are in a level-red operation condition until further notice. I don't need to remind you who you work for and how important it is that absolutely none of what you see or hear today can ever leave this facility.

"I'll be on-site today and personally checking to be sure everyone's system has the access you need to accomplish your mission.

"Go get 'em."

Ken and Everett walked back toward their cubicles.

Everett was the first to speak. "Safeguards have been put in place to protect our national interest. What was that supposed to mean?"

Ken shook his head. "You're a little too inquisitive, but it sounds like the CIA is putting the kibosh on the new currency."

Once at his desk, Everett logged into his computer and retrieved his assignment. He was tasked with monitoring bank accounts and firewalls for Bank of America.

Just before lunch, Agent Jones passed by his desk. "Anything out of the ordinary?"

"Nothing I can detect," Everett said.

"Good. Call me over if anything comes up." Jones started to walk away.

"Sir?" Everett said.

Jones stopped walking and turned around. "Yes, Mr. Carroll?"

"I noticed the price of gold was spiking tremendously. Is that something someone should be trying to get a hold of?" Everett wasn't sure if he was crossing the line, but his inquisitiveness was getting the best of him.

"I wouldn't be concerned, at least not today."

Everett nodded and went back to work.

After Jones left, Everett thought about the way Jones had answered him. *At least not today.*

Everett looked at his phone on the desk and noticed something underneath. "A matchbook," he said beneath his breath.

Everett retrieved the object and opened it to look inside. It appeared to be an ordinary book of matches from McGuire's Pub. The Irish bar was located just a block from his apartment. He pulled the matches out to see if anything was written inside, but nothing was.

It was obvious that Jones had somehow slipped the matches beneath his phone. Since nothing was written inside, Everett assumed he was expected to go by there after work.

Everett proceeded to watch his screen for telltale signs of cyber-espionage attacks against Bank of America. Lunch was served at noon. The cafeteria was closed, and the workers brought pizza and sodas around to each desk on a cart.

"Thanks," Everett said as his slices arrived.

The familiar cafeteria worker smiled. "You're very welcome."

Everett bit into his first slice. *This is probably the best thing I've ever eaten at this facility,* he thought. *If the cafeteria servers didn't know they worked for a government agency before, I guess they do now. I'm sure they had to go through a much higher level of scrutiny to get a job here. And of course, there is the security screen to pass through every day when they arrive and when they leave. They must know something.*

At three o'clock, the cafeteria workers returned with a choice of coffee or energy drink.

Everett selected a Red Bull. "Wow, we're getting the royal treatment today."

Everett sipped the cold beverage. *What's that? Looks like someone is attempting to breach the firewall!*

Right away, Everett picked up the phone and called Agent Jones. "Sir, I have what looks like an attack against Bank of America's Merrill Lynch stock trading server. Are the markets still open, or did the SEC close them early?"

"I'll be right there. Initiate a counter attack against the source and then sever the hard line connection via a direct shut down of the Internet service provider."

Everett did as he was instructed. "Okay, but this is going to shut down a huge chunk of the Internet when I shut down the ISP."

Jones didn't acknowledge the concern, but was at Everett's desk in seconds. "I'll forward this activity to the cyber security team, and they'll handle it from here."

Everett watched as Jones took over his keyboard and entered the forwarding address. *Glister@handm.com, why does that sound familiar?* He thought, *hand m? Oh yeah, H and M, that's where Lisa's friend works. I figured she was a spook.*

Everett smiled. *It will be nice to meet someone who works in the intelligence community. That will make it much easier to understand each other's secrecy regarding work.*

Jones finished up. "Good work soldier; carry on. You'll be finishing up at seven tonight. We've got another team from Northrop Grumman taking over at that time. Shifts will be staggered tomorrow, so check your phone to see what time you're coming in."

"Great," Everett said. "See you later . . . I mean see you tomorrow."

Jones just kept walking away as if he hadn't heard anything.

Seven o'clock came without any other apparent threats to the systems that Everett was monitoring. An instant message appeared on his screen to let him know that an analyst at Northrop Grumman had assumed his security file. Everett headed for the door.

On the way home, Everett sighed. "What a day! Part of me just wants to go home and crash, but I'm sure Jones is going to let me in on what happened. That's definitely worth sticking it out for a few more hours."

Everett scanned the radio for a news station that might be covering the economic events of the day. It wasn't long before he found the local NPR station. He turned up the volume to catch the rest of the report that was being aired.

". . . unprecedented sell-off rebounded dramatically after BRICS Bank President Chau issued a statement saying the bank would be postponing their announcement until a later date. Sources inside the emerging-market, trade-settlement bank stated that a systemic failure occurred inside the bank's main server. The cause of the failure has been accredited to an abnormal level of trading volume and is expected to be resolved soon.

"As all trade between member nations flows through the BRICS Bank, commerce between Brazil, Russia, India, China, and South Africa has come to a screeching halt until the server can be brought back on line. It is estimated that the outage could cost the BRICS nations as much as twenty billion dollars US per day.

"The S&P saw the most dramatic rebound. After being down twenty-two percent just before the announcement, the index closed down seven percent. While still calamitous, the losses were only a fraction of what they were at the day's low.

"Profit taking stepped into the commodities markets. Gold pared its intraday gains to close up ten percent at $3,060.

Silver also closed below intraday highs, but still managed to gain fourteen percent for the day. The white metal closed at a new record closing price of $109.

"US treasuries sustained the brunt of the destruction today. The yield on the ten-year bond shot up to twelve percent. This is dismal news for the housing market. Home prices have struggled to gain traction ever since the collapse of the housing 2.0 bubble.

"In the wake of today's turmoil, talks may resume over merging the Fed, European Central Bank, Bank of International Settlements, IMF, and World Bank with the central banks of Canada, Japan, and England. Several members of the House and Senate affiliated with the Constitutional, Libertarian, and Tea Party Movements of the past decade fought hard against the consolidation of the American central bank with global banking authorities. Those opposing the move cite that such a move would compromise US sovereignty.

"UN Secretary General Angelo Luz has urged President Clay to call an emergency session of Congress to allow the merger or to do it through executive order. Press Secretary Luis Fernandez told reporters that President Clay would consider all options. He added that today's events brought to light the fragility of our financial system and that a global structure was needed to combat such systemic vulnerabilities.

"France, Spain, Germany, the Netherlands, and Italy have all issued statements voicing their willingness to sit down and discuss a charter for a new UN financial conglomerate. The transition would likely be relatively seamless for members of the EU, but it would be quite a shock to American culture.

"Japan and Canada were also on board before the talks broke down. Like the US, England had its share of dissenters in Parliament for the global bank, but the shot across the bow today may silence them."

Everett pulled into the parking lot of McGuire's. He walked inside not knowing what to expect. The clientele was a bit older than the pubs Everett generally frequented. *This is pretty much what I expected. Old furnishings, too many things on the wall, and needs a good cleaning.* He looked around for Jones but didn't see anyone who could possibly be him, even in disguise.

Everett sat down at a booth and grabbed a menu. "Nothing too enticing. I guess I'll try the burger." He looked around for a server but didn't see anyone. He waited for a while but finally came to the conclusion that he had to order from the bar.

Everett walked to the bar and ordered his burger and a Coke.

"I'll call your name when it's ready," the bartender said.

"I'm Everett."

The bartender jotted his name on the ticket. "Okay, Everett."

Everett dropped off his Coke at the booth then went to the restroom. Upon his return, Jones was sitting at the booth.

Everett sat down. "Hi."

Jones pushed the Coke toward Everett. "It's a bad habit for someone in your line of work to leave their beverage unattended."

Everett put his hand on the glass. "I never thought of that, thanks. I haven't eaten since lunch, so I already ordered a burger. Can I order something for you?"

Jones crossed his hands on the table. "I'm having the seafood pasta."

"Oh, alright," Everett said.

Jones looked toward the front of the bar over the top of his glasses. "You wouldn't think seafood pasta would be good coming from an Irish bar, but one thing you learn at the Company is never judge a book by its cover. It's what I come here for. And the garlic bread is fantastic."

"It's great that you still have such a good appetite." Everett wished he hadn't said that as soon as the words left his lips.

"I'm not taking chemo or radiation," Jones said. "It wouldn't buy me that much time anyway, and food is about all I have to enjoy in life."

Everett wanted to change the subject in a hurry. "The radio said the UN is pushing to merge the central banks of the developed economies."

"That's already a done deal."

The bartender walked over to the table and sat a drink on

the table. "Bushmills on the rocks, Mr. Smith."

Everett was waiting for Jones to correct him, but he didn't.

"Thank you," Jones said.

Once the bartender walked away, Jones explained. "Smith is what it says on my credit card."

"Oh," Everett said.

No matter, his name probably isn't Jones either, Everett thought. "So why are the reporters talking like it's something in the works?"

"Theater." Jones took a sip of the whiskey.

"And the market turnaround today?" Everett asked. "Did we have anything to do with that?"

"Dragon had everything to do with that today," Jones said. "Dragon developed a multilayer strategy to take down the BRICS central computer years ago. It began by collecting personal information on high-level political appointees. They're always the most vulnerable because they don't understand how complex computer systems work. They get lax in security protocols because they see them as burdensome. Once their online habits were mapped, Dragon infected their personal devices, which carried the infection inside the secure facility and eventually infected the main server. Once in place, the virus sat dormant until a set of events triggered the activation of the bug.

"The entire BRICS system is garbage. Any piece of equipment that was connected to that network will have to be thrown out. It will be months before the BRICS Bank is operational again.

"In the meantime, things will return to something resembling normal market conditions, if the Russians or the Chinese don't launch a hot war.

"But sometime in the near future, the dollar will be thrown out, the euro will be thrown out, the yen, Canadian dollar, they're all gone. A new global currency will be introduced, but not by the BRICS Bank. It will be a currency controlled by the IMF, UN, and World Bank."

Everett's eyes peered at Jones intently. "When?"

"Soon, at a time of Dragon's choosing."

Everett wasn't sure of what he was being told. "Is Dragon self-aware? What level of artificial intelligence are we talking about? You said Dragon designed the strategy for the virus. Is there human input in all of this?"

Jones took another drink. "Oh, yes, there is a high level of human intelligence and oversight. A committee develops the overall desired outcomes. Those are fed to Dragon and the system develops strategies and courses of action. The committee then approves or rejects the plan. Plans that are approved are implemented through Dragon's electronic actions, and directives are issued to human agents. Plans that are turned down are scraped, and Dragon develops an alternative method of reaching the goal.

"Dragon is not what you would call self-aware. It's simply able to predict, with an astounding rate of accuracy, what will happen when certain actions are taken. What it really does is allow us to see into the future based on known inputs. The only thing it cannot predict is unknown inputs. Things like weather events, earthquakes, terrorist attacks that are planned outside of the communications grid, or other occurrences of that nature are not accounted for. But projections of price movements, market reactions, terrorist attacks planned using communications wired into the grid, and even herd behavior is very precise."

"So Dragon has engineered a smooth transition into the new global currency?"

"No," Jones said. "It isn't meant to be smooth at all. It is specifically designed to create utter chaos. And you need to start coming up with a plan to deal with it when it comes because it will be a tectonic shift that turns the world upside down."

The bartender brought the food over. "Since you are Mr. Smith's guest, I can take care of anything you might need."

Everett was still trying to process what he was being told. "I'm sorry, what did you say?"

The bartender placed the tray under his arm. "Can I get anything else for you?"

"Please, yes," Everett stammered. "I'll have what he's having."

"Bushmills on the rocks?" the bartender asked.

"Please," Everett said.

The barman walked away and Everett searched for a starting point to initiate the barrage of questions forming in his head. "Who's controlling this? The CIA? Why would they want it to be so cataclysmic? What should I do?"

Jones smiled. "One at a time, Mr. Carroll. I'll start with the easiest question. Why would they want it to be so disruptive? That answer is threefold.

"First, absolute disorder means that the masses will accept the new world order without question or protest. They'll be begging for anything that promises to maintain peace and brings control, and they will get control. The infrastructure that comes in to fill the void will blow your mind. You've never seen anything like what is coming in the way of control.

"Second, there will be a massive wealth transfer. If you think you can imagine the money that could be made by insider trading on a global scale, by someone with absolute knowledge, unlimited resources, and no fear of repercussion, you still haven't begun to grasp the magnitude of what will happen.

"Third, it will bring about a titanic global depopulation. Some estimates are as high as forty percent."

"Forty percent of what?" Everett's mind seemed unable to accept what he was hearing.

"Forty percent of human life on earth," Jones said.

Everett just looked at him while Jones paused to take a bite of his food.

Jones finished chewing. "Next, you asked who is doing

this. Yes, the CIA is involved, and at a very high level, but we're not in control."

"The president?" Everett asked as Jones took another bite.

Jones almost laughed. "No son, not the president. The president is a puppet. The Rothschilds, Rockefellers, and a hand full of other people are pulling the strings. I couldn't tell you all of them if I wanted too. I don't think anyone knows all the names on that list. They rule and direct through a select number of organizations. Internationally, the Bilderberg group meets annually to keep the sort of upper-level management briefed on the agenda.

"America has long been the brain center for these global power elite. The Council on Foreign Relations has played the largest role here in America. The CFR members list reads like a who's who of former presidents, cabinet members, Treasury officials, Fed board members, CIA directors, news media, and power elites."

"Like who?"

"Son, we'd be here all day. Unlike Bilderberg and the Skulls, CFR is a matter of public record. Memberships are published on the CFR website. To name a few from the present and the past: the Clintons, Ford, Hoover, Carter, Walter Mondale, David Rockefeller, John Rockefeller, Robert Rubin, Charlie Rose, Katie Couric, Barbara Walters, Tom Brokaw, Walter Cronkite, James Baker, Janet Napolitano, Dick Cheney, Michael Bloomberg, Henry Kissinger, Alan Greenspan, former CIA Directors David Patreus, Michael Hayden, and Robert Gates; the list goes on forever.

"Most of the instructions to the global banking community flow through the Trilateral Commission. Its membership is also public knowledge. Current and former members include Paul Volker, David Rockefeller, Mario Monti, Henry Kissinger, Madeleine Albright, Larry Summers, Susan Rice, and lots of names you'd probably recognize.

"From those three organizations, directives are passed along through government, media, and corporate channels."

Everett looked at Jones's Masonic ring. "What about the Masons and the CIA?"

Jones nodded. "The Masons are probably the bottom rung of the ladder; of course, that all depends which degree a Mason obtains.

"The CIA is a special breed. The go-between for the CIA and several US administrations has been the Skull and Bones. Skull and Bones have a special insight into the elite agenda. It would be my guess that direct contact between the ruling class and the Skulls occur at their Yale tomb.

"If the ruling class was King Arthur, the Skulls would be something akin to the Knights of the Round Table, and the CIA would be an elite class of soldiers responsible for carrying out the king's wishes.

"All the other organizations I mentioned would be diplomatic or political in nature."

Everett sat like a deer in the headlights as Jones calmly unveiled this hierarchy of power and secrecy between bites of his favorite dish. He saw that his drink had been dropped off but hadn't noticed the bartender come by with the Coke. Everett took a sip. "Two names that kept coming up for both groups were David Rockefeller and Henry Kissinger. There seems to be a lot of overlap in membership."

Jones nodded. "Oh yes, lots of overlap. In fact, John D. Rockefeller donated the property that the UN sits on in New York. David Rockefeller and Kissinger were known members of the Bilderberg Group, and both had close ties with the Company throughout their lives."

Everett had finally started picking at his food. "And these groups intend on imploding the economy?"

Jones smiled. "Well, that is an inevitable event, but it will suit their agenda. They'll manage the collapse to better fulfill their design."

"Aren't they rich enough? Why do they need a massive wealth transfer?"

"It's not about money. It is about power. The elite at the top of the pyramid are drunk on power. They're addicted. And like any addict, too much is never enough. If you ask them how much is enough, they'd all say just a little bit more."

Everett took a bite of his now cold burger. He finished chewing. "You said the Rothschilds were involved, but I never heard their name come up in any of the groups you mentioned."

"And you never will. Like a mafia boss, that family never gets its hands dirty. UN Secretary General Luz is a descendant of the Rothschild family." Jones took a sip of his drink. "His mother is a Rothschild."

"And his father?"

Jones shook his head. "He came out of nowhere, sort of like Obama. Suspiciously unconnected to all of these secret groups."

"You mentioned that George H. W. Bush was a member of the Skull and Bones."

Jones finished the remaining garlic bread. "And the son, George W. Bush, he's also a member. The grandfather of George H. W., Samuel Bush, ran Buckeye Steel, which was a Rockefeller corporation. The father of George H. W. was US Senator Prescott Bush, who was a director of Union Banking Corporation. The bank was caught holding gold for the Nazis, but of course, Prescott was never indicted. He was also never indicted for being involved in the conspiracy to overthrow the US government and replace it with a fascist regime in 1933. He'd have been proud of his grandson signing the Patriot Act."

Everett began to slump in the booth. It had been a long day, and the adrenaline from learning about the secret societies was wearing off. "And what should I do to prepare for the chaos?"

Jones chuckled. "I think you've stumbled onto what some of your coworkers are doing to get ready for the event."

"You mean the unauthorized credit card charges?"

"Yes, but more specifically the cryptocurrencies. I suspect

a lot of operatives who are aware of the plot are scrambling to put some wealth into places where it won't get taken out when the dollar, euro, and yen collapse."

Everett poured a bit of his Coke into his whiskey glass. "You think cryptocurrencies are a safe place?"

Jones shook his head. "Not at all. I think you're right. I bet the agents behind the cryptocurrencies are just parking it there. The bankers at the IMF, Fed, and ECB will probably direct Dragon to launch an attack against the gold price. Once it plummets, the CIA operatives diverting funds into cryptocurrencies will likely move the majority of their holdings into gold and silver."

Everett stirred his drink. "Why would they want to take the gold price down?"

Jones handed his plate to the bartender who had come by to clear the table. "It will make it cheaper to accumulate for one. The other reason is to discredit it as a competitor to the new global currency."

"Do the bankers intend to make the global currency gold-backed, like the BRICS currency would have been?"

Jones curled his lip. "No. The new currency will be cryptographic. Bitcoin was the beta test for it."

"So this Nakamoto guy who created bitcoin, he worked for the Company?"

Jones smiled. "Yes and no. Let's just say we made him an offer he couldn't refuse."

Everett nodded. "That's why none of the funds are being converted into bitcoin."

"Bingo." Jones held up his glass to signal for the bartender to bring him another. "Darkcoin, on the other hand, is an effective tool in the hands of someone who knows how to exploit it."

"I'm confused. Bitcoin will be the new global currency?"

Jones shook his head. "No, the bitcoin payment system will be used for the new currency, but bitcoin was just the prototype. Bitcoin holders will have their bitcoins converted to the new currency, but their virtual wallets and cyber vaults will be obsolete. Likewise, the private exchanges won't work with the new currency. The IMF will be the only exchange. Dragon will track and store all payments, balances, and purchases."

Everett was wearing down, but he had to know more. "Then why are CIA operatives stockpiling gold and silver?"

"Because there will be no more paper currency. Black ops run off of the radar. We used paper for everything. There were no credit cards and very few wire transfers. Field agents use cash so nothing can be traced. Gold and silver will be the new black-market currency. Besides that, the CIA has been given carte blanche for decades; it's unclear how much slack we'll have when the new government rolls out. It's sort of like working for a business that is coming under new management. You know what the old bosses let you get away with, but when the new management team shows up, everyone has to get to work on time, stop playing games on the computer, and quit taking an extra twenty minutes for lunch. You know you'll still have a job, but you want to enjoy things the way they are while you can. Do you understand?"

Everett finished his drink. "Yeah, I guess that makes sense. But what should I do?"

The bartender brought Jones's second drink. Agent Jones smiled and nodded at the man as he took the fresh whiskey. "Right, we still haven't covered that, and it's getting late. When you see gold and silver drop thirty or forty percent in the course of five days or less, start putting all of your liquid assets into physical coins. Better stock up on some dry goods too. The stores might be closed down for a while. No payment system means no stores. If you have somewhere outside of the city to lay low for a while, that'd be smart also."

Everett was tired, but this statement sparked his interest. "I thought the bitcoin payment system would work."

Jones sipped his drink. "Stores aren't set up for that. And like I said before, the elite want to see a period of civil unrest. They want people to beg them to come in and save the day. They also want a significant die-off to reduce the population. Less people are easier to control, and the elite don't have to share their planet with as many peasants. These people are absolutely sick. I can see that you're tired, and you have enough to digest for now, but next time we get together, I'll fill you in on the details."

"There's more?"

Jones laughed, "Son, we're just getting started."

CHAPTER 9

Woe to those who call evil good and good evil, who put darkness for light and light for darkness, who put bitter for sweet and sweet for bitter.

Isaiah 5:20

Noah Parker came to in the back of the patrol car. Blood was running down his head and into his right eye. He struggled to wipe it off on his shoulder, but the handcuffs held his arms behind his back and made it an impossible task.

The car drove through the security gate at the county jail. Rodgers put the car in park and walked around to open Noah's door. "You ready to do things the easy way?"

Noah stepped out of the car and stood with the officer's assistance. "Did you have to crack my skull after you tased me?"

Rodgers guided Noah by the arm. "You hit your head on

the desk after you went out. We'll have the nurse clean that up and put a bandage on it while you're in booking."

Noah had nothing else to say. There was no point in it anyway. Noah went through booking where he was fingerprinted.

The nurse did come to clean up his wound. "This isn't too deep. I'll just put some Steri-Strips on there. Leave them alone for a few days. If you pick at them, they'll come off and this might open back up."

Noah glanced up at her but said nothing.

He had to give up his clothes and put on the orange pants and shirt issued by the jail. "How humiliating," he muttered to himself.

Noah sat in a holding cell for nearly three hours before he was taken to his cellblock. Once there, he took the mattress and the linens he was assigned and found a cell with an empty bunk.

He placed his things on the top bunk and nodded at the man occupying the bottom.

The man looked over the top of the book he was reading. "Make yourself at home; I'm Phil."

Noah forced a smile as he put the sheets on the mattress. "Nice to meet you."

"What did you do?"

"Taught creationism in public school."

Phil laughed. "No, seriously, what are you in here for."

"I'm serious. It is a violation of the criminal codes in Community Core to teach creationism."

Phil picked his book back up. "Suit yourself. If you don't want to talk about it, that's fine, but I don't need any BS excuses."

Noah crawled up in the bunk and stared at the ceiling. His mind raced for a while, and then he finally fell asleep.

Phil nudged Noah. "Buddy, wake up. You're on the news. Sorry I didn't believe you. I've never heard of a charge like that."

Noah wasn't sleeping very hard. He jumped out of the rack and followed Phil out into the dayroom to see the television, which was mounted fifteen feet up on the wall.

The field reporter outside of the jail was speaking to the reporter in the newsroom.

"That's right Rick, roughly one hundred miles away from the site of the landmark Scopes Monkey Trial, held in Dayton, Tennessee, in 1925, a historical arrest has once again been made over the controversy of creation versus evolution. Noah Parker was arrested earlier today for teaching creationism at Sevier County High School. The arrest shows how much America has changed in less than a century.

"In the 1925 Scopes trial, John Thomas Scopes was accused of teaching evolution in a Tennessee High School. Although the case was later overturned, Scopes was found guilty of teaching evolution and fined one hundred dollars. The trial turned into a media frenzy, and reporters from all over the country descended on the small town of Dayton, Tennessee. Dayton now holds an annual festival to commemorate the event. During the festival, a musical play entitled, *Front Page News*, which depicts the events of the trial, is performed at the Cumberland County Playhouse. Only time will tell if this case will also gain national recognition. Back to you, Rick."

Phil patted Noah on the shoulder. "Sounds like you might end up as famous as this Scopes guy."

"Lucky me."

Dinner was being served while the news was on. Noah found a seat next to Phil and waited for the tray to be placed in front of him. When it arrived, two boiled hot dogs, two slices of white bread, lukewarm mixed vegetables, and a piece of yellow cake with no icing sat on the plastic section tray.

Noah stared at it.

Phil wrapped one of his hotdogs in a piece of the bread. "You better eat. There won't be anything else until 5:00 AM."

Noah pushed the tray toward Phil. "I should be bonding out soon. Do you want it?"

Phil pulled the tray over and took the hotdogs. "At least eat your cake. It's not too bad, and you're not free until you walk out that door."

Noah nodded and picked up the cake.

After dinner, a voice came over the intercom. "The following inmates have visitors. When you hear your name called, line up at the sally port door: Miller, Gibson, Mills, Dunn, Parker, Alvarez. If you didn't hear your name, you don't have a visitor."

Noah got in the line by the door and waited. Two guards appeared outside of the thick glass and metal door, a buzzer sounded, and the heavy door slid open.

The first guard put on latex gloves, while the second gave instructions. "Line up with your hands against the wall."

Noah complied as the guard went from inmate to inmate performing a pat-down search.

After the search, Noah followed the line to the visitor station. He found an empty booth and waited. Moments later, Cassie came to the glass separation booth and picked up the phone. "What happened to your head?"

Noah held the receiver just close enough to hear. "The officer said that I hit my head on the desk after they tased me."

Cassie's lip started to quiver. She swallowed hard. "I'm so sorry this happened to you."

"Did you call a bail bondsman?"

Cassie wiped a single tear. "They hit you with resisting arrest and assault of a law enforcement officer in addition to the Community Core violation. I think they're trying to make an example out of you. Your bond is $100,000. We need ten grand to bond you out. We're short about $1,500. I sold off some stock from our Roth IRA. By the time the money from the sale is available to transfer out of the IRA account and it clears into our checking, it could be Thursday or Friday."

Noah bit his lip in anger. "He assaulted me! And I never resisted!"

Cassie maintained a calm tone. "I know baby. I called the teachers union to get you a lawyer, but they can't represent you because of the Community Core contract violation.

"I spoke with Isaiah, and he has a friend that's a lawyer. I called the lawyer, and he's filing for a bond reduction hearing. Either way, it could take a couple of days. Will you be all right?"

"I can stick it out. The market looked like it was about to get pummeled this morning before I left for work. The news said it rebounded quite a bit, but I guess we still lost a lot on the stocks you had to sell."

Cassie smiled. "Not as much as we would've if the market hadn't come back around. The proceeds of the sale and our savings will be completely gone once we bond you out. Do you think we should sell off some more so we have a little cash? Besides that, I think something is happening in the markets that they're not telling us about. We could be in for a rough ride."

Noah tried to think. With everything else that was going on today, he wasn't in the best position to be making a decision like this. "What's the total value of the portfolio after today's drop?"

"Roughly $40,000."

"What do you think we should do?"

"I think we should sell everything and take the cash. Since it's a Roth IRA, we won't pay any penalties. What happened today is a very bad sign."

Noah though for a minute. "How about we sell half and think about the rest at a later date."

"Okay, we can talk about the other half after you get out." Cassie filled Noah in on how much Lacy missed him and assured him that everything would be okay.

They said their good-byes, and Noah returned to his cell.

He climbed on his bunk.

"Did your visit go okay?" Phil said.

"A little disappointing. You were right. You're not free until you walk out the door."

"Do you want to borrow a book?"

Noah looked over the side of the rack. "Do you have a Bible?"

Phil rummaged around under his bunk and pulled out a Bible. "They used to give these out free. Now, someone has to order it for you from an approved Internet bookstore. My mom sent me this one."

Noah took the Bible. "Thanks."

Phil laughed. "Of course, they might be banned altogether

if you don't win this trial."

Noah still had not grasped what his trial would mean for religious liberty. For the moment, he was focused strictly on getting out of this cage.

Noah read the soothing words of Psalms until he fell asleep.

Early the next morning, Noah woke to the sound of breakfast being served. The trustees brought around breakfasts in bags and handed them through the cell door. Noah opened the brown bag he had been given. Inside was a boiled egg, a pint of skim milk, and a square piece of bread wrapped in plastic wrap. "Why can't we eat in the dayroom?"

Phil began to remove the shell from the boiled egg. "Budget cuts. The jail doesn't have enough correctional officers to watch us all day, every day. When they're short staffed, we stay on lock-down."

Noah tore into the food. "Is this supposed to be a biscuit?"

Phil removed the contents of the paper bag and used it to put the egg shells in. "That's what they call it."

Noah was famished since he had skipped dinner the evening before. He ate everything without complaining.

Shortly after breakfast, the door to his cell buzzed, and a voice came over the intercom. "Parker, pack it up. You're bonding out."

Phil smiled at Noah. "Congratulations buddy, I thought

you were going to be stuck here with us for a while."

"So did I." Noah wrapped the sheets and the mattress. "Take care."

"You too," Phil said.

Noah proceeded to the sally port door and waited for a guard to arrive to escort him back to the processing area. Forty minutes later, the door opened, and the corrections officer walked Noah down the hall. "We're a little short staffed today. It could take a while to process you out."

"Okay," Noah said.

The guard took Noah to the holding cell he had sat in when he was booked the day before. Noah sat and waited some more.

***

Cassie had just finished cleaning the dishes from breakfast when she heard a knock at the door.

She dried her hands and went to look out the window. "Sevier County Sherriff? Could they have dropped the charges and brought Noah home?"

She opened the door. A deputy in his mid-forties greeted her. "Mrs. Parker, I'm Deputy Donaldson. May we come in to talk with you for a moment?"

"What about?"

Donaldson had three other deputies behind him. This was obviously not a social call.

Donaldson stuck his foot in the doorjamb so Cassie couldn't close the door. "We're escorting Ms. Carrick from Child Services. She's here to do an evaluation."

Cassie tried to close the door but couldn't. "Unless you have a warrant, you need to leave."

Donaldson was a big guy. He pushed the door open and walked in with the other three following him. "We don't need a warrant ma'am. This will all go much easier if you just let us talk with you for a minute. Do you have any weapons in the house?"

Cassie started for her phone. "I'm calling my lawyer."

Donaldson yelled. "Take a seat!"

The second deputy to come in drew his pistol, as did the third deputy. Cassie put her hands in the air.

Donaldson said, "Wooten, check her purse. She was going for it."

Wooten complied. "She has a Kahr nine millimeter in here."

Cassie didn't move. "I was going for my phone."

"Cuff her," Donaldson said.

The Parker's dog, Buster, became very upset and started barking at the deputies.

Donaldson was moving toward Cassie. "Shoot that dog, Puckett."

Lacy walked into the room just as Deputy Puckett fired three shots into Buster. "No! Buster!"

The little girl threw herself on the convulsing animal. Buster had a violent seizure before he expired.

The fourth deputy shouted, "What is wrong with you people? You don't just shoot their dog! He was just barking. This is America. I spent four years in the desert risking my life and fighting for freedom. This is not freedom!"

Donaldson pointed at him. "Starkey, outside. Wait in the car. We'll talk about this later."

Starkey ripped his badge off his shirt and threw it on the floor. "We're not talking about anything. I want no part of this. Killing a dog, searching houses with no warrants, taking kids away from their parents for no good reason. This is on you."

Donaldson yelled. "You vets think you know everything. We've got a war right here. If you walk away, your career is finished."

Starkey kept walking and didn't look back.

Puckett holstered his weapon and helped Donaldson secure cuffs on Cassie. "Should we go after Starkey?"

Donaldson shook his head. "Let him go. He chose his side."

Deputy Wooten grabbed Lacy from the floor where she lay screaming, holding the bloody corpse of her dog, Buster. "I need to put zip-tie restraints on this one."

"Do what you have to do." Donaldson adjusted his utility belt and walked outside to retrieve the Child Services worker.

Cassie sat on the couch. Her face was blood red with fury, but she stayed calm for Lacy. "It's going to be okay sweetie."

The youngster screamed. "They killed Buster. I hate them. I hate them!"

A heavyset woman followed Deputy Donaldson back in the room. "Lacy, I'm Ms. Carrick from the Department of Child Services."

Lacy spit at her. "I hate you!"

Ms. Carrick stepped away from her. "You're just upset right now, but everything is going to be fine."

Lacy kicked her feet. "Nothing is fine. You killed Buster. I hate you all!"

Ms. Carrick walked around the house. "Mrs. Parker, I'm here to do an evaluation. Your husband has been charged with crimes against children. It's routine for Child Services to do an investigation after criminal charges involving minors. I'm going to be honest with you. So far, things don't look good. Deputy Donaldson says you have weapons in the house."

Cassie tried to bite her tongue and be polite, but she was furious. "I have a permit for my handgun."

Ms. Carrick opened the doors on the entertainment center and snooped around. "There was no trigger lock, and the weapon was not secured."

Cassie looked at the body of Buster lying lifeless on the floor. She wanted to lash out just as Lacy had. "I haven't committed a crime. Why am I being interrogated like this?"

Ms. Carrick looked on the laptop computer. "Why do you have Ron Paul Homeschool Curriculum? Tennessee law requires homeschoolers to utilize Community Core materials. Supplemental resources must meet CC standards. I can assure you that this is not on the list of approved sources."

Cassie tried to move her hands, which were cuffed behind her back. "We have the material given to us by the Department of Education. I was just looking at Dr. Paul's materials to compare."

Ms. Carrick handed the laptop to Deputy Donaldson. "Can you keep this in your evidence lock-up?"

Donaldson took the computer. "She has a paperback copy of Ron Paul's, *The School Revolution,* here on the shelf. Should we take that?"

Ms. Carrick picked it up to look at it. "It should be considered hate speech material, but for now, it's not against the law. Are you charging Mrs. Parker?"

"There are no charges at the moment. We'll look through the house before we leave and see if we find anything."

Ms. Carrick headed for the door. "Put the child in the back of my car."

Donaldson nodded at Wooten. "Will do."

"Mommy!" Lacy cried in agony as Wooten picked her up

to take her to the car.

Cassie was as tough as nails. She fought back the tears until Lacy was gone. "Don't worry sweetheart. Mommy will come get you very soon."

Donaldson and Puckett walked throughout the house. Puckett walked into the master bedroom while Donaldson walked upstairs to the office. "Deputy Donaldson, they've got a gun cabinet in here."

Donaldson walked back down the stairs. He saw Cassie's keys on the table by the door. "Is it key or combination?"

"Keyed."

Donaldson smiled at Cassie as he picked up the keys and joined Puckett in the bedroom.

Minutes later, Donaldson walked out carrying a pump action shotgun and a .22 rifle. "We'll hang on to these so you don't get yourself in any trouble."

He handed the weapons, including Cassie's Kahr, to Puckett. "Put these in the trunk with the computer. I'll be out in a minute."

Puckett left and Donaldson took his key ring out. "If I uncuff you, am I going to have any problems?"

She looked at the floor. "No, sir."

Donaldson removed the cuffs from Cassie's wrists. He watched her as he walked toward the door. "Have a nice day ma'am."

Cassie rubbed her wrists as she watched the deputy leave.

The second they left the driveway, she walked out to the shed and retrieved the shovel. She started digging at the corner of the shed. Just beneath the concrete footer was a green ammo box. She pulled it out from under the footer and dusted it off. She opened the box and took out a Glock 26. It was the smallest nine-millimeter Glock manufactured. Despite its small size, the double-stacked magazine still held ten rounds. She took all three magazines from the ammo box and loaded them right there in the backyard. She popped one magazine in the pistol, racked the slide and stuck it in the back of her jeans. She placed the other two magazines in her back pocket. Cassie returned through the kitchen door, grabbed her car keys, stepped over Buster's dead body, and headed toward the front door.

CHAPTER 10

THESE are the times that try men's souls. The summer soldier and the sunshine patriot will, in this crisis, shrink from the service of their country; but he that stands it now, deserves the love and thanks of man and woman. Tyranny, like hell, is not easily conquered; yet we have this consolation with us, that the harder the conflict, the more glorious the triumph. What we obtain too cheap, we esteem too lightly: it is dearness only that gives everything its value. Heaven knows how to put a proper price upon its goods; and it would be strange indeed if so celestial an article as freedom should not be highly rated.

Thomas Paine, *The American Crisis*

Noah waited for several hours before a guard finally came to process him out. "You ready to go?"

"Yes." Noah signed a paper and was given a bag containing the clothing he'd worn in, as well as the rest of his personal effects. He took his things to a changing room and got dressed. He put his phone, wallet, and keys into his pockets and walked out the door.

A burly man with a thick beard was waiting outside of the door for him. "Mr. Parker?"

"Yes?"

"I'm Tom. Your bail bond is with me. I'll need you to sign a few papers before you leave."

Noah followed the man. "Is my wife here?"

Tom shuffled through his papers. "I don't know."

"Didn't she bond me out?"

Tom handed Noah the first form. "Read this over and sign at the bottom. No, Elliot Rodgers bonded you out."

Noah took the pen and scanned the page before signing. "Elliot Rodgers? Doesn't sound familiar."

Tom passed Noah the next form to sign. "He seemed to know who you were."

"Do you have his number?"

Tom looked through the folder labeled Parker and jotted down a number on a scrap piece of paper. "Here you go."

Noah looked at the number. "Thanks."

Tom handed Noah another form. "This is a list of the requirements for your bond. If you need to leave town for any reason at all, give me a call and let me know where you're going and when you'll be back. I'm sure you understand why."

"Absolutely. Thanks."

Tom shook Noah's hand. "Take care, Mr. Parker."

"Thanks again." Noah took out his phone and called Cassie.

***

Cassie had just started the car when the phone rang. "Noah?"

"I'm out. Someone bonded me out. Can you pick me up?"

Cassie thought about what she was about to do.

"Are you there? Can you come pick me up?" Noah asked.

Cassie's mind was spinning. "I'm here. Actually, there's a huge mess all over the rug. I have to get it cleaned up before it stains. Can you call a cab?"

"I don't really want to waste money on a cab. I don't have a job. I can wait. Take your time."

Cassie cut the ignition in the car. "I'm sorry. I'll get someone to pick you up and take you back to the school to get your truck."

"Okay, I love you," Noah said.

"I love you too. I'm so glad you're out. I'll see you in a bit." Cassie hung up, closed her eyes and took a deep breath.

She dialed Isaiah's phone.

"Hello?"

"Isaiah, it's Cassie. Noah is out, and he needs someone to pick him up and take him to get his truck. The Sherriff's department came by a while ago with DCS and took Lacy. They also shot Buster. His body is in the middle of the living room floor. I want to get it cleaned up before Noah gets home. He doesn't know yet. Can you help me?"

"Of course. Don't worry about Noah. I'll take care of getting him to his truck, and I'll follow him home. Is there anything else you need right now?"

Cassie was holding back the tears. She knew, once they started, the flood gates would open. "I just need to get my daughter back."

"We'll get your daughter back. Just be calm and wait for Noah and me to get there. Let's say a quick prayer."

Cassie knew a prayer would make her start crying, but she reluctantly agreed. "Okay."

"Dear Jesus, these are trying times for the Parkers. You assured us in John sixteen that, in this world, we would have trouble. You also said that we could take heart, because you overcame the world. I pray for a sense of peace and protection to cover Cassie, Lacy, and Noah. Hide them in the shadow of your wings, and keep them as the apple of your eye. Give us wisdom to know how to deal with this situation, and grant us victory in this battle. I pray that you'll bring Lacy home soon. Thank you Lord.

"Cassie, I want you to know that God loves Lacy very much and that you can rest in the fact that he is taking perfect care of her while she's gone."

Cassie was sobbing by now. "Thank you."

"We'll be there soon," Isaiah said.

Cassie put the phone down and let the tears flow for several minutes. She had to take a few minutes to be human and let the emotions out. Minutes later, a sense of clarity came over her. She felt a miraculous sense of peace. Suddenly she understood what a mistake it would have been to run after the Sherriff's deputies in a rage.

"Thank you, Jesus." Cassie dried her tears, got out of the car, and went back in the house.

She looked at Buster's lifeless body and bent down to pet him one last time. "I'm not going down without a fight. I'm going to get Lacy back and avenge your death, Buster. I promise; it won't be in vain."

She walked to the bedroom, took the pistol out of her jeans, and exchanged it for her digital camera. She returned to the living room and began filming the crime scene. She narrated the video as she filmed. "This is our dog, Buster. He was shot this morning when the Sevier County Sherriff's Department raided my home and kidnapped my daughter, Lacy. Before Buster died, he had a violent seizure, while my seven-year-old daughter threw herself on his dying body. Deputy Wooten pried her off of her pet's murdered corpse and handed her over to DCS, still covered in the blood of her lifelong friend, Buster."

Cassie walked into Lacy's room. She filmed the line of stuffed animals meticulously placed on the perfectly-made-up bed. "This is my daughter's room. Hours ago, she lived in a world where she felt safe and secure. We're good parents. We always did our best to protect her and keep her from harm. So why was she ripped from our arms? Because my husband dared to mention the word 'creation' in a public school classroom."

She walked into her bedroom and filmed the drawers that had been pulled out of the dresser and the contents dumped on the floor. She filmed the overturned mattress and the emptied-out gun cabinet. "This act of defiance against the great and holy state has resulted in my husband's imprisonment, the abduction of our daughter, the murder of our pet, the confiscation of my personal property, and the theft of our firearms.

"If you count yourself as an atheist that sees Christians as a plague against this nation, glory in this battle that you have just won, but know that the war has only begun. If you consider yourself to be a Christian, you need to pray up and get ready for action. If you sit back in your easy chair and do nothing, you may soon find yourself in my situation. If you are a pastor of a church that doesn't want to get involved in politics, you better change your stance or start training for a new line of work, because the ministry may soon be outlawed if you continue to sit on the sidelines.

"If you are a fair-weather patriot that is not ready to count the cost of freedom, you may soon learn the even greater cost of your inaction. If you are among the blind, the deaf, and the sleeping that have been ignorant of the growth of this totalitarian, police state that we now live in, open your eyes, pierce your closed ears, and wake up. The enemy is at our gates. If you have found a comfortable position straddling the fence, choose a side or else ready yourself for the consequences when a side is chosen for you. And mark my words, when this conflict is finished, either by free will or default, everyone will have chosen a side."

Cassie finished the video and quickly took over one hundred photographs of the crime scene. She took the camera up stairs and put the photographs and videos onto multiple flash drives. Next, she uploaded the video to YouTube. While the video was uploading, she went downstairs to bury her dog.

She went outside to the shed, took the shovel, and walked to the orchard. Buster would always lie under a certain apple tree in the middle of the orchard when she and Lacy would go out to pick fruit. The strategically chosen spot allowed him to keep a faithful eye on them most anywhere in the orchard without moving.

"This was your favorite spot out here, Buster." She began digging just far enough away from the trunk of the tree to miss the majority of the roots. Then, she went back to the house, moved the coffee table, and rolled Buster's body up in the bloody rug. She took him to the grave and covered it up.

"We'll miss you, buddy. You were a good friend to Lacy. Thank you." Cassie started crying again, but more of a soft, sorrowful cry than the violent sobbing that had overtaken her before.

Back at the house, she filled a bucket with water and

started to clean the blood from the wood floor.

***

Noah perused the papers given to him by the bondsman. His phone rang.

"Hello?"

"Noah, it's Isaiah. Cassie asked me to pick you up. I'll be there in about twenty minutes. You must be starving. Why don't you go across the street and get something to eat?"

"Sounds good. There's a Wendy's on 441. Can you pick me up there?"

"Too early for Krystal's?"

"I haven't been in jail that long."

Isaiah laughed. "I'll see you in a bit."

"Thanks." Noah folded the papers and started walking to the Wendy's located just behind the jail.

Once there, he placed a big order. It was ready in a few short minutes. He took it to a window seat where he could watch for Isaiah. While he ate, he took out the number Tom had given him and dialed the phone.

"May I speak with Elliot?"

"This is him."

"This is Noah Parker. I called to thank you for bailing me out. That was a very kind gesture. I don't even know you."

"You know me, and it was the least I could do. This is Deputy Rodgers. Well, former Deputy. I owe you a big apology . . . and a thank you."

"Oh." Noah had no words.

"What you said about the Nuremburg trials forced me to think about who I am and what I'm turning into. Obviously, you struck a nerve. I'm pretty good at shaking stuff off, unless it's true. I didn't join the Sherriff's office to be a foot soldier for an oppressive regime. Most of the guys in the department didn't either. It's been a long, slow metamorphosis that we barely noticed. We've had some huge jumps, but I've never realized how bad things were until yesterday. I've made small compromise after small compromise to keep my job. Individually, they didn't seem to make much of a difference, but collectively, they really add up. I filled out the paperwork for your arrest yesterday, and then turned in my badge.

"I'd like to buy you dinner and tell you more, if you'll accept my apology."

Even after looking at the last name on the paper Tom had given him, the thought that Elliot Rodgers could be Deputy Rodgers had never crossed Noah's mind. "Yeah, sure. Apology accepted. I can't believe you bailed me out."

"Part of doing the right thing is accepting the cost," Rodgers said.

"I'll accept your offer for dinner as well. I'm out of a job, so that would be great. Of course, you're out of a job also."

"I actually have a lead on a new job already. Hickory Creek Lodge is trying to beef up security for the season. They're looking for people with police experience. Once again, sorry for tasing you, and thanks for showing me who I've become."

"I heard the lodge was looking to tighten security. I guess they had a lot of thefts by thugs from Knoxville last year. Thanks for bailing me out. Take care."

"You too."

Noah went back to his meal. What a strange string of events.

Isaiah pulled up minutes later. Noah walked out to his truck. He would soon learn of the assault against his wife, daughter, pet, and home. Cassie followed these types of news events. While nothing could have prepared her for what had happened, she was well aware of the increased militarization of law enforcement and the disregard for individual rights.

Noah, on the other hand, would be completely taken off guard. He typically stayed pretty cool, but when his family was threatened, he could become quite violent.

CHAPTER 11

One day the angels came to present themselves before the LORD, and Satan also came with them. The LORD said to Satan, "Where have you come from?" Satan answered the LORD, "From roaming through the earth and going back and forth in it." Then the LORD said to Satan, "Have you considered my servant Job? There is no one on earth like him; he is blameless and upright, a man who fears God and shuns evil."

"Does Job fear God for nothing?" Satan replied. "Have you not put a hedge around him and his household and everything he has? You have blessed the work of his hands, so that his flocks and herds are spread throughout the land. But stretch out your hand and strike everything he has, and he will surely curse you to your face."

The LORD said to Satan, "Very well, then, everything he has is in your hands, but on the man himself do not lay a finger." Then Satan went out from the presence of the LORD.

Job 1:6-12

Noah closed the door of Isaiah's truck. "Thanks for picking me up."

"Anytime. I bet you're glad to be out of there," Isaiah said.

"Yeah, and that was the best Wendy's meal I've had in my life."

Isaiah kept his eyes on the road. "You made the local news."

"I saw. We had a television in the cell block."

"Did Cassie tell you I have a friend willing to represent you?"

Noah looked over at Isaiah. "She said something about someone you knew who was going to file for a bond reduction hearing, but that was it."

"Well, he's willing to fight this thing for you. Pro bono, too. I think he probably expects to get some serious exposure from the case, but it won't cost you anything. He's a Christian, so his heart really is in it. His name is Leo Cobb."

Noah's face lit up. "That's fantastic!"

Isaiah nodded his head. "But remember, Leo is also a shrewd business man. I would expect that he'll be pushing for maximum exposure."

"I really appreciate any help I can get. Our savings would get depleted pretty quickly if I had to hire a lawyer to fight this. I'll be happy to help him get exposure or add value in any way I can. I won't mind at all; in fact, I want people to know about my case. I had no idea what America had become until yesterday morning.

"Cassie has been talking about the loss of freedom and the police state for years now, but I have to admit, I only half listened. I never said it, but I thought she was overreacting. I guess I owe her an apology."

Isaiah smiled. "You know Cassie isn't the I-told-you-so type. She wants everyone to be aware so they can defend against the threats to our way of life."

They soon arrived at the school parking lot. Noah opened the door. "Thanks again for the ride. I don't know if we'll be at the study Thursday night or not. Can you give me Leo's number?"

Isaiah said, "I'm going to follow you back to your house. We'll call Leo together from there."

"Oh, okay." Noah didn't quite know what to make of that, but Isaiah had just picked him up from jail. He couldn't very well turn him down.

Noah started his truck and headed home with Isaiah close behind.

Cassie came out to greet him with a big hug when he pulled up to the house. "Noah, I'm so glad you're home."

He held her tight. "Me, too. Where is Lacy?"

Isaiah parked behind Noah, got out of his truck, and walked up to Noah and Cassie.

Cassie started to tear up again. "Child Services came by this morning with the police. They took Lacy."

"What? Why?" Noah shouted.

Cassie held Noah's arm tightly. "They said it was because you were charged with a felony against children."

Noah pulled away and headed into the house. He ran straight for the gun cabinet and saw that it was open and missing the weapons. He immediately headed toward the shed to dig up the pistol Cassie kept buried in the back. It had already been dug up. Cassie came around the side of the house with Isaiah close behind her.

Noah shouted in anger, "Where are the guns, Cassie?"

She stood a few feet back because he was so loud. "The police took my Kahr, the shotgun and the .22."

"Where's the Glock?" Noah demanded.

Cassie walked a little closer to him. "Noah, this is not the way to fight this battle. You'll get yourself killed."

"I'll take some of these criminals with me, too!"

Cassie tenderly took his hand. "What about Lacy? She'll be

left behind as a prisoner of the state."

Noah pulled his hand away. "You'll still be here. I can't let these crooks take my little girl and get away with it. I'm going to kill someone. Give me the pistol, Cassie!"

Cassie took both of Noah's hands and held them tighter. "I can't do this without you. Please, Noah."

Isaiah put his arm around Noah. "We're going to do this together. We're going to do this right. No one is getting away with anything."

Noah pulled away from Isaiah. "You knew about this and didn't tell me?"

Isaiah said, "For one thing, it wasn't my place to tell you; it was Cassie's. The other reason is that you had to drive your truck home. Look at you. You're shaking like a leaf with anger. You couldn't have driven home like this. What good would it have done for you to have known fifteen minutes ago?

"I called Sharon Beck on the way to pick you up. She is a certified foster parent. She's already working to get custody of Lacy. The crisis center where they first take the kids is filled to capacity, so she may have her by tonight. The best thing you can do is relax and trust God for a little while.

"I understand that you're angry. I'm mad, too. I can only imagine the rage inside of you right now. I'd be the same way if it was my child, but you have to let it go for now and trust God."

Noah clenched his jaw but said nothing.

Cassie said, "They shot Buster, also."

Noah groaned and bit his fist. He could not handle one more thing. He felt like Job, abandoned by God, given over to Satan to sift like wheat. Noah thought about how Job had fallen down to worship God in the midst of his trials. The best Noah could do was not to shake his fist at God for allowing this to happen.

Cassie prayed, "God, please take this rage from my husband's heart. Help us to trust you, Father. We don't know what to do. Thank you for Isaiah and the help that you are giving us through him. Give us peace and wisdom."

Noah sat down on the ground near the hole where Cassie had dug up the pistol. He began to bawl. He cried hard and loud. He wailed with a deep, soul-filled sorrow and violent anger as he had never before cried in his life.

Isaiah and Cassie knelt beside him and tried to comfort him.

Noah's crying eventually died down into soft sobs. Cassie held him tight. Isaiah went into the house and brought everyone a glass of ice water.

Cassie walked Noah out to Buster's grave. "He liked this spot."

Noah just nodded.

After a few minutes, they walked back to the house. Isaiah was in the living room talking quietly on the phone. Noah walked past him to Lacy's room and sat on her bed. He took her favorite bear and held it to his nose. He could smell Lacy on the stuffed animal. Cassie sat next to him and adjusted the other toy animals on the bed.

Isaiah walked in a few minutes later. "Sharon pulled some strings at the crisis center. She is getting custody of Lacy tonight or first thing in the morning. She also got an update on Lacy. She's safe, and she'll be okay."

Isaiah's phone rang. "Hello? Just a second. Noah, it's Leonard Cobb."

"Who?" Noah said.

"Leo Cobb, the lawyer. Do you feel like talking to him right now?"

Noah nodded.

Isaiah sat the phone on the dresser next to Lacy's bed. "Leo, you're on speaker. I'm here with Mr. and Mrs. Parker."

Cobb's voice came over the speaker. "Noah, I'm so sorry for your trouble. I filed a motion to dismiss. It is a shot in the dark, but we have to try. I'm going to be super honest with you. The way the law reads, you're guilty. The prosecutor will drag every kid from every class you've taught this year until they find one that says you mentioned creationism. Our best hope is to create a national media frenzy so that no one on the face of God's green earth could not know about it. Once we do that, we'll shame the jury into finding you not guilty."

Noah leaned forward toward the phone. "How will they do that if I'm guilty?"

"It's called jury nullification. This is still the Bible Belt, and

I'll make sure this trial stays right here in Sevier County," Cobb said.

Isaiah said, "Leo, DCS took custody of their daughter. Any chance you can help with that?"

"What happened?" Cobb said.

Cassie gave him an abbreviated account of the raid and abduction, as well as the killing of Buster.

Cobb said, "Did you get pictures?"

Cassie said, "Yes, and I made a video. I already posted it on YouTube."

Cobb said, "Good job, post it on every social media site you can think of, and start emailing the link to everyone you know. Ask them to send it to everyone they know. Send me a copy first, though."

Isaiah said, "Cassie works for the Mountain Press. She used to work for Channel Ten."

Cobb said, "Can you talk to the editor, maybe get him to let you write a piece on what happened? Do you still have contacts at Channel 10? The more public outrage we can stir up, the better."

Cassie said, "I'll do everything I can."

Leo Cobb said, "I know you will. And so will I. We're going to win this thing."

Everyone said their good-byes. Noah took a long, hot shower and plopped down on the couch.

Cassie did the same. They talked until late and prayed for Lacy.

Isaiah called Cassie's phone at 11:30 that night. "Sharon just got home with Lacy. She's making her some macaroni and cheese and putting her to bed."

Cassie said, "Thank you for everything, Isaiah."

With that, Noah was able to go to sleep.

CHAPTER 12

Education should aim at destroying free will, so that, after pupils have left school, they shall be incapable, throughout the rest of their lives, of thinking or acting otherwise than as their schoolmasters would have wished.

Bertrand Russell, *The Impact of Science on Society*

Thursday was Everett Carroll's first day back to a normal work schedule since the flash crash. He'd been running full steam ahead the past three days, so he slept an extra half hour. Everett wanted to make a quick appearance at the gym before work but didn't have time for his usual full workout. He jumped on the treadmill and watched CNBC while he ran. The reporter covered the early-morning market data.

"Gold and silver were hit hard overnight. Both metals have given up nearly all of the gains they made earlier this week when market fear caused prices to spike. Goldman Sachs has dropped their price forecast to $1,500 for gold.

This statement alone could send gold spiraling into a free fall.

"In other news, the BRICS Bank has been unable to bring their mainframe computer back online. This level of financial disruption is proving to be very hard for the less developed members to absorb. Brazil's Bovespa is down twenty-five percent, and India's Mumbai Sensex is down thirty-seven percent since Monday.

"The Johannesburg Stock Exchange saw losses approach fifty percent Tuesday afternoon. Regulators closed the trading floor early Tuesday, and it has not yet reopened. Several cities in South Africa have seen rioting over the past two days after shopkeepers closed their doors. Like the JSE, the South African rand is in free fall, and store owners fear they won't be able to restock their shelves using the collapsing currency.

"Russia and China, on the other hand, seem well poised to withstand the fallout. Each of those markets have fallen less than five percent since the failure of the system responsible for trade settlement among BRICS member nations.

"BRICS president Changlie Chau said in an interview yesterday that cyberespionage was the catalyst for the failure of the bank's system. He went on to say those responsible will have blood on their hands. More than sixty deaths have been accredited to the riots in South Africa. Brazil has enacted martial law and curfews to prevent similar disorder in São Paulo and Rio.

"If the BRICS nations are able to reorganize and roll out a

common currency, they will have to do some serious recalculations to account for the currency collapse in the South African rand and massive devaluations in the Indian rupee and the Brazilian real."

Everett shook his head. "I'm really helping to make the world a better place, aren't I?"

He finished his workout, showered, changed, and stopped by Starbucks. Everett could have hit the Dunkin' Donuts drive-through instead of Starbucks. That would have allowed him time for a full workout, but everyone has their priorities.

Once at work, Everett passed by John Jones's office. "Not here yet. He's been here early every day since Monday's flash crash."

Everett sat at his desk and logged in. He opened his inbox and read the memo. "Agent John Jones will be out for the day. Please report all concerns and forward all potential threats to Agent Tom Doe." *Doe. That sounds like another company-issued name*, he thought.

Everett's day passed without incident. Northrop Grumman took over the watchman protocols for the Bank of America system he was assigned to monitor, and Everett went home. He checked the prices of gold and silver on his phone while he walked toward the parking lot.

Ken caught up with him right after they cleared security. "What'cha looking at?"

"Nothing."

Ken peeked at Everett's screen. "You buying gold?"

"I don't know. I'm really just watching the price action. It's been all over the place in that past few days."

Ken smirked. "Pretty much exactly like the rest of the markets."

Everett stuck the phone in his pocket. "Yeah, you've got a point."

"I see your buddy didn't come in today," Ken said.

"What buddy?"

"Jones."

Everett became defensive. "He's not my buddy. Why would you say that?"

"Chillax! It was a joke."

"Sorry, I'm just a little edgy."

Ken slapped Everett on the shoulder. "We all are. This week has disrupted everyone's schedule."

Everett bade his friend farewell and got in his car. He stopped by the coin shop in Ashburn on the way home.

A peculiar old man with shaggy eyebrows and bushy gray hair stood behind the display case. "Can I help you?"

Everett peered through the case. "I don't know what I'm looking for. I was just thinking I'd like to buy some gold and silver. You know, just in case."

"Ah, bullion. Those are all numismatic coins. You'll pay a higher premium for those. Many of them are rare. Some are quite old. This case over to the right has modern bullion coins and bars."

Everett walked over to the other case. "Do you take credit cards?"

"There's a five percent surcharge on top of the price for Visa and MasterCard. We don't take Amex."

Everett pointed at the tube of one-ounce Silver American Eagles. "How much are these?"

"Twenty-five hundred for the tube. If you only want a few, they're one hundred thirty each."

Everett opened his wallet and looked at the five one-hundred-dollar bills. He pulled out three of them. "I'll take two of the one-ounce Silver American Eagles."

The man took Everett's money and presented him with the two coins in protective plastic sleeves along with his change.

Everett placed the coins in his pocket and the change in his wallet. "Thanks, I'll probably be back."

"See you soon," the old man said.

Everett went home to shower and change before going out to get something to eat. He rarely cooked. Most evenings he would grab some takeout, but he would also go out to eat by himself on occasions. He didn't mind being alone in a restaurant. He certainly preferred it to poor company.

As he was walking out the door, he heard a phone ringing. It wasn't his phone. "Where is that coming from?" He isolated the noise to the area around the couch. He looked in the cushions but found nothing. He knelt down and peered beneath the couch. "There it is." He pulled the phone out from under the sofa.

Everett looked at the inexpensive prepaid phone. "This looks like a burner. No way. This guy has been in my house? He certainly isn't retired."

Everett opened the message icon on the burner phone. A string of numbers appeared. "Looks like latitude and longitude. I'm not looking this up on my computer."

Everett proceeded out the door. Rather than going to the restaurant, he stopped by the storage shed to retrieve his tablet. He took it to the car, drove around the corner to a hotel where he could get Wi-Fi access from the parking lot, and typed in the latitude and longitude. Next, he mapped out the route. It was near the Virginia–West Virginia border. "Better get something to go. Looks like this is going to be a long night."

Everett kept his tablet with him as he sped off. He stopped by the upscale grocery in Ashburn and picked up some fried chicken, macaroni, mashed potatoes, and biscuits to take with him. It wasn't his first choice, but it was already cooked, and it was better than the fast-food options in Ashburn. For a normal driver, it would have been about an hour-and-a-half drive. Everett figured he could push it and be there in an hour. He ate one of the drumsticks as he drove, being careful not to get crumbs or grease on his seats. The engine in his BMW 550i was made for speed. It felt good to get on the road and open it up.

He exited the highway at Woodstock and drove out to a small country road called Wolf Gap Road. The road snaked around the foothills of the Appalachians then up into the mountains. Everett finally reached the coordinates and found a humble cabin.

He turned off the car and brought the food to the door.

Jones opened the door. "You found me."

Everett was taken aback by his appearance but tried not to show it. "I brought fried chicken. I hope you're hungry."

"That was very kind. I'm actually very hungry." Jones stopped to put the oxygen mask on his face and took a deep breath.

As Everett followed Jones into the cabin, he suddenly appreciated the ability to breathe a deep breath of air.

Jones rolled the oxygen tank over to a chair in the kitchen and sat down. "I couldn't breathe this morning when I was getting ready for work. I went to the hospital, and they gave me a shot of prednisolone. They also chained me to this contraption. I can't blame anyone but myself. It scared the heck out of me, though. I've always been ready to take a bullet, but you don't want to experience what it feels like to suffocate because you can't breathe."

Everett took the chicken to the small dining table. "Wow, that was all of a sudden, huh?"

Jones picked up a cup and spit tobacco in it. "Yeah, all of a sudden. There are some plates in that cupboard. The good news is that I quit smoking."

Everett took the plates and sat them on the table. "And started chewing?"

Jones snickered. "I won't be around long enough to get mouth or throat cancer. I don't want to spend my last days going through nicotine withdrawal."

Everett got himself a glass of water and sat down to eat.

Jones picked up a piece of the chicken then paused. "Do you mind if we pray?"

Everett was surprised. "Uh, sure, go ahead. I didn't know you were religious."

Jones bowed his head. "God, thank you for this food . . . I don't know what else to say. Amen."

Everett looked up and started eating his food.

Jones spooned some of the potatoes onto his plate. "I take it you don't believe in a higher being."

Everett shrugged. "I don't know. No."

Jones smiled. "I never counted myself a believer before. But being in my present condition has caused me to ponder what comes next. Some of the things I've run across working for the Company have also given me reason to reconsider."

Everett couldn't imagine what Jones could have found at the CIA to make him believe in God. "Like what?"

"Are you familiar with the Christian concept of the Rapture, Mr. Carroll?"

"Vaguely. Doesn't some radical sect of Christianity believe they're going to disappear?"

Jones finished chewing and wiped his mouth. "Oh, it's quite mainstream theology for Christians."

Everett fought back a chuckle. "That sounds crazy to me. I can't imagine anyone believing such a thing."

"I would have agreed with you 100 percent a couple of years ago. You have to realize though, for people who believe that God created everything in the known universe from nothing, what would they find impossible for such a God?"

"That sounds ludicrous as well."

"But, Mr. Carroll, your belief system, as an atheist, says the same thing happened, only without anything to set the chain of events into motion. Is that any less ludicrous?"

"Yes, but we know everything happened very slowly over billions of years."

Jones looked over at the wooden cuckoo clock on his kitchen wall. "If I tell you that the clock on my wall formed over millions of years, would you believe me?"

Everett glanced at the clock. "Of course not."

"Why?"

"Because it's obvious that it was made by a clockmaker."

"Have you seen the clockmaker? How can you be sure?"

Everett recalled a scientific argument from his recent

college days. "The second law of thermodynamics says that an isolated system will evolve to its maximum state of entropy. It is impossible for something to evolve into a more ordered state without outside influence. For a complex system like your clock, an outside influence had to fabricate it. "

"Impressive answer. Now why does that hold true for something as simple as a cuckoo clock, but not for a system as complex as the human body? The eye alone is a vastly more complex system than your computer tablet, yet you're willing to accept that it simply happened with no outside influence? How do you reconcile that notion with your second law of thermodynamics?"

Suddenly, Everett didn't feel so smart. "Well . . ."

"Complexity is evidence of design, Mr. Carroll. But I digress. Back to the main topic, one of the things I stumbled upon while working on Dragon was a propaganda campaign to craft a cover story for a mass disappearance. It was an active campaign that had been going on for decades and was being integrated into Dragon. The narrative is fostering a belief in extraterrestrial life forms through documentaries, news, entertainment, and other information channels. When the disappearance occurs, those remaining will be told by government leaders that the disappearance is a massive abduction by alien life forms. The people left on earth will be led to believe that they were chosen to take part in a new utopian experience led by extraterrestrial advisors."

Everett was sure that Agent Jones was losing his mind. He thought, *I'll humor him because he's dying, but the cancer is obviously clouding his reason.*

"I've made a career out of reading people, Mr. Carroll. I can't say that I blame your look of disbelief, but consider what I've been right about. The BRICS Bank withdrew their announcement of a new currency, and gold prices took a very steep dive this morning. And precious metals prices will continue to fall, just as I said."

Everett lifted his eyebrows. "You were right about that. I'm not saying I don't believe you, but it sounds very far-fetched that the CIA would be crafting a cover story for a mass disappearance based on a myth from the Bible. And aliens? That's really a tough sell."

Jones said, "Let's say you awoke to a massive disappearance tomorrow morning, and you switched on the news to find out what happened. One channel said it was an alien abduction, and the other said it was the Rapture. Who would you be most inclined to believe?"

Everett rolled his eyes. "For the sake of argument, I would be more likely to believe the alien story."

"That's because you've been conditioned through grade school, college, movies, television, and news media to accept evolution and thereby regard God as a fairy tale. On the other hand, regarding aliens, you've been conditioned by the same information channels to wonder if we are alone in the universe."

Everett was a bit put off at being told that he'd been manipulated. "I don't know that I was conditioned, Agent Jones."

"Please, call me John. I'm rather certain that my days serving as your supervisor are finished. At any rate, whether it is for the Rapture or some other event resulting in a mass disappearance, the Company is involved in crafting this cover story. It's a classic tactic for the CIA to get out in front of a story so they can control the narrative."

"So it's not necessarily the Rapture that they are planning for?" Everett said.

"No, there was nothing in the files that I read calling the event the Rapture. But the cover story seems to be configured for the dictionary definition of this event predicted by the Evangelical Christian Church."

"Is there a timeline for the disappearance?"

Jones paused to take a deep breath from his oxygen tank. "No, like I said, the cover story has been ready, as if it was awaiting an imminent event, for several decades."

Everett looked back at the cuckoo clock on the wall. "But this cover story, it's made you reconsider your belief in God?"

Jones nodded. "Among other factors. One of the reasons I always dismissed the existence of God was because of bad examples I've seen from so-called believers. Yet I work for an organization that infiltrates the ranks of our enemies, uses disinformation, and conducts character assassinations on a regular basis. If there is some type of otherworldly battle between good and evil, it would make sense that similar tactics would be employed."

Everett understood why Jones would be contemplating the afterlife in his current predicament, but Everett wanted to focus on tangible facts. "You were right about the metals prices. I stopped by the coin shop today on the way home. I bought two ounces of silver, just to look at it and familiarize myself with the process. I do believe what you said about the managed collapse. I respect your thoughts about God as well. I just need things I can see and touch."

"Very well, Mr. Carroll. About your silver and gold purchases, it was smart to dip your toe in the water, but wait a few days before you go all in. There will be a bigger drop in the prices. If you scout out some online dealers, you might find better prices."

Everett took the two coins out of his pocket. "Won't it be more anonymous if I pay with cash at a coin shop?"

Jones nodded. "Yes, but if you go over ten thousand dollars, the coin shop will have to fill out a form 8300 to send to the IRS. It was part of the Patriot Act. Same thing with the online dealers. They don't want to do any more paperwork than they have to. You'll likely have to mail in a paper check to the online dealers. It's traceable, but it sets off less alarms than a credit card transaction. How much do you have in cash?"

"Do you mean in the bank?"

"Liquid," Jones said.

"Maybe thirty thousand."

Jones shook his head. "On your salary? You should have

more than that."

Everett thought saving up thirty thousand dollars was quite an accomplishment. "I have a car lease, rent, food, clothes. All that stuff adds up."

"You should put all your savings into silver and gold. Do you own a good firearm?"

Everett put his hand up. "Wait, all of it? And no, I don't own a gun. I'm an analyst."

Jones had finished eating and got up to put his plate in the sink. "Well, put in whatever amount of wealth you want to survive the crash." Jones washed the plate, dried it, and stuck it back in the cupboard. "Everyone should own a gun, Mr. Carroll. The world is a dangerous place. Did you think any more about a place to lay low when it hits the fan?"

Everett was still digesting being told to put all of his cash into gold and silver. "No, I don't really have anywhere else to go. My parents are divorced and both live in DC with their new families. I didn't take too well to the blended family thing. Both of my stepparents are nice enough, but they both have kids of their own. It's just not me. My apartment building in Ashburn is really nice. We have a security gate with a guard, and I'm on the third floor."

Jones laughed. "That rent-a-cop and aluminum gate won't last ten minutes if society melts down, son. If things get tough, you come on up here. Even if I'm gone. The deed to this place is under an alias."

Jones opened the other side of the cupboard and jiggled

the shelf for a few seconds. The shelf acted as the handle for a false wall, which he pulled out. He stuck his hand inside and extracted an old metal coffee can. He opened it and retrieved a checkbook and a folded piece of paper. "Here is the deed and bank account I use to pay the taxes on this place. I have enough in here to cover taxes for about two years, but I doubt it will be worth anything after the crash. Here's a spare key. I probably have enough provisions in the loft for a year. You should bring some food up here for yourself while you can. I don't think I'll be around for another year, but I'd rather have too much than not enough."

Everett didn't know what to think. This man, whom he hardly knew, was showing him more concern and attention than his own father. "That's very generous of you."

Jones returned the coffee can to its hiding place. "Get yourself a couple hundred pounds of white rice, some peanut butter, canned vegetables, soups, and canned meats. And learn how to cook. It is a lot less detrimental if you burn a few meals now, than after it all comes crashing down."

Everett placed the key on his key chain. "Thank you, John."

"I'm going back down to my house in Fairfax. I'll be back and forth between there and here until it hits. Don't be shy; come on up whenever you want. And find yourself a wife. Don't be like me, married to the Company. She won't love you back."

Everett looked at the old wood floor. He knew Jones wouldn't want him to, but he couldn't help feel bad for the dying man. If John Jones was offering to share his cabin with

Everett, he was determined to be his friend for the little bit of life he had left, no matter how unpleasant the cancer would become.

Jones rolled his oxygen tank back into the living room, put some tobacco in his mouth, and sat down.

Everett followed him. "Should you have your oxygen tank near the open fire?"

Jones joked. "It's okay as long as I don't stick it in the fireplace."

Everett found a place to sit on the couch. "Where is your Freemason ring?"

Jones shook his head. "I'm done with the lot of them. No one from my lodge has even called since I was diagnosed. Not that I was ever a great friend to most of them. Just as well. I've wasted enough time on the occult."

"Occult? You make it sound like a cabal of Satan worshipers."

Jones sat back in his chair. "Well, that might not be too far from the truth. Occult is derived from the Latin *occultare*, which simply means secret. By definition, that places all secret societies in the category of occult. All of them have practices or traditions that I would consider darkly ritualistic, probably what you think of when you say satanic."

Everett looked at Jones's face, half lit by the light of the fire. It made the subject all the spookier. "Like what?"

"During initiation, members of Skull and Bones are buried

in coffins and resurrected into the order. It is almost an anti-baptism. The Bohemian Grove in California has a ritual they call the Cremation of Care. It mimics a human sacrifice being burned alive at the foot of a towering owl statue."

"Why an owl?"

Jones took a deep breath from the oxygen mask. "The owl has been a symbol of the dark arts for centuries. It's a carnivore, a stealth hunter."

Everett interrupted. "So is an eagle."

Jones nodded. "But the owl hunts at night, in secrecy. Its ability to see in the dark gives it an advantage over the creatures of the light. Darkness is symbolic for the hidden knowledge of the secret societies, which allows them to prey on those who are not privy to their confidential understanding. The owl is also a symbol of wisdom. That's where we get the saying 'wise as an owl.'"

"The *G* in the center of the Masonic compass and square stands for *gnosis*, the Greek word for 'knowledge.'"

Everett got up to put a log in the fire, which was burning low. "What's wrong with knowledge and wisdom?"

"Nothing, inherently, but the biblical account of the fall of man is based on Adam and Eve eating the forbidden fruit, which gave them the knowledge of good and evil. The Lucifereans see knowledge as something that they can shake in the face of God, especially when it can be used as a sort of forbidden fruit to lure people away from God. Genesis chapter three, verse twenty-two speaks of God's disappointment when Adam had become like a god because he had the knowledge of good and evil. While the Christians see this event as the fall of man, the Lucifereans see it as the ascent of man."

"Wow, you know the Bible pretty well for a recent convert."

Jones laughed. "Genesis chapter three, verse twenty-two is the source of the 322 on the bottom of the Skull and Bones seal. More than a few people in secret societies are familiar with that verse. Other than that one, I couldn't tell you too many Bible verses. I remember a few Bible stories that my grandmother tried to teach me when I was young. It's funny how many of those seemed to come back to me as I moved higher up in the Masons."

Everett looked at the time on his new burner phone. It was getting late, but he was intrigued by the stories. "And what about the Freemasons. Do they have any dark rituals?"

Jones paused for a moment. "We . . . I mean they have a reenactment of the murder of Hiram Abiff. According to the legend, Hiram was the lead architect in charge of building Solomon's temple. He was the only person who knew the Tetragrammaton, the name of God."

"Tetra what?"

"Tetragrammaton. When God gave his name to Moses, it was regarded as too holy to be written. The Jews dropped the vowels when writing the name of God and simply wrote the consonants, YHVW. That's why you'll often hear Christians or Jews refer to God as Jehovah or Yahweh. They're trying to fill in the blanks left by the vowels that were dropped when writing the name of God.

"Long story short, Hiram was attacked by those who wanted to know the name of God, which would have made them master masons. Being a master mason would have allowed them to earn more money. Hiram refused to tell them, and they murdered him. The true name of God was lost forever. And substitute words were incorporated for master masons."

"That doesn't sound so satanic."

Jones leaned forward. The light from the fire lit his aging face in a way that made Everett's arm hair stand up. Then Jones spoke. "Until a mason achieves the thirty-third degree. Then he learns that Hiram was resurrected by King Solomon, and the true name of God is . . . Lucifer."

Everett stared at Jones. "That sounds satanic. Even as an atheist, I find that frightening."

Jones said, "I always thought of it as a sort of folklore or allegorical, but most of the thirty-third-degree Masons believe in this as much as the most devout Christian or Jew believes in their God."

"And they believe Lucifer is god?"

"They do," Jones said. "They believe that the Creator wants to keep humanity ignorant, and that Lucifer, which means light bearer, wants humanity to embrace knowledge and wisdom."

"Seems like a common ideology throughout the secret

societies."

Jones nodded. "And they are the ones orchestrating the new global government. You can bet that once it is in place, they will do whatever they see as Lucifer's will. All of this was predicted in the Bible. The people at the very top are reading it like God's playbook. They're trying to take preventive steps to mitigate and control public perception of the events predicted in the Bible. You might not believe in the Bible, Mr. Carroll, but I can assure you that the Luciferians controlling the New World Order take it very seriously."

Everett took in everything he was being told. He believed that Jones was giving him honest information and that the man was still in control of his mind. While not yet ready to denounce his atheist beliefs, he was much less sure of them than he'd been only hours ago. "Thank you for the information, John."

"Thanks for listening. I wasted most of my life learning about all of this. A tidbit here, a morsel there. Now that the pieces of the puzzle are coming together, it's about time for me to cash in my chips. I hope you'll keep pursuing the truth. I see that same curiosity in your eyes that I held as a younger man."

Everett looked Agent Jones in the eye. "I will."

Jones picked up a Bible from the table beside his chair. "I also hope you'll dedicate some time to investigating what you believe about the existence of God. Now that I'm certain He exists, I have the great task of getting to know Him through this book before I come face-to-face with Him. I wish I'd started sooner."

Everett didn't know why, but this subject always made him uncomfortable. He could debate most anything with an open mind and loved to learn about other cultures, but when it came to the Bible, there was something that touched him inside. It was as if his very soul was being confronted. "Well, good luck with that. Thanks for everything. I need to get home. It's late."

Jones got up to walk Everett to the door. "Remember what I said. Bring some provisions up here, buy a gun, and get your ducks in a row so that you're ready to move when the gold and silver markets look like they're down by roughly forty percent. Never bring your regular phone up here, even with the battery out. You should take the GPS navigation out of your car also. If you don't know how, I'll show you."

"I already took it out. I was a computer science major in school, remember?"

Jones smiled. "I remember, but I don't know what they teach kids anymore. I know the entire education system is ninety percent propaganda. That doesn't leave much room for useful skills. You're a smart kid. You'll figure it out, and you'll get through. It won't be easy, so get yourself ready for it. This collapse is going to be worse than anything you can imagine."

Everett listened with his full attention. His paradigm was shifting at warp speed. "Okay, I feel like I should try to learn as much from you as possible. I know I'm going to have questions."

Jones nodded. "I'll teach you all I can. Keep that burner somewhere handy. Not in your house. Check it every day. I'll be in touch."

Everett waved good-bye as he opened his car door.

Jones waved back. "Thanks for the chicken."

"Please, it was the least I could do." Everett closed his door and drove away.

As he drove home, he started making a mental list of all the things he had to do. *The silver and gold, I think I can figure out. Groceries, that won't be a problem. It'll be easier than learning to cook. The gun, that's going to be the challenge. I need to buy something that will be off the record.*

CHAPTER 13

Two are better than one, because they have a good return for their work: If one falls down, his friend can help him up. But pity the man who falls and has no one to help him up!

Ecclesiastes 4:9

Noah anxiously prepared to leave for Bible study. Sharon would be bringing Lacy. It would be the first time he or Cassandra had seen her in two days.

Noah brought Lacy's favorite bear. "Stick this in the bag you're taking to Sharon."

"I can't believe I forgot to pack her bear." Cassie took the bear from Noah and placed it in the bag.

Noah grabbed his jacket and opened the door. "I hope it doesn't upset Lacy to see us and not be able to come home."

Cassie walked out the door to the car. "She'll just have to adjust. We're doing everything we can to get her back."

Noah locked the front door and got in the car. "I guess it could be worse. Thank God that Sharon was able to get custody of her."

During the drive to Isaiah's, Cassie said, "I think we should buy another shotgun and a rifle."

Noah shook his head. "We need to really watch our money."

"We still have our savings and the money from the stocks we sold. I spoke with Carl at the paper. They'll give me as much work as I want. When they don't need me for writing or editing, I can work in ad sales. We'll be fine with money. Something will come up for you. In the meantime, you can homeschool Lacy."

Noah glanced over at Cassie. "Why do we need a shotgun and a rifle?"

"They took us off guard this time, but I'm not going to sit idly by and let something like this happen again."

Noah turned onto Isaiah's road. "I may have a felony conviction in a month from now."

"Then we'll stash a gun or two in the yard like before. That's the only reason we have a gun now. The federal government is tightening the noose on our freedoms more and more. I know I've been harping on this for years, but I really feel like things are about to come to a head. I don't want to be unarmed when it all goes down."

Noah nodded. "And you were just proven right. I'm sorry if I was dismissive all the times you tried to talk to me about the tyrannical police state. But I'm with you now. If something happens, you're right, we should have the ability to fight back."

"Great, so we can get a battle rifle?"

Noah opened his eyes wide. "A battle rifle? Are we going to fight the Army?"

"I don't know who we're going to fight, Noah. But I'd like to be ready. The way things are going, AR-15s and AK-47s will be banned soon. I think we should get one while we still can."

Noah pulled into Isaiah's driveway. "I'm going to start trusting your instinct, Cassie. Over the years, I've watched the things you've talked about come true. I'm the cautious type. God made me that way. Be patient with me, but I'm on board. Yes, you can get a battle rifle."

"Awesome, I'll pick it up tomorrow."

"You already have one picked out?"

Cassie got out of the car and grabbed the bag she'd put together for Lacy. "Come on, Lacy's waiting."

Noah smiled. He'd been set up and had fallen right into Cassie's trap, but he didn't care. He loved her deeply and all the more so since this nightmare had begun. If he had to walk through the valley, he was glad he could go through it with her.

Noah got out and walked hand in hand with Cassie to the front door.

Isaiah opened the door and let them in. "Lacy's in the kitchen."

Noah patted Isaiah on the shoulder. "Thanks."

Once in the kitchen, Noah grabbed Lacy and hugged her tightly. "Daddy missed you so much."

Lacy gripped him fast. "I was afraid the police killed you. Did the police shoot Sox?"

"No, honey, the police didn't kill Sox," Noah said.

"I brought your bear." Cassandra handed the stuffed animal to Lacy.

Sharon walked into the room. "I told you mommy and daddy were alright."

Cassie handed the bag of clothes to Sharon. "Thank you for taking care of our little girl. You don't know how much this means to us."

Sharon hugged Cassie. "It's no trouble at all."

Noah pulled Sharon to the side. "Her eyes look glassy. Is she okay?"

Sharon sighed. "The crisis center put her on medication for PTSD. They love doping kids up. I've been through this before with other kids. They prescribed her Zoloft and Klonopin. She slept most of the day yesterday. I'm giving her children's chewable aspirin so when the social worker asks her if she's taking her medication, she'll say yes. Isaiah said that we're welcome to meet up over here as often as we like. I was thinking, you'll see her every Sunday at church and Thursdays for Bible study. Would you and Cassie like to come by here on Mondays and Fridays?"

Noah said, "That would be fantastic. Thank you."

Sharon poured herself a glass of water. "Becky is keeping her on Saturday nights when I go to the restaurant. She said you'd be welcome to come over there as well. I'm so sorry about all of this, but we'll do everything we can to help out."

Noah took Sharon's hand. "We really appreciate everything you're doing."

Noah and Cassie sat and talked with Lacy for the first hour, while the others held Bible study.

Lynette Ray came in the kitchen with a neatly wrapped gift and presented it to Lacy, who was sitting in Noah's lap. "Mom and Dad said I should let you all be alone for a little while, but I wanted to bring this to Lacy to make her feel better. We pray for your family every night."

Lacy took the gift and opened it. "A baby doll! Thank you, Lynette."

Noah patted her on the head. "That's very sweet. You two can play for a while. Cassie and I are going in the living room with the others. Lacy is coming to your house on Saturday."

Lacy's eyes lit up. "I am?"

Noah put her down from his lap. "Yes, and Mom and I

are coming over to visit."

"That will be fun!" Lynette said.

Noah and Cassie joined the adults in the living room and left the two girls alone to play.

Isaiah stood up. "Come on in; you didn't miss much. It's hard to stay on topic when everyone's hearts are preoccupied with your ordeal. I'll leave it up to you whether you feel like discussing the subject or not, but we're all concerned and want to know how we can help."

Noah found two seats next to the Taylors and motioned for Cassie to sit next to him. "We can talk about it. First, I'd like to say thank you so much for all the prayer and support you folks have given us. Especially the Rays, Sharon, and you, Isaiah. We'd be in a lot worse shape if it wasn't for you folks."

Isaiah said, "What else can we do to help?"

Cassie jumped in. "I emailed a video link to everyone in our small group. Did you all get it?"

Everyone in the room acknowledged receiving the email.

Cassie stood up. "We need you to share that video with everyone in your email list. Ask them to share with everyone they know. I spoke with my editor at the Mountain Press, and he is pretty much giving me carte blanche on writing about our experience as long as I provide in-depth coverage of Noah's trial. I contacted my old boss at Channel 10 in Knoxville, and they came out this morning to interview Noah about the trial. As soon as the other local stations heard about that, they started calling. Fox News wants to do a Skype interview tomorrow. That will be the big one. From there, it will depend on whether or not CNN and MSNBC pick up the story. If they don't, it will just be a blurb on Fox and die out after a day or two. If anyone has time to reach out to alternative media sites, that's our best bet. They're small, but there are literally thousands of them. More and more people are starting to go to alternative media for the real news, especially folks in the Liberty movement."

There was a knock at the door, and Cassie sat back down to grab her purse.

Noah figured she was thinking exactly what he was thinking. *Could it be the Department of Child Services? Had they followed Sharon to see if she was bringing Lacy to see them?* He looked over at Cassie's hand, which was in her purse, resting on the handle of the Glock. A pang of guilt shot over Noah as he realized his wife was stepping into the void he had left as the protector of his family. If he lived through the next five minutes, he vowed to step up and provide for his family's safety and security. He recalled first Timothy five, verse 8.: "*If anyone does not provide for his relatives, and especially for his immediate family, he has denied the faith and is worse than an unbeliever.*"

Noah looked over at David Ray who had stuck his hand behind his back. *Is he going for a gun? This is really shameful,* he thought, *everyone is doing my job but me.*

Isaiah looked through the peephole before opening the door. "It's Pastor Mike."

Noah sighed and gave Cassie a look that begged for forgiveness.

Cassie smiled back and grabbed Noah's hand.

Pastor Mike Barnes walked in the door, followed by his wife, Lynn. They were both carrying a dish. "I'm sorry we're late, but I had a meeting this evening. I brought one of Mrs. Barnes's blackberry cobblers, as well as her famous cherry dump cake. I just know you'll forgive our tardiness as soon as you take a bite. Jim Taylor forwarded a video link to me yesterday, and I just had to come by to express my sincere condolences and pledge the support of the church to the Parkers."

Isaiah and Sharon got up to take the dishes to the kitchen so that the pastor's hands would be free.

Pastor Mike sat next to Cassie. "We're going to announce what happened to you at church at the end of the service Sunday. I'm going to give a ten second warning that what I'm about to show is graphic, then we're going to show your video of the crime scene on the big screen, if that's okay with you. What you said in the video about pastors who didn't want to be involved in politics shot straight to my heart. I'm not sitting on the sidelines anymore."

Cassie said, "Of course it's okay if you show the video. Thank you very much!"

Pastor Mike continued, "The video is going to stir up a lot of emotion. We need to make a call to action right after. I was thinking about starting a petition and organizing a protest on the courthouse steps. Do you have any thoughts on that?"

Cassie took Noah's hand. "That would be wonderful."

Pastor Mike said, "I'm good friends with George McConnell. His talk show is nationally syndicated on Christian radio. He said he'd love to have you two come on the show to talk about what's now being called the Parker Monkey Trial and your home invasion. And Noah, you've always tithed to Faith Church. Now it's our turn to help you in your time of need. I want to help you out with a stipend, so you can focus on your case until it's over, and you can get back to work."

Noah shook his head. "I can't do that, Pastor."

Pastor Mike's voice turned serious. "Noah, Faith Church supports missionaries and has several different ministries that try to fulfill our mission. I can't think of a more important ministry right now than for you to win this case. If you lose, we all lose. This isn't just about you; this is about freedom. It's about the First Amendment. If you lose this case, a precedent has been set for every Christian in America to be told to sit down and shut up. Are you refusing to accept this calling that God has so clearly placed on your life?"

Noah hadn't expected such a scolding. "I accept the calling Pastor, but . . ."

Pastor Mike cut him off. "But what? First Timothy five, verse eighteen says, 'a worker is worth his wages'. Do you know more than the inerrant Word of God, Noah?"

Noah sat quietly for a moment. He'd been put in his place. He thought about how Pastor Mike had just quoted a verse from the same chapter of the Bible he'd thought about not five minutes ago. *Maybe that was confirmation.*

Pastor Mike looked at Cassie. "The head of our new Defenders of the Faith ministry is going to need an assistant. Do you need a sermonette?"

Cassie put her hands up. "No, sir. I surrender."

Pastor Mike stood up. "Good, let's get some pie."

Benny Loomis came up to Noah on the way to the kitchen. "Congratulations."

Noah shook his hand. "Thank you, Benny."

Noah said to Pastor Mike, "If Benny needs help with any projects around the church, I'll be happy to help out. I'm fairly handy."

Pastor Mike looked at Noah. "You're pushing it, but I'll keep that in mind. Thank you."

Lynn Barnes came up to Noah and Cassie in the kitchen. "I hope Mike isn't being too aggressive. He's very passionate about what you two have been through. Let me know if he's too overwhelming, and I'll have a chat with him."

Noah said, "Not at all, Mrs. Barnes. And this cherry dump cake is fantastic."

Cassie said, "We need all the exposure we can get. Trust me; it's not too much. This type of thing happens all the time. The news covers it, and people go back to sleep. If you remember the Justina Pelletier case, it took her family sixteen months to regain custody of her after she was abducted by the Massachusetts Department of Children and Families. One doctor said that she was misdiagnosed by another doctor and accused her parents of medical child abuse because of that. Then there was the California couple, the Nikolayevs, whose child was abducted at gunpoint by the police and Child Protective Services because the parents wanted to get a second opinion before they admitted their baby, Sammy, into surgery.

"Both of those cases got national media attention, but nothing changed.

"If you search YouTube for 'dog shot by police', you'll get over 204,000 results, but the police state has continued to grow. Even after the public outcry several years ago from the flash bang grenade that almost killed a Georgia toddler, nothing was done about the militarization of the police. The baby's family, the Phonesavahns, incurred roughly $800,000 in medical bills, and Habersham County refused to lift a finger to help the toddler, even though no drugs or weapons were found in the raid.

"The list of tragedies is too long to recite. Seven-year-old Aiyana Jones of Detroit was killed in a police raid. John Adams, from right here in Tennessee, was killed by police who raided the wrong house. None of their murderers were ever convicted. That's why it keeps happening. If some folks start getting prison time for manslaughter, things will change. But the trend is certainly moving in the wrong direction."

Lynn pulled Cassie close. "We're all with you on this one. Maybe we can make a difference."

Cassie hugged the pastor's wife. "We'll tell our story to everyone who'll listen."

Henry Whitaker motioned for Noah to follow him out to the porch.

Noah kissed Cassie on the cheek. "I'll be right back."

He walked outside where it was only him and Henry.

Henry leaned over the railing of the porch. "I bet you're livid about all of this."

Noah stood nearby. "It's been a rough couple of days."

Henry glanced at Noah. "If you want to hit these guys hard, let me know. I'm in."

"Thanks. We can use all the help we can get. If we can get enough people together, I'd like to start protesting on Monday. I'll need people for mornings and afternoons. I think it would be good if everyone could commit to specific time slots so we can keep the momentum going. Can you come down to the courthouse Monday morning?"

Henry shook his head. "That's not what I'm talking about. I know some guys with great technical skills, IEDs, that sort of thing."

Noah stepped back. "We've got a lot of support to do things the right way. I'll admit that I was furious, but like Pastor Mike just said, this is bigger than my case. It's about our freedom of speech and freedom from religious persecution."

Henry turned and looked at Noah. "You're dealing with violent people, and the only thing they understand is violence. Cassie hit the nail on the head in her video. They locked you up, murdered your dog, and abducted your daughter. They owe you a pound of flesh."

Noah said, "Thanks, but I have to try the high road."

Benny Loomis walked out and joined them on the porch.

Henry looked at Benny then back at Noah. He turned to go back in the house. "My offer is always open."

Benny leaned against the rail. "What did he want?"

Noah rarely heard Benny talk. He thought it was curious that he'd come outside to speak with him. Of course, everyone was offering support in their own way. "He had some ideas on how to help out."

"I don't trust him."

"Oh?" Noah said.

"He just started coming around all of a sudden. He shows very little attention in the actual Bible studies. I'd be very careful around him if I was you."

Noah was very surprised to hear Benny talking like that. "Is it just a hunch, or do you know something specific?"

Benny said, "He reminds me of some folks I used to work with. Bad people."

"Before you worked at the church?"

"Yes."

"Where did you used to work?"

Benny turned to go back in the house. "I went through something similar to what you're going through. We'll sit down and talk when we have a little more time."

Noah was getting to know a different side to some of the people in the Bible study.

CHAPTER 14

An ounce of prevention is worth a pound of cure.

Benjamin Franklin

Everett went to his storage locker Saturday morning. He turned on his new burner phone to see if there were any messages. There was nothing. He took the burner and his tablet and headed to Dunkin' Donuts. Everett bought a large coffee, powered up his tablet, and sat down to work.

Everett navigated to Armslist.com and selected Virginia. Rather than select a specific category of firearms, he scrolled down the page to see what was available.

Armslist.com was an online source for firearm classified ads. They featured private sales, which required no formal filing of paperwork in most states.

He found several nice-looking handguns but wasn't well versed in which ones were high quality and which ones weren't. He'd been given only an abbreviated introduction to firearms during his orientation with the CIA. Since he was an analyst, very little time was spent on weapons training.

"This looks familiar. I think one of the trainers at orientation had something like this. Kimber Eclipse Pro 2, $1,200. Only eight rounds in the magazine."

Everett continued perusing the ads. "This looks a little more like a good middle-of-the-road pistol. I don't need a Cadillac, but I don't want a piece of junk either." He read the ad to himself, just below a whisper. "Sig Sauer P229 .40 caliber. It comes with two 12 round magazines. That's more like it. And it's almost half the price, $625. But it's all the way in Stafford. I wanted to take some food to the cabin. Looks like I'm taking a road trip today."

Stafford was sixty miles south of Everett's apartment. The cabin was one hundred miles west of Stafford, and then he still had seventy-five miles to get back home. Even with Everett's heavy-footed driving, he was looking at three hours total drive time.

Everett called the seller from his burner phone and arranged a time to pick up the pistol.

The man answered. "Hello?"

"I'm calling about the Sig. I'll take it."

"I'm running a couple of errands right now. I should be home in two hours."

"I can be there in two hours," Everett said.

"Do you have a concealed carry license?"

"No, but I have my law enforcement ID; will that work?" Everett didn't flash his agency ID too often, but he understood its value.

"That'll work. I'll text you the address," the man said.

His first stop was the bank. Everett asked to withdraw $9,000. He was told that $5,000 was the maximum.

"Why is that?" he asked.

The teller said, "It's our policy. We don't keep that much money on hand. If you want to make a larger withdrawal, you have to fill out a request form and schedule ahead of time. It's for your security."

Everett shook his head. "Thanks for looking out for me."

The teller just smiled.

Everett filled out a new withdrawal slip and handed it to the teller, who gave him the money.

Next he headed to the grocery. He threw several bags of dried beans and white rice in the cart, followed by lots of pasta and canned pasta sauce. He also loaded up on peanut butter, crackers, and cookies. Noting that his cart was now full, Everett checked out and placed the contents in the back of his car. Before he left Ashburn, he returned to the coin shop.

The old man greeted him as he walked in the door. "You came back fast."

"I heard there was a sale."

The old man laughed. "You might say that. Silver lost another twenty percent by the time the market closed yesterday. Premiums are down, too."

"How does that work? The premiums, I mean," Everett asked.

The old man walked over to the case with the modern coins where Everett was standing. "The mints charge a premium over the spot price of the metal. Might be five, ten, or twenty percent. It depends on demand. On top of that, when the market starts making wild swings, the secondary buyers and sellers assess their own premium or discount. If the price is shooting up, lots of buyers chase the market higher, and the secondary market will tack on an extra five or ten percent. When it starts tumbling, people generally run for the exits, and they want out, even if they have to take a bigger hit because there are no buyers. That's when I buy."

Everett looked at the selection of silver and gold coins in the case. "So you're buying now?"

"Are you here to sell those two coins back already?"

Everett chuckled. "No, I'm actually looking to buy a few more."

"Good time to buy. Tubes of the Eagles are only $1,920 today."

"Wow! That's a big drop from Thursday."

The man took a tube of the Eagles out and handed it to

Everett. "The combined drop in the metal price and the premium really adds up."

Everett inspected the tube of twenty Silver American Eagles. "How much are the gold coins?"

The man took out a tray of the coins. "The one-ounce Gold American Eagles are $2,740. A little less for a Gold Canadian Maple Leaf."

Everett picked up the half-ounce Gold Eagle. "And these are half of that?"

"No, the smaller denominations have a higher premium. That's $1,450."

Everett tried to quickly calculate the increase in the premium. "A little over twenty percent premium. What's the premium on the quarter-ounce Eagles?"

"Roughly twenty-five percent. They're $750."

Everett pulled a stack of hundreds out of his pocket. "I'll take one of the quarter-ounce Gold Eagles and a tube of Silver Eagles."

The man slid the coins toward Everett and placed the others back in the case. "$2,670. Looks like you still have a lot of paper in your hand. Are you sure I can't get you anything else?"

Everett counted out the money. "I'm sure. I'll be back, but it looks like the price might keep falling. I want to keep a little powder dry."

Everett stuck the coins and change in his pocket, returned

to his car, and headed to Stafford.

An hour later, he arrived. It was a nice house in a good neighborhood, so he felt less nervous about the transaction.

The man walked outside to meet him. "Nice car."

Everett figured the seller must have been relieved to see that he wasn't some junkie. "Thanks."

"What branch of law enforcement pays well enough to afford that?"

Everett knew he'd have to have this conversation sooner or later, so he took out his CIA credentials and handed them to the man.

The man took his ID. "Oh! That one!"

Everett followed the man into the house. The pistol was sitting on the kitchen counter. "Looks brand new."

"I take care of my guns. Here's the sales form for you to fill out. I filled out the seller's info. I'll photocopy it so you can have a copy for your records."

Everett filled out the form and handed it back.

The man took the form and turned to go copy it. "I've got a Remington 870 if you're looking for a shotgun."

"How much?"

"$350. I put a tactical stock on it and a nice sling. I'll throw in two boxes of shells."

Everett considered the fact that he was still under $1,000

for both guns. "Okay. Do you have any ammo for the Sig?"

"I'll give you a box of fifty full metal jackets and twenty-five rounds of hollow point if you take both guns at the price I'm asking."

It hadn't occurred to Everett that he could have negotiated the price lower. No matter, it seemed like an honest deal. He counted out the money. "Wrap it up."

The man returned with the shotgun, ammo, and sales form. He added the serial number of the shotgun to both copies of the form and handed one to Everett. "Nice doing business with you."

"You too, take care." Everett collected his new purchases and headed to his car.

Everett sped down the road toward the cabin. Once he arrived, he knocked to see if Jones was there. No answer, so he let himself in.

He found the ladder that led up to the loft and headed up to scope it out before trying to lug his supplies up. "Wow, look at that."

Jones had several shelves filled with assorted canned goods, MREs, and dry foods. There was also a large black safe. "I wonder what he's got in there."

Everett went back to the car and started hauling his groceries inside and up the ladder. He was in great condition, but by the third load, he started feeling the strain of lugging the heavier food items up the ladder. "I wonder how he got that safe up here. I guess, being a Mason, he probably knows the secret method the Egyptians used to build the pyramids."

Once the supplies were unloaded, Everett walked around and looked over the property. The leaves were changing colors, and the smell of fall was in the air. He breathed in the serenity and remembered what Jones had said about complexity being evidence of a designer. Everett looked at one of the orange leaves on the ground. He picked it up. He looked at the individual veins and considered how they all worked together with the branches and roots of the tree to form a complex system. Then he thought about the way the fall colors looked like a painting. "Maybe it is silly to think this all just happened by itself. I don't know."

Everett decided today was not the day to think about such things. He got in the car and headed home.

He arrived back in Ashburn in record time. Everett stopped by the storage locker and returned the tablet and burner. He also left the shotgun and ammo in the locker. *I'll keep the pistol at the apartment,* he thought. *It might be nice to have around. The gold and silver, I'll keep those at home too, but I need to find a better way of securing them besides my sock drawer.*

Once he arrived home, he checked his phone, which he had purposely left on the charger by his bed. "Three texts from Ken. 'Are we still on? Where are you? Don't leave me hanging.'"

Everett snickered as he dialed the phone. "Serves him right for pushing this on me."

Ken was loud. "Bro! Where you been? I've been texting you all morning!"

Everett turned the volume down on his phone. "I'm here. Chill out. I've got like two hours."

"Yeah, but it'll take you an hour to get downtown."

Everett looked up at the ceiling and sighed. "Downtown?"

"Yeah, I got reservations for Groove. It's that new place on H Street."

Everett shook his head. "I thought we were doing something around here. I don't want to drive into DC. That place is a war zone. Parking, traffic – what are you doing to me?"

"Give me one shot, bro. Trust me, you're going to like Courtney."

"One shot." Everett made sort of a growling noise to show his displeasure as he hung up.

He jumped in the shower, shaved, and put on his nicest clothes . . . just in case.

He was ready on time, but had to have a quick look at his new pistol before he left. He loaded the magazines and practiced working the slide to load and unload the chamber. Then he looked around the house for a good place to stash the gold and silver. He decided to hide them in the freezer. He opened one of his frozen dinners, took out the plastic pouch inside, and placed the silver and gold in the box. He super-glued it closed and stuck the box back in the freezer. "Not exactly the right weight for a frozen meatloaf dinner, but it will have to do for now." He checked the time on his phone. "Great, now I'm late."

Everett ran to his car and headed downtown. When he arrived, there were no parking spaces. He finally found a garage four blocks away. He checked the time. "I'm twenty minutes late." He decided against running to the restaurant, as he didn't want to show up sweating.

He arrived at the hostess desk. "I'm with the Gordon party."

The hostess smiled. "Oh yeah, they're waiting for you."

Once at the table, Everett greeted Ken and his girlfriend, Lisa.

Ken introduced Everett to Courtney.

Everett was surprised. She really was beautiful. She wore stylish glasses and had long blonde hair and an hourglass figure.

"Nice of you to join us," Courtney said.

He suddenly wished he'd made more of an effort to be on time. Rather than apologize, he went for the joke. "Ken's been trying to find someone to cook for me."

Courtney peered over the top of her glasses, leaning in toward Everett. "Are you sure you want to open with that one?"

Everett repositioned himself. He'd already lost his tactical advantage. He'd have to start over and regain lost ground. This was bad, but he'd come back from worse situations. He took her hand. "Hi, I'm Everett Carroll."

"Pleased to meet you, Mr. Carroll. I'm Courtney Hayes."

Everett kissed her hand and sat down.

Courtney cracked her first smile. He thought he might have seen her blush, but he kept his head in the game.

Appetizers arrived, and Ken said, "We ordered some starters. I knew you'd be here soon."

"Great," Everett said.

The server asked, "Can I take everyone's order?"

The others started ordering, and Everett looked at the menu to make a quick selection. By the time the server got to him, he was ready. "I'll take the lobster ravioli."

The server collected the menus and Everett took a few appetizers.

Everett looked at Courtney. He still couldn't believe how pretty she was. "What area do you live in?"

"South Laurel."

Everett took a drink of his water. "In Maryland. You're on the other side of DC. Isn't that near Fort Meade?"

"It's near Laurel."

Everett knew exactly where it was. It was minutes away from NSA headquarters in Fort Meade. Her attempt to redirect him was as good as confirmation. "Ken tells me you work for H and M. That's a cyber-security firm, isn't it?"

"Yes."

"You know, the government has a big cyber-security

facility over that way."

Courtney lowered her eyebrows and tilted her head. "Oh, really?"

Everett remembered the files that Jones had forwarded to H and M. "Yeah, it's all top secret. That's probably why you haven't heard of it." Of course, the NSA headquarters in Fort Meade wasn't secret at all.

Courtney stirred her drink with her straw and took a sip. "That's probably why."

The main courses arrived and they continued talking. They talked about where they had gone to school, family life, hobbies, and interests. Courtney was really into the outdoors, while Everett was into movies. It wasn't a perfect match, but they found common ground in exercise. As the night moved on, Everett could see that Courtney was letting her guard down.

Courtney and Lisa excused themselves to go to the ladies room.

Ken moved over to sit next to Everett. "What do you think? Was I right?"

Everett fought to hold back his smile. "You were right."

"Nice recovery, bro. I thought you blew it in the first thirty seconds. Looks like she's coming around."

"Yeah, I've got to try to completely redeem myself somehow. I'll order dessert. What does Lisa like?" Everett asked.

"Anything chocolate."

Everett motioned for the server to come over. "What are your best desserts?"

The server replied, "We have an incredible crème brûlée, chocolate ice cream cake, and a cherry cheesecake."

"We'll take one of everything," Everett said.

The girls returned, and Everett informed them of the dessert selection.

"That's very sweet, but I can't have dairy," Courtney said.

Everett's face dropped. "Would you like a coffee?"

"No thanks."

The desserts came, and Everett served a small portion of each one to everyone except Courtney. He felt like a complete loser. *Why didn't I wait and ask? Now she has to watch everyone else eat while she has nothing.*

Courtney stuck her spoon onto Everett's plate and took a huge bite of his ice cream cake. "I suspected that you might work for the intelligence community since you work in an office park out past Langley, but I guess I was wrong."

Everett was stuck. "Why is that?"

Courtney took a bite of his cheesecake. "You obviously can't read a bluff. There's no way the Company would ever hire someone like you."

No one called it the Company except people who worked

in the intelligence community. Everett had met his match. She could take a joke, and she could dish it out.

Everett grabbed the check when it came and paid the server. He took out his phone and said to Courtney, "Can I have your number?"

"Why?" Courtney asked.

He couldn't believe how hard she was making this. She evidently knew he was hooked. "In case something happens to Ken and Lisa. I'd like to have an emergency contact."

"Good answer." She proceeded to give him her number. "Can you cook?"

Everett was caught off guard. "What?"

"Lisa said she was going to find someone to cook for me. You better know how to cook." Courtney grabbed her purse, said goodnight to Ken and Lisa, kissed Everett on the mouth, and walked away.

Everett sat like a deer in the headlights.

CHAPTER 15

He said to them, "But now if you have a purse, take it, and also a bag; and if you don't have a sword, sell your cloak and buy one."

Luke 22:36

Noah was typing the sign-up sheet for next week's protests when Cassie came home Saturday morning.

"I'm home."

"Okay, I'm upstairs in the office," Noah yelled.

He finished the sign-up sheet and started drafting a petition to have the Sevier County Sheriff removed from office. He'd spent most of Friday morning calling and complaining to the sheriff's office about the way Buster was shot and trying to get custody of his daughter. He had also tried to find out about getting their firearms and laptop returned. He was stonewalled at every turn. As for his daughter, Noah was told it would require a court order from a judge to get her back. Leo was working on that.

Regarding Buster, he was told shooting the animal was standard practice; an officer could shoot any time he or she felt threatened by a barking dog. He was told he could not retrieve his firearms until he was cleared of the felony charges against him, and about the computer, it was evidence in the custody case.

Noah's interview aired on Fox News as well as Channel 10. The other local stations had vowed to cover the protests at the county courthouse. Noah was ready to fight to get his life back.

His phone rang. "Hello?"

"Mr. Parker?"

"Yes?"

"I'm George McConnell. I do a radio show called *Faith and Freedom*. Mike Barnes gave me your contact information."

"Yes, George. Pastor Mike told me to expect your call. My wife and I love your show."

"That's fantastic. I wanted to know if tomorrow would be a good time to record an interview with you and your wife. I saw your story on Fox. You did a great job. It's terrible what's happening to you."

Noah said, "We'll probably go out to eat after church tomorrow. As you know, we lost custody of our daughter over this. We only get to see her at church and social functions. The lady who is keeping her is meeting us for lunch so we can see Lacy. It might be five or so by the time we get home."

"I totally understand, Noah. How would six be for an interview?"

"That would be fine. Is it audio only? And should I call in?"

George said, "I'll call you on Skype if you'll give me your screen name. And yes, it's audio only."

"My Skype screen name is parker.monkey.trial."

"That's a good one!" George McConnell said.

"My wife came up with it. She built a website for us, ParkerMonkeyTrial.com. It's what the media has labeled the trial, and the name makes it easy for folks to find the site, so they can see the videos and stay up-to-date with the trial."

"Are you offering sponsorship banners?"

"No, our attorney is representing us for free, and our church is helping out with our day-to-day expenses, so we're pretty well covered."

"But there's a lot of value for people who want to advertise on your site. With all of the media attention you're getting, you'll probably get tons of views on that site. I'd give you $500 to place a banner that advertises the *Faith and Freedom* show on your site."

"That's very generous. Email my wife, Cassie@ParkerMonkeyTrial.com. She handles all of that."

"Great, I look forward to speaking with you tomorrow, Noah."

"Talk to you then." Noah hung up and started to call Cassie to tell her the news when the phone rang again.

"Hello?"

"Noah, it's Leo. We have your emergency custody hearing set for next Tuesday. Judge Malone is handling it. He's a solid conservative. Nothing is ever guaranteed, but I'm sure he'll throw this nonsense out."

"Do you know which judge is assigned to my criminal case?"

"Harriet Flynn. Not really who I'd have picked if it was up to me. Of course, I don't get to pick judges. I'd say the chance of her granting a dismissal is almost nil. For the case, though, it won't matter. We'll get a jury from around here, and we'll beat this thing."

"Thanks, Leo. I appreciate all you're doing for us. Hey, I have an interview on the *Faith and Freedom* show tomorrow. You're welcome to sit in if you want."

"Great, what time?"

"Six."

"I'll be at your house around 5:45."

"See you then. Thanks again." Noah hung up and ran downstairs to fill Cassie in on the latest developments.

Noah didn't see her in the house and went outside to look

for her. "Cassie!"

"I'm in the shed."

Noah walked over to the shed and found Cassie with a length of twelve-inch PVC pipe, end caps, and pipe glue. "What's all of this?"

"I'm making a cache tube for the shotgun."

"What shotgun?"

"The one I bought yesterday."

"You bought an AR-15 yesterday."

"And a shotgun. That was our conversation Thursday evening. I was buying a rifle and a shotgun."

Noah shook his head. "What are these .38 shells for?"

"I bought the shotgun from a guy who was selling it at Tim's Guns. He was also selling an old .38 service revolver. It was a package deal, and it was about the same as the cost of a new shotgun."

"Tim didn't mind you stepping in on his business?"

"Tim offered to let me have first dibs on the deal. He was happy to sell me the AR."

Noah threw his hands in the air. "What am I going to do? There isn't really a support group for men whose wives buy too many guns."

"I got a good deal. You should be happy."

Noah kissed Cassie. "I'm very happy to have you as my wife."

She smiled and continued her project. "I'm sorry, I should have told you. I'm still not used to you being on board with everything."

"I understand. I'm sorry I was so hardheaded."

Cassie pulled the revolver out of a box on the shelf. "It's nice, isn't it?"

Noah took the pistol and inspected it. "Very nice. You're putting it in the cache tube?"

"Yes, with the ammo the guy threw in, the shotgun, and a couple boxes of buck shot."

"It's a good idea. Thanks for taking care of all of that for us, Cassie. I just talked to Leo, and the custody hearing is set for next Tuesday. He's pretty sure the judge will give Lacy back to us."

Cassie stopped what she was doing and hugged Noah. "I hope so. My soul aches without her."

Noah hugged her back then handed the pistol to Cassie. "By the way, George McConnell wants to place an ad on ParkerMonkeyTrial.com. He thinks he'll get some good exposure from it. He said he'd pay $500 to run a banner."

"$500 a month?"

"I guess. Is that how that works?"

Cassie placed the pistol in a vacuum-seal bag and sealed it.

"That's great! We can buy another pistol for you."

Noah didn't argue. "Okay."

"Okay? I was kidding, but if you're going to be that easy, I'll find something nice for you."

"You've been right about everything so far. If what you said about the New World Order and the UN confiscating guns turns out to be true, we should probably buy what we can now. I have to get my daughter back, and that's taking all of my focus right now, but once we get her back, we should probably start developing a strategy to deal with all of this. Whatever's coming, we need to be ready for it."

Cassie looked at Noah as if she couldn't believe what he was saying. Noah could hardly believe it himself. After years of trying to reel Cassie in from the fringe, now he was becoming a conspiracy theory nut too.

Cassie finished packing the weapons and ammo into the cache tube. "Can you bring me about a half-pound of white rice in a sock?"

"For what?" Noah asked.

"It will help absorb any moisture that seeps into the cache tube."

"Won't the vacuum seals protect the guns from moisture?"

She nodded. "Yes, and the tube should be airtight, but redundancy is a good thing."

"Okay, be right back." Noah turned to go back in the house.

Cassie caught him before he was out of earshot. "And take out a package of ground beef."

"For the tube?" Noah was really confused.

"No, silly. I'm making meatloaf to take over to the Rays' tonight."

"Oh, yeah."

Cassie and Noah finished their project. Afterwards, Cassie looked over the Mountain Press editor's revisions to her article. Noah went to purchase copies of local papers to see what coverage their plight was receiving.

On his way back, his phone rang.

"Hello?"

"Noah, it's Elliot Rodgers. Can I buy lunch for you and your wife this afternoon? I don't have to be at the lodge until six."

"I'm on my way home. As soon as I get there, I'll ask her. Can I call you right back?"

"Sure thing."

Noah was soon home. He went upstairs to the office where she was working. "Cassie, I told you about the deputy who arrested me and quit his job over it."

"Yeah, Rodgers, right?"

"Right. He invited us to lunch this afternoon."

"That was nice of him, but I want to see how much

coverage we're getting online. I just Googled Parker Monkey Trail and got 80,000 results."

Noah's eyes opened wide. "No way!"

"All the results aren't us, just the first few pages are. After that, it's just things where those three terms appear together. I want to see who's covering us, and then find similar sites, podcasts, and aggregators to send articles to. But you go have lunch with . . . what did you say his first name was?"

"Elliot."

"Right, you go have lunch with Elliot."

"Okay, see you in a bit." Noah went down the stairs and called Elliot.

"Hey, Cassie is busy, but I'm available for a couple of hours."

Elliot said, "Great, do you like barbeque?"

"Sure," Noah replied.

"Meet me at The Pit Stop in thirty minutes."

"See you then." Noah hung up, scanned over the newspapers he'd bought, and then headed out the door.

***

Noah walked into The Pit Stop and saw Elliot waving at him from a booth near the back. He walked over to the table. "Thanks for the invitation."

Elliot stood to shake Noah's hand. "Thanks for coming.

And thanks for accepting my apology."

Noah sat down, and Elliot handed him a package from the booth where he'd been sitting. "This isn't from me. The deputy that walked off the job when your daughter was taken, Kevin Starkey, wanted me to give this to you."

Noah took the package and opened it. "A new laptop."

"Yeah, he filed a formal complaint against the other deputies before he handed in his badge. He got a copy of the report and saw that your laptop was taken in the raid. We can't replace your dog or your job, but we'll do anything we can to help you get your daughter back. Your case is becoming very polarizing within the department. Some of the guys are hardliners who'll do whatever they're told, and the others are dead set against what's going on. Some are ready to walk off the job. Several of them are like I was; they don't agree with it, but they need the paycheck. Me and Starkey are trying to convince them to take a stand when it comes time.

"So, rumor has it that you're organizing a protest for Monday morning."

Noah was still looking over the new laptop. "We are. Can you come?"

"I'll be there. So will Starkey. Maybe a couple of other guys from the sheriff's department that aren't on shift. It'll probably cost them their job, though. Sherriff Gregory has let it be known that insubordination won't be tolerated."

Noah looked up. "Aren't they allowed to have their own opinions?"

"As long as their opinion is perfectly in sync with the official opinion of the department, absolutely." Elliot Rodgers picked up his menu.

The waitress walked over. "Do you need more time?"

Noah said, "I'll have the pulled pork sandwich with chips and a Coke."

Elliot handed the menu to the waitress. "Ditto."

"Thanks, I'll be right back with your drinks." She turned and walked away.

"Do you always get the same thing?" Elliot asked.

"Always. You mentioned that you've been witnessing a gradual decline in the department last time we spoke."

Elliot pulled some napkins out of the dispenser against the wall and handed half to Noah. "Yep. I didn't like it, but I did what I saw everyone else doing. Going along to get along, you know? It started after September 11th. We were instructed to be more intrusive. Orders were to frisk anyone we came into contact with. Look around more during traffic stops, that kind of thing. Considering what had just happened, it seemed like an appropriate response. If it had stopped there, maybe it would have been reasonable. Now that I look back, those measures seem to mark the initial stage of a conditioning campaign – one to make people more complacent.

"Next, we were asked to report suspicious behavior that could potentially be terror-related to the Feds, which also seemed like a normal response to stopping terrorism. The first thing that made me take notice was what DHS considered suspicious activity. It was stupid stuff like people who store up food, buy guns, or have prior military service. We live in the mountains. Anyone who ain't dead from the snowstorm we had two years ago must have been storing food. Am I supposed to turn them all in for being terrorists? At some point, the terrorists went from being the mujahideen to being you and me.

"After the first housing bubble, the department's budget got hammered. We all took pay cuts, chipped in more for our retirement and health care, and still saw about a third of our coworkers get pink slips. It looked like more of us were going to be out of a job. Then DC rode in on a white horse with money from the magic unicorn. Of course, that money had strings tied to it. We became obligated to the federal government. All sorts of federal grants popped up, which the department could apply for. Every grant we received was tied to training us to be a more militarized police force.

"One grant was called the Public Safety Grant; we trained with our new assault rifles provided by DHS to deal with active shooters and got several thousand dollars. Another grant was called the Mobile Response Grant; DOD donated a mine-resistant armored personnel carrier, we trained with DHS, and we got more money. Every time we needed a bailout, we got the money plus training from the government and some type of military equipment.

"I don't want to sound like a conspiracy theorist, but the federal government is getting us ready for something. A lot of the guys in the department agree."

The waitress arrived with their order. Noah took the basket containing his food. "Thanks."

Elliot did the same. "This looks good. Thank you very much."

The waitress smiled. "Give me a wave if you need anything else."

Noah turned his attention back to Elliot. "I think you're right. My wife has been following this stuff for several years."

Elliot nodded. "She believes in the New World Order and the whole bit? What about you?"

Noah took a sip of his Coke. "I'm a recent convert. And yourself?"

"I've had a front row seat. I'd have to be blind not to believe it."

Noah tittered. "And I've been thrust into the arena."

"That about sums it up." Elliot paused. "But know that I'm getting in there with you. Whatever happens, I've got your back."

"That means a lot, Elliot, thank you. But you've done enough. I don't hold the arrest against you personally."

Elliot wiped his mouth with his napkin. "I'm glad I was able to make it up to you. But I want to get in the arena with you because this battle is just as important to me. As you reminded me, I took an oath. We take our oath when we first get sworn in, and then it kind of goes to the back of our minds, behind all of the department policies and bureaucracy.

I went home and looked over the oath I took."

Elliot pulled out a folded piece of paper from his pocket. "'I do solemnly swear that I will perform with fidelity the duties of the office to which I have been appointed, and which I am about to assume. I do solemnly swear to support the constitutions of Tennessee and the United States and to faithfully perform the duties of the office of deputy sheriff for Sevier County, Tennessee.'"

He laid the paper down on the table. "I didn't lay down my badge because I was giving up on the oath. I laid it down because it was hindering my ability to perform with fidelity my primary duties, which are to support the constitutions of Tennessee and the United States.

"But this isn't going to end with me. Starkey and I are holding every man in the department accountable to this oath. We're challenging them to lay down their badge the minute they're asked to violate this oath. If they don't, we want them to know that they're liars and criminals. Treason is defined as betraying your country, especially by trying to overthrow the government. If a man puts on a badge and uses that badge to usurp the laws of the land, especially the Bill of Rights, that's treason. I don't care if the government is overthrown by an overnight military coup or a multi-decade-long conspiracy designed to systematically destroy our founding principles one by one. Both are treason, and anyone who is party to either act is guilty of treason."

Noah was genuinely inspired by Elliot's speech. "Wow! I'm honored to fight at your side. If you explain it like that to the men in your department, they'll either come over to our side or be well aware of what they're guilty of."

The two men finished their meals, and Elliot paid the check.

Noah said, "Thanks again for lunch. And please tell Kevin that I said thanks for the laptop. Did he find a job?"

Elliot counted his change and left a generous tip. "I got him on at the lodge. They have several openings for third shift. Did you find a job yet?"

"My pastor wants me to focus on this trial, so he basically put me on staff at the church while I fight this. He thinks it's an important battle for Christians everywhere."

Elliot nodded. "A fight for freedom anywhere is a fight for freedom everywhere. He sounds like a smart man. Where do you attend?"

"Faith Church. The pastor is giving a special message tomorrow about freedom and duty. You should come."

Elliot gave Noah's shoulder a squeeze. "I'll be there. Mind if I bring my wife?"

"Bring anyone you want."

"Okay, I'll bring Starkey too. He could use a trip to church."

The two men said their farewells, and Noah headed home.

***

Noah walked in the house and handed the new computer

to Cassie.

"A laptop?" Cassie was so excited. She took it straight to the table and hooked it up.

"The deputy that walked off, Kevin Starkey, bought it for us."

"He was a Marine; we should be the ones buying something for him to thank him for his service. How did he know they took our laptop? He left before they stole it." Cassie continued the setup process on the new computer.

"He read the report before he quit. It mentioned that the laptop was taken. I'm going upstairs to send an email to George to let him know that Leo will be joining us for the interview tomorrow evening."

"Okay, I'll be here."

Later that evening, the Parkers took their meatloaf over to the Rays' house, where they shared a meal and visited with their daughter. After dinner, the trial and the upcoming protest were the main topics of conversation.

Becky Ray brought coffee around to the adults in the living room. "I think it's so great that Pastor Mike is putting the full weight of our church into this battle."

David Ray followed her in with a container of milk and a bowl of sugar. "It's like he said, 'if you lose, we all lose.' I hope you both know that Becky and I are committed to this. It could have just as easily been us that all of this happened to. If you need anything, don't hesitate to ask."

Cassie sipped her coffee. "Actually, you could show us how to operate an AR-15. I just bought one. I could probably fumble around and figure it out, but you can get me through the learning curve a little faster."

"Did you bring it?" David asked.

"Yes." Cassie set her coffee on the table and went to the car to retrieve the rifle.

When she returned, Cassie handed him the case. David opened it. "DPMS, this is a good rifle for the money. They won NRA Gun of the Year a couple of times. I've probably got a few extra parts lying around if you'd like me to trick it out for you."

Cassie clasped her hands together. "Wow! That would be fantastic."

Becky caught David before he left the room. "And give her some of those metal magazines. They're taking up too much room in the closet."

"Okay." David left to retrieve his tools and some attachments for the Parkers' new rifle.

Becky rolled her eyes. "During the last magazine scare, Magpul thirty-round Pmags completely sold out for months. David went crazy and bought all the metal thirty-round magazines he could find before they were out of stock. A year later, when the market normalized, he bought a bunch of Pmags. Now, the metal ones are just collecting dust and filling up my closet."

David came back in the room with a large toolbox and

seven metal magazines. "These are great magazines; I just like Pmags better."

Cassie took the magazines. "Thank you so much."

David opened the toolbox. "I have an aluminum four-rail handguard if you want it. It adds a little weight, but you can mount a light, forward grip, and backup sights."

Cassie looked at the handguard. "Okay."

David placed the D-ring tool on the front of the rifle and quickly changed the handguard. Next, he put on a set of backup sights, an inexpensive reflex sight, and a forward grip. "I don't have an extra tactical light, but you can buy a good one online."

Noah looked on in amazement at how quickly David had totally changed the appearance of the AR-15. "Very cool. Thank you so much. What do we owe you?"

David passed the rifle to Noah. "You can pay me back by learning how to use it."

Noah took the rifle and followed David's instructions on how to change the magazine, operate the safety, and deploy the backup sights.

David scratched around in the box a little more and dug out a single point sling attachment. "I'll put this on and try to find you an extra sling. Bring it over here next Saturday morning, and we'll go over some shooting techniques."

"Am I invited, too?" Cassie asked.

David laughed. "Of course."

There was a knock at the door.

"That must be Sharon." David got up to peek out the peephole before opening the door.

David opened the door and Sharon Beck came in.

"What a night at the restaurant," she said.

"Busy?" Cassie asked.

"Yes! I thought we were ready for the season, but we still need a couple more cooks and a server. I was doing everything tonight." Sharon plopped down on the couch next to Becky.

"That's a good problem," Noah said.

"Hmm. If I could find decent help, it would be. You'd be surprised how hard it is to get good workers. Especially with unemployment so high. But the government makes being unemployed so easy, people don't see why they should make any effort. I guess Cassie thinks it's part of a conspiracy to make people easier to control. I never would have believed that before, but why else would the government want people to be totally dependent on handouts?" Sharon looked at Cassie as if she thought Cassie would explain it all.

Cassie just shrugged.

Becky said, "You're blessed to be so busy. A lot of the local restaurants might not make it through the season. Overall, tourism is way down."

Sharon unbuttoned her coat. "Most of them are way overpriced. In this economy, you have to offer people value.

A restaurant is just a business. You have to deliver a good product that folks can afford. To make it around here, you have to show people that you can hang on. We have people that come back every year; they like the food and know we offer a fair price.

"Hickory Creek Lodge is still doing well because the rich folks love that place. We still get plenty of them every fall. The high-priced places like that do okay if they can put out good food. A few other inexpensive places like The Kettle do all right, too. It's the places in the middle that are getting squeezed. Pretty much like America. We've got rich and poor, but there ain't much in between these days."

Lacy and Lynette walked into the room.

"Are you ready to go, sweet pea?" Sharon asked.

Lacy nodded. "Mom and Dad, am I going to see you at church tomorrow?"

Noah grabbed his little girl and hugged her tightly. "Of course."

Cassie gave her a kiss on the head. "You be a good girl for Ms. Beck."

Lacy put her coat on. "I will. I love you. Goodnight."

Noah and Cassie left the Rays' house shortly after Lacy and Sharon.

***

The next morning, Noah and Cassie arrived at church a little early.

"There's Elliot and his wife. Let's go say hi." Noah led Cassie toward the Rodgers.

Noah waved when they got close. "Elliot, this my wife, Cassie."

Elliot shook her hand. "Pleasure, ma'am. This is my better half, Caroline."

"Very nice to meet you," Noah said.

Caroline grinned widely and hugged Elliot's arm. "You're the man responsible for turning my husband into Sam Adams?"

Noah put his hands up. "Oh, I think that rabble rouser has always been in there. If I had anything to do with waking him up, I do apologize."

Caroline looked at Elliot. "Actually, I kind of like it."

Cassie said, "We have to go say hi to our little girl, but why don't you two sit with us?"

"That will be fine," Elliot said. "We'll save you a seat."

"Where's Kevin?" Noah asked.

Elliot said, "Probably shooting some espresso. He worked third shift at the lodge last night. Said he was going home to change."

"Okay, see you in a bit," Noah said.

The Parkers went to see Lacy, then met the Rodgers back in the sanctuary. Kevin Starkey had arrived and looked very alert. Introductions were made, and Cassie said, "Thank you very much for the laptop."

Kevin grinned. "Glad I could help."

The service started, and the choir sang a few worship songs. Next, Pastor Mike began teaching.

"John Adams said, 'Liberty must at all hazards be supported. We have a right to it, derived from our Maker. But if we had not, our fathers have earned and bought it for us, at the expense of their ease, their estates, their pleasure, and their blood.'

"I've avoided politics from the pulpit for years. I thought I was doing the right thing by focusing on the Bible. Now, I see what has become of our nation, where thousands upon thousands of pastors, just like me, avoided politics. We've missed, perhaps, our greatest calling.

"Proverbs thirty-one, verses eight and nine, say, 'Speak up for those who cannot speak for themselves, for the rights of all who are destitute. Speak up and judge fairly; defend the rights of the poor and needy.'

"Who are those who can't speak for themselves? Isn't it our children who will be left with the world we leave them? Who are the poor and the needy that need their rights defended? Isn't it us? Compared to a federal government with unlimited resources, aren't we all poor? If any one of us has his or her rights violated by the state, isn't that person the needy?

"I've asked permission to share the Parkers' story with you

this morning. I think most of you are aware of their plight, but I'll elaborate. Today, I'm going to explain what they've gone through in the past week. We'll watch a video made by Cassie at the end of the service, and then we'll have a call to action.

"In first Corinthians twelve, verses twenty-six and twenty-seven, Paul says, 'If one part suffers, every part suffers with it; if one part is honored, every part rejoices with it. Now you are the body of Christ, and each one of you is a part of it.'

"As I tell you what happened to the Parkers last week, I want you to visualize that all of these things are happening to you. Because if we are all one body, as Paul said, then these violations happened to each and every one of us."

Pastor Mike continued to describe in graphic detail everything that had happened to the Parkers. He left out no fact and pulled no punches. He described Lacy's screaming; the bloody corpse of Buster, the family dog; and Noah's arrest.

Afterwards, Pastor Mike played Cassie's narrated footage of the crime scene. When the video finished, he asked, "If that had just happened to you, what would you be willing to do to make it right? What are you willing to do to make sure this doesn't happen again? Whatever you'd be willing to do if that had been you is what you need to do tomorrow, because that just happened to each and every person in this room. I was just arrested. That was your dog that was murdered. Every one of our children was abducted when Lacy Parker was forcibly taken from her mother's arms.

"Ephesians says, 'be angry and sin not.' Sitting back and

letting this happen when you have the power to stop it is a sin."

It was very uncharacteristic for Pastor Mike to raise his voice, so the congregation was caught off guard when he shouted, "Now who's angry?"

Elliot Rodgers was the first person to stand up and start clapping. Kevin Starkey was next. Soon everyone in the sanctuary was standing and clapping.

Pastor Mike calmed everyone down. "We're holding protests at the county courthouse starting tomorrow. We'll be petitioning to get Sherriff Gregory to step down, and we'll be asking for the support of our county commissioners. I want you to ask for the support of every person you know. Either people are with us or they are against us. It's time to draw a line in the sand. Everyone who stood up and said they're mad, I expect you to walk the walk. No excuses! The church is providing lunch after the service, so no one has any reason to leave. You'll have plenty of time to sign up for the protests and get copies of the petition, so you can start collecting signatures.

"I don't want to live in a country where this kind of stuff happens. You shouldn't either."

After Pastor Mike prayed, he said, "God bless, and I'll see you all outside for the picnic."

At the picnic, Noah's time slot sign-up sheet for the protest was soon filled, and people began writing their names on the back. His stack of forty petitions soon dwindled down to only two, so Lynn Barnes took one to the church office and made more copies. Most all of the congregants of Faith Church offered their support to Noah and Cassie.

Jim and Sandy Taylor came to say hi after the crowd started to thin out. Jim took a petition sheet. "God is with you on this, Noah."

Noah nodded. "I think you're right, Jim."

Jim said, "I spoke with Commissioner Laurence. You already have support from the majority of the county commissioners. Once the protest and petition hit the news and people start calling them, it will probably be near unanimous."

Noah was happy to have a friend like Jim who was well connected. "Good to know. I trust you'll keep your finger on the political pulse."

Jim smiled. "You can count on me."

***

Noah and Cassie arrived home from church just in time to get ready for the interview. Leo Cobb pulled into the drive only minutes later.

Noah opened the door for him. "Come on in. Can I offer you some coffee or water?"

Leo removed his overcoat. "Can I have a cup of coffee for now and some water for the interview?"

"Sure thing." Noah went to the kitchen to start a pot of coffee.

Cassie entered the living room, greeted Leo, and set up the laptop. "This computer has a better camera built in than what we have connected to our desktop in the office. Besides, we can position it so we can all sit side-by-side on the couch."

Leo said, "Sounds good to me."

Cassie fidgeted with the computer for several minutes, trying to get a good camera angle. "Let's put the laptop on a chair, and it will give us a wider view while we chat with George."

Noah reappeared with coffee and water for everyone. He set the drinks on the coffee table. "Is everyone ready?"

"Ready." Cassie directed Noah to sit on her right and Leo on her left.

George McConnell called on Skype and briefed everyone on the format of the show. He instructed Cassie to cut the video feed to save bandwidth and thereby increase the audio quality. The interview began, and the first few questions went over the events of the past week.

Next, George directed his questions to Leo Cobb. "Mr. Cobb, it was very gracious of you to represent the Parkers pro bono. Did you have to compete against the ACLU to get the case? I know that organization represented John Scopes in the 1925 Scopes Monkey Trial. I know they're for freedom of speech, no matter which side of the evolutionary argument a person happens to stand on."

Leo laughed. "The ACLU would certainly have you believe that. Their actions tell a different story. Back in 2004, members of the school board in Dover, Pennsylvania, wanted intelligent design to be offered in addition to evolution. When the material was made available, the ACLU was on the side of suppressing the county's freedom of speech. The ACLU won the case, and intelligent design could no longer be mentioned."

George said, "It sounds like the ACLU might have some agenda other than the civil liberties of Americans."

George continued the interview, covering the particulars of the case. He wrapped up the interview with a call to action. "For Sevier County residents, please stop by the courthouse, show your support, and sign the petition to have Sherriff Gregory removed from office. This has to start at the local level. We have to send a message to our elected officials in our communities. If they won't stand up for our constitutional rights, they'll be handed a pink slip. If we won't take action to change our communities, how can we ever hope to address the corruption in Washington?

"If you're a listener outside of Sevier County, visit the Parkers' website, ParkerMonkeyTrial.com, and share the videos on social media, send links to your pastor, and call your local news stations. Let's get this message out there. Hopefully, your local elected officials will get the message that a police force can't walk into people's homes without a warrant and abduct their child when the child is perfectly safe, and you can't have a policy that has no other way of dealing with family pets than shooting them. There is no reason the deputies who shot Buster couldn't have allowed Cassie to put him in the other room if they felt threatened. We're going to tell Sherriff Gregory that since he won't change those policies, we'll find someone else who will."

Once the interview was finished, everyone said their goodbyes, and Leo left. Noah made a pot of tea to share with Cassie to help them unwind. While he had no idea of the drama to come, he did know the following day would be a big day.

CHAPTER 16

In the beginning of a change the patriot is a scarce man, and brave, and hated and scorned. When his cause succeeds, the timid join him, for then it costs nothing to be a patriot.

Mark Twain

Noah awoke to the smell of coffee and pancakes. He rolled out of bed and followed the enchanting aroma to the kitchen.

Cassie was setting the table. "You slept in this morning."

Noah poured his coffee. "It took me a while to go to sleep last night. I was thinking about the protest. I should have gone for a run last night, but I was so tired from all the activity."

Cassie placed the plate of pancakes on the table. "And you'll probably be too tired to run tonight after standing up all day."

"We'll wrap up the protest at 5:30. The courthouse will clear out by then. I'll come straight home and go for a run." Noah brought the syrup to the table as he sat down. He prayed to bless the food, and they began eating.

Cassie said, "I was going to pack us a lunch to take, but Becky texted me and said she'd make sandwiches and drop them off around noon."

"That's nice of her. Is she coming to the protest?"

"For a little while, but she has Lynette, so she can't stay long. What time do you want to be at the courthouse?"

Noah poured a little extra syrup on his pancakes. "No later than 8:30. That's when everyone starts showing up for work."

The Parkers finished breakfast and got dressed for the day ahead. Noah finished getting ready first and flipped on the financial news while he waited for Cassie.

The reporter was giving an update of the recent turmoil in the global markets.

> "One week after the computer glitch that paralyzed the BRICS nation's ability to use their independent system for international trade, the problem still has not been solved. Asian stocks took a steep decline this morning at the market open.
>
> "India's financial regulatory agency, SEBI, has closed all markets in the country. The DICGC, the depository insurance arm of India's central bank,

issued strict limitations on withdrawals this morning. The announcement has triggered a massive run on the banks in India. Fearing a similar response, South Africa has declared a banking holiday for the next three days. This will only intensify the rioting in the major South African cities.

"Brazil's Ministry of Finance has pledged a fresh infusion of reals in order to keep the Brazilian economy operational, even if it is seriously wounded. Rioting in Sao Paulo turned the city into a total war zone this weekend. Police are completely outnumbered by rioters and gangs. Merchants and suppliers are no longer able to conduct business within the city. If stores are not able to reopen soon, the death toll in Sao Paulo is expected to rise dramatically in coming weeks due to starvation. International aid agencies are setting up relief camps outside of Sao Paulo. Those who are able to flee the city are taking part in a mass exodus, but many of the city's twelve million inhabitants are too poor and have no resources even to get to the relief camps.

"Gold and silver have dropped precipitously since the metals market opened last night. Silver is now at sixty-five dollars per ounce, representing nearly a forty-five percent drop since last week's high. Gold seems to have found a temporary support level at $2100. The yellow metal now sits just above support at $2108. It has fallen thirty-four percent since last week."

Cassie walked into the room. "Wow! That is a huge drop

in one week. We should think about buying some silver."

Noah looked at her. "It's in freefall. Who knows how low it could go."

Cassie finished putting her earrings on. "That's not normal market activity. Someone is pushing the price lower for a reason. Probably so they can load up on it at a cheap price. The world markets are in turmoil. Gold and silver always skyrocket when there's this much fear in the markets. The precious metals are going to turn around, I promise."

Noah remembered that he'd vowed to start trusting her instincts, but it was still an internal fight for him. "We can talk about it."

Cassie smiled. "I'll take that. What else did the news say?"

"Things are really breaking down in South Africa and Brazil. Riots, bank runs, market crashes, I hope it never gets that bad here."

Cassie grabbed her jacket. "Oh, I think it will get a lot worse. The global economy is interconnected. This is probably the first domino. Remember 2008?"

Noah turned off the television and grabbed his coat. "Yeah, what about it?"

"The meltdown started in subprime mortgage debt."

"I remember, but that's what caused the meltdown in the first place."

Cassie followed Noah out the door. "True, but those types of market events always start in the most volatile fringe markets and work their way into the mainstream."

Noah stuck his key in the door to lock the dead bolt. "So you think what's happening to the stock markets in South Africa, Brazil, and India will spread to America?"

"I do."

Noah stopped. "Maybe we should sell the rest of our stocks."

"Okay."

Noah turned to go back in the house. "Are you coming?"

"You want to sell right now?"

"Don't you think we should?"

Cassie followed Noah back to the front door. "I don't know that the contagion is going to spread that fast. In fact, the Plunge Protection Team could very well push US markets higher before a crash comes."

"That sounds like another one of your conspiracy organizations." Noah walked in and walked upstairs.

Cassie started laughing as she trailed behind him. "The Plunge Protection Team is the official nickname for the President's Working Group on Financial Markets. That's mainstream news."

"And they get away with manipulating markets in broad daylight?" Noah logged into their Roth IRA trading account.

"It's the government; they get away with anything they

want. Who's going to stop them? The American people? They're all asleep at the wheel. Most have no idea what's going on. What do you think the Fed does when they set interest rates? That's blatant manipulation of markets."

Noah started entering sell orders for all of their holdings. "Yeah, I guess that is manipulation of the interest rate market."

"And everything is tied to interest rates: housing, stocks, commodities, gold, silver, the auto industry. What market can you think of that isn't affected by interest rates?"

Noah strained to think of something. "I don't know."

"Neither do I. Are you going to let all of the proceeds sit around in cash? That's almost as risky as having it in the market."

"We should buy some gold and silver?" Noah turned around to look at her.

"I think we should, but you're the leader of the family."

Noah paused for a second to wonder if he'd earned that title. "Yes, but you're the one who's taken the time to get educated on all of this, so as leader of the family, I delegate this area of decision-making to you."

Cassie beamed at the compliment. She kissed him on the head. "Hop up; let me get on the computer for a minute."

Noah gave her the chair, and Cassie went to an online gold and silver dealer that she'd obviously researched ahead of time.

Cassie quickly placed an order. "We just put $5,000 in silver and $5,000 in gold. We'll watch the market and buy a little more later."

"That's it?"

"I have to write a check for the order and drop it in the mailbox on the way to the courthouse." Cassie took out the checkbook and quickly filled in the amount and appropriate information.

Noah grabbed an envelope, placed a return address sticker and a stamp on it, and then handed it to Cassie. "Why did you split it down the middle?"

Cassie addressed the envelope. "Gold is more stable, but the silver is in smaller denominations, in case we have to use it as a currency someday. I'll tell you all about it on the way to the courthouse. We gotta hustle; we're running late."

Seconds later, Noah and Cassie were on the road. Noah pulled over near the mailbox and Cassie jumped out to drop off the check.

They arrived at the courthouse at 8:25 AM. Isaiah was there with Benny Loomis and around twenty other people from church.

Noah looked on in amazement that so many people were already there. Some had homemade picket signs with various patriotic messages. One man held the Gadsden flag, which was the familiar yellow flag with a coiled serpent and the words, don't tread on me, written across the bottom. "Thank you all for coming out. I really appreciate it."

Isaiah said, "You two almost missed out on the donuts. Benny brought Krispy Kremes."

Noah looked behind him.

Benny handed him a full box of donuts. "I put this to the side for you. I know Cassie likes chocolate glazed."

Cassie was greeting some of the other protestors when Benny said the word chocolate. She made an abrupt about face. "Oh, I shouldn't." She opened the box and took two of the chocolate glazed donuts.

Elliot Rodgers and Kevin Starkey were next to arrive.

"Glad you could make it. Donut?" Noah handed the box to Elliot.

"I hate being stereotyped like that." Elliot took a donut and handed the box to Starkey, who also took one.

Kevin Starkey handed the box back to Noah. "Four guys from the department are coming by in uniform."

"To protest?" Noah asked.

"Yes."

"Won't they get in trouble?"

Rodgers said, "They'll be fired. I already got them jobs at the lodge."

Noah shook his head. "I hope I'm doing the right thing. I don't want everyone to ruin their lives because of me."

Starkey said, "It's not because of you. It's for freedom and liberty. But you have to be fully convinced that you're doing the right thing. You can't second-guess yourself. This might get very difficult, and if you waiver, everyone is going to see it, the patriots and the tyrants. If you give up, the tyrants will get bolder, and the patriots will lose heart. No sacrifice is too big as long as we see this thing through to the end."

Noah understood what Kevin was saying. "Yeah, thanks."

The crowd continued to grow and consisted of over forty people by nine o'clock. Leo Cobb showed up around 9:15. "Noah, good turnout. Is this about what you expected?"

Noah shook his head. "I expected four or five people. I was just hoping we could keep enough people around to collect signatures."

Cobb looked around. "I'm expecting Channel 8 to be here any minute. They're coming down to do an interview with us and run it at lunch. That should bring out some more people. I'll make sure I plug your website and ask folks to come down to sign the petition."

Isaiah walked over to shake hands with his friend, Leo. "Is he taking good care of you, Noah?"

"Leo is great. I really appreciate you introducing us, Isaiah."

Cassie tugged Noah's arm. "You gotta see this."

Noah turned around to see a chimpanzee with a derby hat, three-piece suit, black-and-white leather shoes, and a cane. "No way!"

The lady escorting the chimp walked over and asked for Noah. She was quickly pointed in Noah's direction. "Mr. Parker?"

Noah looked at the monkey, then back up at the lady. "Yes, hi."

"I'm Margaret, and this is Joe. He plays Joe Mendi over in Dayton at our Scopes Monkey Trial Festival every year. I'm sure you're familiar with the trial and the festival."

"I'm learning about it as I go." Noah wasn't as well versed in the historic trial as folks assumed he was.

"Well I heard about your ordeal and started following your website. I wanted to bring Joe out and show our support. I hope that's okay."

Noah tried to process the effect that a monkey dressed in a suit would have on the protest. "Sure. Yes, thank you."

Leo seemed to have run the same analysis. "Thank you very much for coming out, we're so glad to have you. I know all about the Scopes trial. I went to the festival several years back. I'm Mr. Parker's attorney, Leo Cobb."

"Pleased to meet you, I'm Margaret Simmons."

Cassie pulled Noah to the side. "This is pure gold."

Noah whispered. "It's not too gimmicky?"

"You're trying to get attention, there is no such thing as too gimmicky," she said.

Four sheriff's deputies showed up at ten to support Noah,

right around the time that Jim and Sandy Taylor arrived. Introductions were made, then Leo pulled Noah and Cassie away to do the interview with Channel 8. The interview was short, but Leo made sure the message was clear and that Joe, the monkey, was visible in the background.

By noon, the crowd had grown to over sixty people, and it was difficult to navigate the sidewalk in front of the courthouse. Leo told Noah the good news. "I spoke with Margaret, and Joe is going to hold a sign that says ParkerMonkeyTrial.com. I called the print shop, and they're rushing the sign. It should be ready by 1:00. Every kid that walks by or sees the monkey on television is going to tell their parents to look at the monkey."

Noah laughed. "Good idea. Thanks. People don't see a monkey dressed in a suit every day in Sevierville. He's a good attention-getter."

Leo patted Noah on the back. "You've really pulled off a world class protest, Noah."

Noah looked around. "I had nothing to do with this. I have to give all the credit to God. I could have never put this together."

Jim Taylor walked over to give Noah an update. "We've collected four hundred signatures already. This is really going to happen."

Cassie came by with some lunch. "Becky just dropped off some sandwiches. She said they're praying for us, and she's sorry they can't stay longer. David is going to come by right after his shift ends. Maybe around 4:30. Lynette loved the little monkey. I wish Lacy was here to see him.'"

Noah's heart sank. Even though he saw her regularly, he missed his daughter so much. "Me, too."

By one o'clock, the crowd had swelled to well over one hundred. Protestors were on the sidewalks running along both Bruce Street and Court Avenue. They were gathered on the walkway in front of the courthouse and on the lawn. Pastor Mike stopped by with his wife, Lynn. "Noah, this is absolutely fantastic. I'm so glad you have such a big turnout."

"Thank you pastor. The signatures are pouring in as well. I guess Channel 8 aired their piece at 12:00. The other local channels from Knoxville are showing up now."

Pastor Mike gave Noah's arm a squeeze. "They better hurry up. We had to park three blocks over. The parking lot is completely full. Do you mind if I say a few words and offer a quick prayer?"

Noah nodded. "I'd be honored."

Pastor Mike walked up the stairs to the courthouse door and stood looking out over the crowd. "Folks, I'm Pastor Mike Barnes of Faith Church where Noah attends. I see a lot of people here today from Faith Church and several others that I haven't met before. I want to thank you all for showing up today to show your support for Noah and for liberty. This is how our country started. It was people just like you who'd had enough of being told what to do and how to live their lives. In 1776, Pastor John Peter Muhlenberg gave a sermon to his congregation from Ecclesiastes three. He read, 'To everything there is a season, a time for every purpose under heaven: a time to be born, and a time to die; a time to plant, and a time to pluck what is planted.' At the end of his sermon, he said 'In the language of the holy writ, there was a time for all things, a time to preach and a time to pray, but those times have passed away.' He went on to remove his robe and reveal the military uniform he was wearing underneath.

"It is my hope that the time to preach and the time to pray have not yet passed for our present crisis, but that season is certainly waning. If we are to avoid another period of violent revolution, then we must act swiftly. Time is short. Pastors, like myself, have sat quietly by as the winds of tyranny have slowly eroded the foundations of liberty. I regret the time I spent being quiet, but that time is over. I'm ready to do whatever it takes to turn back the tide and regain our lost freedoms. I hope you are as well."

The crowd applauded Pastor Mike's short address. He bowed his head and prayed aloud. "Father God, through the blood of our forefathers you have granted us a land of unprecedented freedom. We've been complacent and derelict in our duty of preserving that freedom. We pray that you'll forgive us and grant us the strength to regain what has been lost. Amen."

The crowd clapped loudly as Pastor Mike stepped down. Soon a chant spontaneously arose. "God gave us our rights, so you can't take them."

Over and over, and louder and louder, the chant grew to a roar. "God gave us our rights, so you can't take them."

By 2:30, the crowd easily exceeded four hundred people

on the grounds of the county courthouse. Additionally, people were driving around the surrounding streets and honking their horns.

Several deputies walked to the courthouse stairs, and one called out over a bullhorn, "This gathering is creating a safety hazard, and we're going to have to ask you to disperse."

Six other deputies made their way to the center of the crowd. The one who appeared to be in charge addressed the four uniformed deputies who'd come with Rodgers and Starkey. "Gregory said you guys are all fired. You need to go to his office and hand in your badges and your service weapons immediately."

One of the four, Kyle Harding, said, "You've got no authority to fire me. If Gregory wants to fire me, tell him to bring his cowardly tail down here and do it himself."

The leader of the six said, "If I have to call him, he's going to have us arrest you."

Harding's face changed. "If you assault me, I will be forced to defend myself. You have absolutely no reason to arrest me. I've done nothing in violation of the law. You, on the other hand, have just threatened a law enforcement officer."

The other three deputies participating in the protest fell in close behind Harding and placed their hands on their weapons.

The leader of the six deputies looked Harding up and down. As he turned away, he said, "You'll regret that." He changed his attention to Noah. "Do you have a permit for this protest?"

Noah looked at Cobb.

Isaiah spoke up. "I do; it's right here with my concealed carry permit."

"Let's see it." The man demanded.

Isaiah handed the leader a copy of the Constitution. "The Bill of Rights is on the back. The First Amendment guarantees my God-given right to peaceably assemble and petition my government for a redress of grievances. That's precisely what we're doing here today."

The man threw the Constitution on the ground and pointed his finger in Isaiah's face. "You're a freakin' smart aleck. I'll make sure you're first in line when we start locking people up. You have ten minutes to clear out, or you're all going to jail."

Cobb grabbed Noah. "We need to get you out of here. Tell Cassie to get her things."

Noah shouted. "No! I'm not going anywhere!"

Cobb said, "Noah, if you're arrested, they'll revoke your bond. I might not be able to get you back out. You've got a lot of momentum going, and we need you to be free so you can fight this."

Pastor Mike backed him up. "Listen to him, Noah. You go on and get out of here. We'll hold down the fort."

Cassie walked up with her jacket in her arm.

Isaiah nodded. "Noah, go home. Let us take over. Cassie, in my kitchen, I have the combination to my safe taped underneath my silverware tray. It's in the drawer next to the sink. The safe is in my bedroom closet. If we get locked up, bail Pastor Mike and me out with the money in the safe."

"Okay," she said.

Cobb escorted Noah and Cassie through the crowd. "Gregory knows you're trying to get him fired, so you need to not give him a reason to arrest you today."

Noah and Cassie walked to their car in the adjacent parking lot. The shouts from the crowd grew louder, and the deputies yelled over the bullhorn. "Disperse. This is an unlawful assembly."

As they drove away, they saw two protestors lying face down in the courthouse lawn being handcuffed.

Noah shook his head. "This is bad."

Cassie put her hand on his leg. "This is necessary!"

CHAPTER 17

Then let those who are in Judea flee to the mountains, let those in the city get out, and let those in the country not enter the city. For this is the time of punishment in fulfillment of all that has been written.

Luke 21:21-22

Noah paced back and forth as he watched the scenes of Isaiah and Pastor Mike being arrested play over and over on the local news channels.

Cassie came back in the room. "Tom said they still haven't been processed in. He can't do anything until they show up in the system."

Noah turned to face her. "Maybe we should go ahead and get Isaiah's money from his safe."

"We don't know how much to take out."

Noah rubbed his chin as he thought for a moment. "Disturbing the peace. It couldn't be more than ten grand each."

Cassie rolled her eyes. "Unless they get assault on an officer and resisting arrest tacked on."

Noah grabbed his keys. "That's true, but if we know where the safe is and figure out how to open it, we'll be that much closer to being ready when we get the call."

Cassie's phone rang. "Hello?"

Noah went to put some food in the bowl for Sox while Cassie was on the phone. He looked at Buster's bag of food, which was still in the closet beside Sox's. The pang of sorrow hit him again. He sighed. It would be a long time before he completely got over losing Buster. Sox came into the room at the sound of the cat food container. The cat seemed to know the pain Noah was feeling and rubbed his leg before he started eating.

Noah scratched Sox behind the ear while he ate. "We're going to get through this, Sox. We'll get Lacy back, and we'll be a family again."

Cassie walked into the room. "I'm ready to go."

Noah got up and headed toward the door. "Who was that?"

"Sharon Beck."

"Is Lacy okay?" Noah asked.

Cassie followed Noah to the car. "Lacy's fine. Sharon is a

mess. She just saw Isaiah getting locked up on television. It really took her off guard. She wanted to make sure something was being done to get him out. I promised that I'd keep her updated. If you ask me, there is something more than just a platonic, friendly concern."

Noah shut the door and started the car. "Oh yeah? You think something is goin' on between the two of them?"

Cassie smiled. "I don't know about Isaiah, but judging by the way Sharon acts, I'd say she has a crush on him."

They arrived at Isaiah's and found his safe. Noah opened it. "Nice gun collection!"

Cassie said, "Wow! What's this?"

Noah picked up the box on the top shelf. "Don't play with his guns."

Cassie didn't listen. She picked up the first battle rifle in the safe. "HK, this is cool!"

Noah shook his head as he opened the top box. "No money in here."

"What is it?" she asked.

"Look." Noah held up several gold coins in plastic sleeves. "Somebody else believes precious metals are a good thing to have around."

Cassie put the HK rifle back in the safe and took out an AK-47. "What do you think about this one?"

"I think you need to focus on what we came here for."

Noah looked in the box below the one with the coins.

Cassie put the AK back and took out the Armalite AR-10. "This is what I need."

Noah pulled out a stack of fifty-dollar bills. "It looks just like the rifle you just bought."

Cassie put it back. "No, this one is chambered in .308."

Noah counted through the bills. "I'll take $5,000 for now; we'll come back if we need to."

Cassie closed the safe and spun the combination dial to make sure it was locked.

On the way home, Cassie called Tom to see if there had been any progress on bailing out Isaiah and Pastor Mike.

After she hung up, Noah asked, "What did he say?"

"No news yet. He said over fifty people were arrested, so it could be late tonight by the time everyone is processed in."

They went home and waited patiently by the phone. They fell asleep on the couch watching the eleven o'clock news.

At 1:30 AM, Cassie's phone rang. "Okay, we'll meet you there."

Noah rubbed his eyes and yawned. "Are they out?"

"We have to meet Tom at the jail with the money and sign some papers."

"Okay, let's do it," Noah said.

Cassie called Sharon during the ride to the jail. "They should be out within the hour."

"Yeah, you're right," Cassie said.

"Great, see you then." Cassie hung up.

Noah glanced over at his wife. "What did Sharon have to say?"

Cassie said, "She thinks they'll be hungry when they get out. She's going over to the Kettle and opening it up, just for them. She wants us to bring them by there. Lacy will be there."

Noah yawned. "Alright."

Cassie tussled his hair. "You can have some coffee when we get to the Kettle."

Noah laughed. "Then I'll never get back to sleep."

Two hours later Noah and Cassie were in a booth at the Country Kettle with Lacy, Pastor Mike, and Isaiah.

Pastor Mike ran his fingers through his hair. "What an experience!"

Noah said, "Jail is a nice place, isn't it?"

Isaiah said, "Thanks for picking us up."

Noah nodded. "I think I owed you a jail pickup."

Lynn Barnes showed up at the Kettle. Pastor Mike stood up to hug his wife, and they embraced for several minutes.

Shortly thereafter, Sharon came to the table with a plate of roast beef, a bowl of mash potatoes, a bowl of gravy, broccoli casserole, and warm rolls. "I hope y'all don't mind eating family style."

When Sharon squeezed into the booth next to Isaiah, Cassie shot Noah a look that said I told you so.

Pastor Mike said a quick prayer, and they all filled their plates.

After dinner, they talked about the protest, the trial, and how terrible things had become.

***

Noah awoke from a deep sleep Tuesday morning, just after nine o'clock. His phone was ringing. By the time he got to it, he'd missed the call.

"Jim. I better call him back." Noah pressed the number, and the phone began to ring.

"Noah."

"Hey Jim. Sorry I missed your call. What's happening?"

"You sound tired. Did I wake you up?" Jim asked.

Noah stretched his free arm. "Late night. It was almost five when we went to bed. We took Isaiah and Pastor Mike over to the Kettle after we bailed them out."

"Go back to sleep; I can tell you later."

Noah said, "I'm up. We've got stuff to do today. Tell me

what's going on."

"The county commissioners held an emergency meeting this morning. They took a vote and are unanimously asking Sherriff Gregory to step down."

Noah lit up at the news. "That's fantastic!"

"They've asked me to be the interim Sherriff," Jim said.

"No kidding!"

"Yep, Gregory is supposed to be out of the office by noon. I want to do some house cleaning. Do you have Elliot's number? I'd like him to help me decide who stays and who goes. Needless to say, the charges against everyone for disturbing the peace will be dropped. The charges you got for resisting and assault will be dropped also. Sorry I can't do anything about the Community Core charges; those are with the state."

Noah nudged Cassie to wake her up. "Thanks so much, Jim. That is absolutely great!"

"I guess your protest did the trick. I took the petitions by early this morning, but I think they'd already made up their minds. Most of the county commissioners have some type of business interest tied to local tourism. National news coverage of jack-booted thugs pushing around citizens in front of the Sevier County Courthouse didn't go over well at all."

Noah beamed over the news. "I can't thank you enough for all of your help, Jim."

"Don't thank me; you did most of the work. But it's like Pastor Mike said, we're all in this together. The war ain't over, but this battle was a major victory."

"Talk to you soon." Noah hung up and tried once more to rouse Cassie.

"Baby, wake up." It was a vain effort. Cassie was dead to the world.

Noah kissed her on the back of the neck and relented to let her sleep. He went to the kitchen, fed the cat, and started a pot of coffee. Once the coffee was ready, he poured a cup, sat quietly at the kitchen table, and took a few minutes to be thankful for God's help in the protest. He opened his Bible to Psalms 9 and started reading to himself.

"I will praise you, O LORD, with all my heart; I will tell of all your wonders. I will be glad and rejoice in you; I will sing praise to your name, O Most High. My enemies turn back; they stumble and perish before you. For you have upheld my right and my cause; you have sat on your throne, judging righteously. You have rebuked the nations and destroyed the wicked; you have blotted out their name for ever and ever. Endless ruin has overtaken the enemy, you have uprooted their cities; even the memory of them has perished. The LORD reigns forever; he has established his throne for judgment."

CHAPTER 18

It is well enough that people of the nation do not understand our banking and monetary system, for if they did, I believe there would be a revolution before tomorrow morning.

Henry Ford

Everett Carroll headed out to the cabin after work Friday evening. He let himself in, as Jones's condition was deteriorating. "I stopped by McGuire's on the way out here and picked up something to go. I didn't think you'd be hungry, so I didn't bother to get you anything. However, I bought myself two orders of the seafood pasta. I think my eyes were bigger than my stomach, so if you want one of them, help yourself," Everett said with a wink.

Jones winked back. "You're right. I'm not hungry, but I hate to see food go to waste. You might as well get me a plate out of the cupboard, too."

Everett laughed as he took out two plates and silverware

to place on the table. "I brought your data card."

Agent Jones now kept the tubes from his oxygen tank attached to his nose at all times. He rolled the tank over to the table and sat down. "Let's see it. And hand me that tin on the top shelf over the coffee cups."

Everett handed Jones the tin and a nickel from his pocket. Jones took a small tool in the shape of a ring from the tin. He placed the coin face up on top of the ring. He slammed the ring against the table two times, and the bottom dropped out of the nickel, revealing a secret compartment that held a micro SD card.

Everett chuckled. "I can't believe they still fall for that. You say it's been around since the Cold War?"

Jones inspected the SD card. "Yeah, and data storage technology has grown by leaps and bounds since then. The security guards who check you in and out at IT aren't well trained at all. They're essentially glorified TSA agents. They don't know what to look for. Can you bring my laptop over here? I hate to make your dinner get cold, but I'm curious to see what we've got here."

Everett went to the living room to retrieve the laptop. "Trust me; dinner was cold a long time ago."

Jones stuck the SD card in the adapter and plugged it into the USB port. The files were in an encrypted folder and a password-protected zipped file. He opened the encryption program, and then extracted the compressed files. "They could have never fit four days' worth of DHDBs in a nickel during the Cold War."

DHDBs were Department Head Daily Briefings. They aggregated all pertinent intelligence and information. Each day, the DHDBs were passed to each department head within the intelligence community. The amount of data contained in one daily briefing was astounding. It was sifted through each day to distill down the Presidential Daily Briefing, or PDB. The PDB went to the president, first thing each morning.

Jones selected the folder containing the raw financial data. "The Chinese are dumping their US debt."

Everett stuck the plates of food in the microwave. "Is it in retaliation for the attack on the BRICS bank?"

Jones shook his head. "No. It's a heavy dump, but they are doing it in a way that the market can absorb. The dollar is up because of everyone looking for safe havens after the real, rand, and rupee fell off the cliff. I think the Chinese are taking advantage of the brief surge, but that doesn't mean that they don't have something else up their sleeve.

"It's also possible that China has intelligence on a retaliatory attack planned by Russia. Whatever it is, they're getting out of US debt as fast as they can without tipping their hand to what they're doing."

Everett rubbed his brow. "Once the capital from the failing currencies dries up, do you think the Chinese will keep selling US Treasuries at this rate?"

Jones looked up from the computer. "If they do, we'll know a major economic event is on the horizon."

Everett took the food from the microwave and placed it on the table. "I can stop by Monday with the latest set of briefings if you're going to be up here."

"You're a young man. I'm sure you have better things to do than run up and down the road every day." Jones took a bite of the pasta.

Everett dropped his eyebrows and put his hand over his open mouth. "You're right! If I miss an episode of the

Kardashians, I'll be a social outcast! And what about my gaming skills? The talents one acquires playing video games are highly perishable. As they say, use it or lose it. Even so, I can squeeze in a few evenings to keep up with the events that are likely to put an end to the world as we know it."

Jones fought back a smile. "Suit yourself."

The two ate quietly for several minutes.

Jones was first to break the silence. "People still watch the Kardashians?"

Everett chuckled and shook his head. "No. I was just trying to be relatable."

Jones faked a look of anger. "You calling me old? 'Cause I'm not. I could take you."

After dinner, Jones combed through more of the files. "Are you still monitoring those cryptocurrency accounts?"

Everett cleaned up the dishes. "I am. Not much action. It's like you said; the account holders have been buying some gold and silver, but nothing significant. The Darkcoin accounts are completely blacked out. I can't trace any activity after the initial purchase, even using the black-box code you gave me to access Dragon. I thought Dragon was omniscient concerning events that occurred on the Web."

Jones adjusted his glasses. "Darkcoin popped up right when the NSA began construction on the Utah facility. It may have been developed by insiders who purposely designed it for themselves to circumvent Dragon, or so they would have a marketable product for those wanting to transact outside of the all-seeing eye of Dragon."

"Should I open a Darkcoin account?" Everett gave his full attention to Jones.

Jones tilted his head from side to side. "It could work either way. Someone is probably monitoring Darkcoin transactions. You could meet the man who designed the program. He could be your best friend and explain all about how anonymous it is. But at the end of the day, he might be CIA deep cover looking for rogue agents, he may be Russian intelligence, or it could be a program developed by China, meant to entrap US intelligence actors. If you decide to open an account, keep it small, use heavy identification cloaking measures, and only use it when you have no other choice."

"Is now a good time to buy more gold and silver? Gold closed below $2000 today, and silver is down by more than fifty percent since its high, two weeks ago."

Jones nodded. "I think so. I believe we're getting close to the end of the line. Keep some cash on hand, though. Right before it all blows up, we'll see the stars align. Those cryptocurrency accounts you're watching will all start moving into gold, and we'll see the supplies of gold and silver dry up. We'll also see stock prices surge and hear rhetoric out of Washington that things have never been better."

Everett sat back down at the table. "If the supplies are going to dry up, why should I keep cash around?"

Jones said, "When the supplies first dry up, you'll still be able to buy, but the premiums will be through the roof. Your cash will mainly be for the first phase of the collapse. Cash will still be king during the first week or so. Once people figure out that the dollar has been abandoned, it will quickly be phased out. After that, there will likely be a barter stage where people won't give up goods for anything except other goods."

"But they'll take gold and silver?"

Jones shook his head. "Probably not. If there aren't any

stores to buy more food, why would you give up the food you need for something that won't keep you alive? People who have farms and the ability to produce excess milk, eggs, or meat might trade with someone for honey, fuel or candles. At that stage, gold and silver won't do them any good."

Everett scratched his head. "So should I be buying things to barter with, like fuel and honey?"

"The best plan is to lay low until the initial phase blows over. If you think folks are nasty and conniving now, wait till you see how they act after the crash. You should prepare well enough to avoid contact with the general public for a year or two. After the die-off, when the new global currency is established, your gold and silver will have preserved the value of your savings. It will also be the underground currency for those who want to operate outside the control of the New World Order. Everyone from drug dealers to political dissidents will use gold and silver for black market transactions. There'll be a huge opportunity for profiteers who don't mind working in both worlds; they'll be able to sell products on the black market for double and triple the price in gold and silver."

"If you want to put aside a few items to barter with during the initial stage, think about the things that no one around here will be able to produce – things a farmer might like to have and would trade for fresh eggs or milk."

Everett though for a second. "Whiskey?"

Jones sighed. "Folks willing to give up life-sustaining food in the middle of a crash for a drink are exactly the type of people you want to avoid. They have serious addictions, and they'll be dangerous. That being said, alcohol has a variety of medicinal uses. That's a good reason to have a few bottles of alcohol around.

"In general, things people can't produce around here are coffee, toilet paper, and sugar. Rice is extremely cheap to buy in massive quantities right now, and you can't grow it in this area. It also takes very little fuel to prepare. You can cook it in a solar cooker, which means you don't have to send up smoke signals to tell everyone in your area of operation that you're here, and you have food."

Everett tried to envision the world Jones was describing. It sounded nothing like the one he lived in now. It was clear that he had a lot of preparations to make. "And the catalyst to the meltdown will be blamed on China or Russia selling too many treasury bonds?"

Jones put some chewing tobacco in his mouth. "No. It will be something much worse."

"Like what?"

"A terrorist attack or a biological threat. It could be a viral outbreak like Ebola, or it could be another 9/11. The top echelon of elites has several scenarios drawn out. When the time comes to pull the trigger, Dragon will decide on the catalyst."

Everett still had trouble believing that a small group of men held the fate of the world in their hands. "And if it's an outbreak, would it be a real virus or a hoax propagated by the media?"

"Oh, it will be real. There's no shortage of weaponized viruses sitting around in DOD-controlled research centers. And the elites have the cures and the vaccines for their personal use."

Everett thought for a few seconds. "And what do you mean by another 9/11? Would the Illuminati orchestrate a false flag attack? Or would it be something the CIA was instructed to allow to happen at the hands of an existing terrorist organization?"

Jones spit his tobacco into a plastic cup. "Could be either. Could be both. We've got a lot of experience with creating boogiemen.

"The CIA created Al Qaeda. Company operatives openly funded the Afghani rebels to fight against the invading Russians in the eighties. You could say it was buffoonery, or you could say it was done with malicious intent. The outcome remains the same.

"Fast forward to 9/11. The case for ISIS being created by the US government with malicious intent is much stronger, not only because of the obvious steps we took to create them, but also because of the connections of the major players in the story."

Everett said, "I'm listening."

"After the invasion of Iraq, everyone in the intelligence community thought the war was over. It should have been. There was some looting and low-level criminal activity, but the Iraqis could have handled that. We'd toppled Sadam's regime and were ready to pull out."

"Why didn't we?" Everett asked.

"Skull and Bones member, George Bush, sent Council on Foreign Relations member, Paul Bremer, to Iraq to be the Presidential Envoy. He was given complete authority over the affairs of the country. He rejected the advice of General Tommy Franks, who'd just run a successful invasion and had a good handle on the situation. Besides that, Franks was well versed in the local politics and had a working relationship with the Iraqis.

"Bremer initiated his de-Ba'athification campaign and alienated the Sunnis from a role in the new government. That was the move that triggered a decade of insurgency fighting and radicalized the Sunni Muslims in Iraq. General Tommy Franks washed his hands of the whole affair and resigned over the quagmire created by Bremer."

Everett said, "Maybe Bremer was just an idiot."

Jones shook his head. "It's unlikely. Bremer was Henry Kissinger's chief of staff. You'll remember that Kissinger is a member of the CFR, Trilateral Commission, and Bilderberg Group. Everything he does is a move to advance toward a one-world government."

Everett laughed. "You make Kissinger sound like the godfather of the New World Order."

Jones smiled. "The book he wrote in 2014 was called World Order. He doesn't try to hide it.

"Back to the radicalized Sunnis in Iraq. Bilderberg member David Petraeus handed out over four hundred million dollars to the alienated Sunni militants, the Sons of Iraq. Years later, this group of Sunnis, battle-hardened by their insurgency fighting against US forces and funded by the US government, was given more training and more weapons to fight against the Assad regime in Syria. They later became known as the Islamic State. Today, the dividend is still paying off, as the administration and the media have the perfect boogieman to keep the American public quaking in their shoes. As long as we promise to keep them safe from ISIL, Americans will sign over their last stitch of freedom without question."

Everett was learning more than he wanted to know. Two weeks ago, he felt like a true patriot who was serving his country. Now, he was feeling more like a member of the old East German Stasi. "Any other signs that the elites are about to pull the trigger?"

Jones nodded. "Whether it's a false flag terrorist attack or an engineered outbreak of Ebola, I think we'll see heavy troop and supply movements across the country. Tons of stuff is already prepositioned, but they'll start moving boots and equipment just before the event. That's one of the things I'm watching for in the daily briefings."

Everett stood up. "You've given me a lot to think about. I've got to get home now, though; I still have a long drive. Would there be a good place for me to hide some of my coins around here?"

Jones got up to see Everett to the door. "Bury them out back in the woods. Pick a tree that you won't forget, and dig a hole. Just make sure your silver is sealed tight. It'll tarnish if it gets any moisture around it. Not gold though. It won't tarnish or corrode."

Everett took the nickel that contained the SD card and stuck it back in his pocket. "Thanks. I'll see you soon."

Jones said, "Bring that little NSA girl up here if you like. There are some nice trails around here for the two of you to enjoy. I'd love to meet her."

Everett took a deep breath. He liked thinking about Courtney. "Yeah. I'm hanging out with her tomorrow night. I'll see what she's doing Sunday afternoon. It's a long trip for her, though. She's way out in South Laurel."

Jones smiled. "Whenever is fine. If you do come, introduce me as Uncle John. She doesn't need to know my work history just yet."

"Okay, but don't address her as the little NSA girl. We're still playing the game and denying that either of us works for the intelligence community."

CHAPTER 19

"We should move toward an international currency because the speculation and conflicts of currency has caused some of the irritations not only among the trading nations but among individuals."

Evelyn Rothschild, 2012 Bloomberg Interview.

Everett pulled into Courtney's driveway Saturday night. He turned off the engine, walked to the door, and knocked.

Courtney answered the door. "Hey. I wasn't expecting you so soon. Come on in; I'll be ready in five minutes."

Everett came in and closed the door. "Oh, am I early?"

Courtney went into her room. "No, but last time you were really late. I thought maybe that was just how you rolled."

Everett was glad she wasn't in the room to see him blush. "Are you ever going to let me live that down?"

"Maybe." Courtney walked back through the living room

and into her kitchen.

Everett looked around at her furnishings and made a mental note. She keeps her stuff neat. Everett was no clean freak, but he could never be happy with a slob.

He looked at a picture of Courtney with her family. "Nice looking family. Do they live nearby?"

She came back in the room, dropped her shoes on the floor, and slipped her feet into them. "California. They couldn't really be any farther away and still be in the same country. What about your folks?"

Everett didn't like talking about his family. He certainly didn't want to tell her about his stepfamilies this soon; he thought it might make him sound dysfunctional. "I was raised by wolves."

They walked outside, and Everett opened the car door for Courtney.

She smiled at the gesture. "At least the wolves taught you good manners."

Everett laughed. He walked around the car, got in, and started the engine.

Courtney looked over at Everett. "I'm not the type of chick who's impressed by cars, but if I was, a BMW 550i would definitely do it."

Everett chuckled. "Thanks . . . I guess."

"So where are you taking me?"

"Kent Island, if that's okay. I like out-of-the-way kind of places."

"Why? Are you married? Is someone going to see us?"

Everett fought back a grin. "No. I just don't like crowded environments like downtown DC. I've never been to this place, but it has great reviews. It's called the Crab House. It's right on the water; it looks really peaceful in the pictures."

"Sounds nice. It should be fun."

The two of them were quiet for a while, but it wasn't an awkward silence. It was okay. Everett was content to be in the car with her, and she didn't seem to be uncomfortable about the silence either.

They made small talk during the hour drive out to Kent Island. Everett thought of it as a test; if he couldn't stand to be in the car with someone for an hour, there wasn't much use in pursuing the matter.

They arrived at the restaurant and were seated right on the water. The cool fall air would soon bring an end to dining al fresco, but today, the weather was pleasant. They both ordered crab legs, which were excellent.

After dinner, the conversation moved to more substantive topics.

Courtney sipped her latte. "So, what did you think of the action in the markets two weeks ago?"

Everett tried to figure out her angle. At the very least, she knew about the attempted attacks from sovereign actors. After all, H and M was taking over the threats that Everett's team had identified. "I don't know. It seemed like bad luck for the BRICS bank. Imagine them having their server meltdown hours before they were to announce a new reserve currency."

Courtney winked at Everett. "Yeah, imagine that."

Everett decided to see what she'd admit to. "So, did H and

M see any activity that would suggest that the meltdown was more than a coincidence?"

Courtney craftily dodged the question. "Like what?"

Everett shrugged. "Like cyber-attacks from hackers who could have been acting on behalf of the BRICS nations in retaliation for the meltdown."

Courtney started to say something, but then didn't. Finally, she said, "IT has a cybersecurity division. You would have surely seen something if that type of activity was occurring."

"Actually, when we identify a threat, we outsource it to another company."

"Who do you outsource it to?"

Everett locked his gaze on Courtney's eyes. "H and M."

Courtney looked down at her latte and rolled her tongue to one side of her mouth. Seconds later, she flipped her hair and looked back up at Everett. "So you've been toying with me for a week now. You know where I work, and now I know where you work. I'm sure you have the same confidentiality policies that we have. I trust Lisa, and I'm sure she would never set me up with an undercover agent who's trying to get me in trouble, so I'm fairly confident that you're all right. I have a curious streak too, and I'd be willing to talk about work, but you're going to have to start."

Everett took his phone out of his pocket and removed the battery. He gave Courtney a nod to do the same.

She complied. "If you don't trust me, that's okay. We can talk about movies or whatever you like."

Everett sipped his espresso. "I trust you, but it's a regular practice to run audits on intelligence personnel by remotely activating their phones, tablets, and laptops. That can't be done to a device with no power source."

Courtney pursed her lips as if she'd just had an epiphany. "That's why all of the devices we're issued at work are Apple products. Have you ever tried to take the battery out of an iPad?"

"I was a computer science major. I'm pretty good with computer hardware, but it would be a hassle, even for me."

"Tell me what you know about the BRICS server."

Everett contemplated what he would say. He was the one who'd pushed the issue. He could have avoided the subject for weeks, but he didn't. Now, he'd crossed the Rubicon, and there was no going back. "I know that the US caused the meltdown."

Courtney looked away from him. "Too shallow. That's obvious. Who did it, and how did they do it?"

"The Company infected the system with a sleeper virus, which activated upon specific market criteria."

Courtney looked back at him. "Now we're being honest. I like that. As a show of good faith, and to answer your question from earlier, yes; several US banking institutions were hit with attempted hacks, which tried to launch an assault on US markets. They were designed to crash all of the major indices by mimicking market orders. If the attacks had been successful, they would have made counterfeit trades until panic selling took over and obliterated the equities markets.

"But we're not out of the woods yet. The BRICS nations hold over two trillion in US debt. Since the cyber-attack didn't work, they can launch outright financial warfare against the US and the dollar by dumping all US debt held among them. We have actionable intel that suggests China is already unloading some of their debt to reduce their cost in such an attack.

"Your turn."

Everett smiled. "Good stuff. But China and Russia won't be the ones to bring down the US economy."

"What makes you so sure?"

"There is a cabal of major power brokers who are planning to take down the existing financial infrastructure, so they can replace it with their own system."

Courtney looked at Everett out of the side of her eye. "Then why aren't the CIA and NSA working to take them down?"

"The CIA and NSA are taking orders from this group."

Courtney sat back and tinkered with her napkin for several seconds. "You know that sounds crazy, right?"

Everett sighed. "Yep."

"And where are you getting your information?"

Everett nodded cryptically. "From a reliable source."

Courtney's response dripped with sarcasm. "Well that makes me feel better."

"Do you think I'd make something like that up?"

Courtney smiled. "No. You seem like an honest person, and I'm pretty good at . . . I'm a good judge of character. I believe you're telling me the truth."

"You're a profiler?"

"I didn't say that."

"How does that fit in with cybersecurity?"

Courtney spun her water glass between her fingers. "If a person – not me, of course – but a person, was a profiler in cybersecurity, she'd be able to advise what type of hacker could be flipped for information or turned into an asset. A profiler might also know which individuals in a foreign intelligence service or corporation would be most vulnerable to entrapment or bribes."

Everett found this devious side of Courtney intriguing. "So you believe that it's at least possible that our employers might use subversive means to achieve their goals?"

Courtney smirked. "I think you've just defined clandestine services."

"Then what is so farfetched about a group that acts on a completely clandestine level with its own agenda? The secret infrastructure is there for the taking. Given the shortcomings of our species proven over and over by history, it seems closer to inevitable than improbable."

Courtney looked at her empty latte and took a drink of her water instead. "You're shattering my paradigm."

"I'm sorry. Do you prefer the bliss of ignorance?"

Courtney pointed at him. "I'm going to let you get away with that one. And no, but it would be nice to have a little warning.

"Would you mind elaborating on your source's theory?"

Everett laid out a much-abbreviated version of what Jones had told him. The two talked late into the night and were eventually asked to leave by the manager so the restaurant could close for the evening.

On the way home, Everett said, "My Uncle John has a nice cabin up in the mountains. I know you like the outdoors, and the leaves are beautiful at this time of year. Would you like to go up there and explore a trail tomorrow?"

"Sounds charming, but it would be a long day. Maybe some other time."

"Sure." Everett was positive that he'd scared her off with this conspiracy talk.

But then she rekindled his hope. "Are you spending Thanksgiving with the wolves?"

Everett laughed. "No, both sets of the wolves have new families that I never really integrated with."

"Then maybe we can have Thanksgiving together. We could ask Ken and Lisa over, and Uncle John, of course."

Everett quickly did the math on Jones and Ken being together for Thanksgiving. He could at least offer. If Jones didn't want to do it, he could make up an excuse. "That'd be great." Then Everett considered the likelihood of Jones still being around by Thanksgiving. It was a sobering thought.

CHAPTER 20

The horse is made ready for the day of battle, but victory rests with the LORD.

Proverbs 21:31

Noah straightened his tie as he was getting ready for court Tuesday morning. "Cassie, we should get a move on. I do not want to be late."

Cassie called out from the bathroom. "Relax. Court doesn't start for another hour and a half. Besides, if I rush to put my makeup on, I'll look like a zombie. Then the judge will never let us get custody of Lacy."

Noah tried to lighten up, but he was very stressed about the custody hearing. He sat down in the living room for a few minutes to pray and ask God for peace.

Cassie was ready to go soon after. "Let's go!"

Noah led the way out the door.

Once they were in the car, Cassie turned the radio on. She scanned the channels until she found an NPR station airing a news brief. The reporter said,

"After an emergency meeting of the FOMC this morning, the Federal Reserve announced an unprecedented bond buying program. The Chairman indicated that the Fed would make a one-time purchase of 2.5 trillion dollars of US debt. Not only will this be the largest one-day balance sheet increase for the US central bank in history, it will also be the largest annual increase.

"The move is said to be a countermeasure to offset severe spikes in interest rates caused by a massive sell-off in US Treasuries. China and Russia alone have sold nearly 2 trillion in US debt since the market opened yesterday morning. A spokesperson for the Treasury said the two countries were forced to sell because of the breakdown in trade among member nations of the BRICS trading block. He went on to say that the decisive action by the Fed will be the best thing for the US, as well as for Russia and China.

"Critics of the Fed's move claim that while interest rates may be curtailed, inflation is likely to jump out of control. The rapid rise in food and energy prices over recent years are accredited to the Fed's bond buying programs back in 2012 and 2013, which were adding just over 1 trillion dollars annually during the peak.

"This argument was debunked by proponents of the Fed's decision. They point out that this massive infusion of US dollars will go directly to the countries selling their US debt. Since nearly none of the 2.5 trillion dollars will end up in America, the effect on domestic prices will be next to nonexistent."

Cassie shook her head.

Noah said, "I take it you disagree."

"NPR is a government shill. Of course, most of the other media outlets are also. Their mandate was to tell the story in a way that keeps people calm. If folks knew the truth, there would be bank runs and rioting in the streets. China isn't dumping US debt because they need the money; this is a deliberate attack. If they were dumping it because they needed the money, they would have done it slowly, over time. By dumping it, they crushed the prices of US treasuries."

Noah said, "Maybe Russia started selling and spooked China."

Cassie replied, "Russia holds less than 200 billion. It isn't enough to crash the US debt market. China, on the other hand, holds close to 2 trillion. Together, they caused a panic in the market and triggered selling by other large holders."

Noah thought for a moment. "If they did it to try to crush America, they wasted all the money lost by pushing down the prices. It sounds like this move by the Fed has stemmed the tide."

Cassie laughed. "Yeah, until hyperinflation sets in. The Fed bought some time; that's all. When we look back on this, we'll see it was a life-changing event for America."

Noah was still buying what he'd been told by NPR. "How will it create inflation here, if all the money goes overseas?"

Cassie said, "Because they'll take those dollars and buy US assets. China and Russia can buy US factories, real estate, gold . . . 2.5 trillion will buy a lot of stuff! No one wants to hold US dollars anyway. Especially after this move. I think we should buy more gold and silver now."

Noah processed what Cassie was saying. "Do you have a connection with your phone right now?"

"Let me check." Cassie took out her phone. "Not yet, but I should in a minute or two."

"Can you place an order on your phone?"

Cassie nodded. "Yes, we have a little time to drop off the check. Our account is already active, and they have our credit card info."

"Okay, do what you think is best."

Cassie studied the signal indicator on her phone. "I also think we should buy some of the things we know are going up in price. We can lock them in at today's prices. Stuff like peanut butter, coffee, and other dry goods that have skyrocketed over the past few years. It's the equivalent of buying a stock that you know is going straight up. We have plenty of storage space."

Noah chuckled. "It's almost insider trading."

"It would be, but any consumer who goes to the grocery and follows monetary policy should know what's about to happen to prices, regardless of what the media tells them."

Cassie started typing in the metals order. "I have a signal. I'm entering the order now."

"Great," Noah replied.

Minutes later, they arrived at the courthouse. They were still over half an hour early. They walked across the street to get two coffees, then came back to sit on the bench in front of the courthouse and wait for Leo.

Noah nervously looked around.

Cassie patted him on the leg. "Leo will be here on time; don't worry."

"I probably should have gotten decaf."

Leo arrived shortly thereafter. "You guys ready?"

Noah stood to shake Leo's hand. "We're ready!"

***

Inside the courtroom, the Parkers' case was the fifth to be called. Noah, Cassie, and Leo approached the defendant's podium, while Ms. Carrick, from the Department of Child Services, stood at the other podium.

Judge Malone looked over the papers and shook his head. "This is absolute nonsense. Mr. Parker, like many people all around this country, I've been following your case. On behalf of the justice system, I want to apologize. The rule of law has failed you, sir. I can't do anything about your case with the Department of Education, but I can restore custody of your daughter. I'll do that today, and furthermore, I'm issuing a no-contact order against the Sevier County DCS."

Noah tried to contain his emotion. "Thank you, your honor."

The judge peered at Ms. Carrick. "I trust you'll relay my no-contact order to your office."

Carrick placed her hands on her hips. "Unlike this court, I followed protocol. You shouldn't try to demonize me or DCS for following the law. I don't appreciate being made out to be the bad guy for doing my job."

Judge Malone replied, "Then maybe you'd appreciate a three-day vacation from your job. Your next display of contempt for this court will land you in the county jail for the next seventy-two hours."

Carrick grabbed her folder from the podium and turned

her back. "Oh, please!"

Judge Malone looked at the bailiff. "Harry, take Ms. Carrick into custody. She just earned three days."

Noah squeezed Cassie's hand. The broad grin on her face showed that she was enjoying this too much.

Cassie put her hand over her mouth to conceal her elation. "Sorry."

Judge Malone redirected his attention back to Leo. "Mr. Cobb, your clients are free to go. I wish them the best in their ongoing judicial proceedings."

Leo escorted the Parkers to the area outside. "Go ahead and pick Lacy up from Sharon's. I'll drop off the paperwork from court later this evening."

Cassie blotted the tears from her eyes as she hugged Leo. "Thank you so much."

Noah patted Leo on the back. "We really appreciate your hard work. You don't know how much getting Lacy back means to us."

"I'm glad I could help. I'll see you later." Leo headed back to his office.

Cassie called Sharon right away to tell her the news. Noah tugged her toward the car while she chatted with Sharon.

Once in the car, Cassie said, "I'm so happy right now."

"Me, too." Noah held Cassie's hands for a second before he started the car.

Cassie said, "Sharon wanted to have a party at the Kettle tonight and invite everyone from Bible study and a few other people from church. I told her we wanted to be alone with

Lacy tonight, and tomorrow would be better."

Noah agreed. "Good call."

Cassie took out her makeup mirror to fix the running mascara from her tears. "She really is a sweet person. I'm so glad Lacy has been with her through all of this. I know it's been rough on Lacy, but it could have been so much worse."

Noah added, "It's been a tough time, but God has blessed us with good friends to help us through."

When they pulled into Sharon's driveway, Noah saw Isaiah's truck. "Look who's here."

Cassie playfully slapped Noah's leg. "I told you so! I can't wait to tell Becky."

Noah cut the engine. "Gossip is a sin."

Cassie flung the door open. "It's not gossip. I'm happy for them, and I want to spread the good news."

Noah teased her, "Justify it any way you want. You don't have to answer to me on Judgment Day."

Cassie gave Noah a look that said watch out.

Sharon's door opened before they reached the porch. Lacy shot out the door. "Mommy, Daddy, am I really going home?"

Noah bent down to hold her. "Yes, princess. You're coming home with us today."

"Forever?" she quizzed.

"Forever!" Cassie affirmed as she bent down to join in the hug.

Isaiah was the first to congratulate them. "We're all so happy for your family, Noah. Everyone has been praying nonstop this morning."

Sharon said, "I called the Taylors and the Rays to tell them the good news. I hope you don't mind."

Cassie hugged her. "Not at all."

Then she pinched Noah and whispered, "See, girls like to share good news."

Noah curled his mouth to one side to show that he was unconvinced by her convoluted reasoning.

Sharon brought Lacy's things to the door. "Is eight o'clock too late for the get-together tomorrow night? I want to close the Kettle early after tomorrow evening's rush."

Noah said, "Eight is fine, but we can't stay too late. We're taking Lacy and Lynette to the Fall Homecoming at the Appalachia Museum over in Clinton Thursday morning. It's an all-weekend event. Thursday is Fall Heritage Day, which is especially for school groups. A lot of people from our homeschool network will be there. The exhibitors show the kids lost arts like butter churning, wool spinning, sorghum making . . . they even have a blacksmith set up."

Isaiah smiled. "What fun!"

Cassie added, "Yeah, and they'll have great bluegrass music, as well as gospel. The Rays will be there; you and Sharon should come."

Isaiah looked at Sharon. "Would you like to go?"

Sharon blushed. "I'd be delighted."

The Parkers said their farewells and headed home to begin rebuilding their family.

Sox met Lacy at the door. Lacy lay down on the floor and hugged her surviving pet. "Sox! I missed you so much! I'm so happy that you're okay."

For their first meal together after being reunited, Cassie made Lacy's two favorite dishes: macaroni and cheese and chilled shrimp with cocktail sauce.

After lunch, Noah asked Lacy, "Would you like to go put some flowers on Buster's grave?"

Lacy looked up at him and bit her lower lip as her eyes began to well up with tears. She nodded her head and stretched out her arms for her daddy to hold her.

Noah picked her up and held her in his lap while the floodgates opened. Soon, they were all crying. Cassie knelt beside Noah and put her arms around them both. Sox even rubbed Cassie's leg, as they were finally able to mourn Buster's death as a family.

CHAPTER 21

You will hear of wars and rumors of wars, but see to it that you are not alarmed. Such things must happen, but the end is still to come.

Matthew 24:6

Tuesday evening, Everett Carroll was happy to get out of work only an hour later than normal. With the obvious attack on the dollar by China and Russia, he knew it could have been another all-nighter. He'd spent the day watching for cyber-attacks against critical US infrastructure.

This time, his workload was passed to a private military intelligence contractor called CACI. With the location of CACI's administration offices near DC, it was common for people to work for a government intelligence agency for ten years, and then take a job at CACI for triple the pay. The justification for higher earnings in the private sector was hard to make. Like all private companies, they did operate at a higher level of fiscal efficiency than any government agency, but CACI was also able to charge ridiculously high fees. One reason for this was that CACI obtained results; the other reason was the incestuous relationship between DC and corporations. DOD and DHS administrators who signed big private contracts were guaranteed well-paid positions on the boards of those companies, as well as exorbitant speaking fees. It was a sort of delayed kickback.

Everett had once considered the private contractor career path for himself. He ruled out CACI after only an afternoon researching the contractor.

They had earned their reputation for obtaining high quality intel during the wars in Iraq and Afghanistan. CACI operated prisons, like the infamous Abu Ghraib, which were immune to the laws in the country of operation. Neither were they held accountable to US or international laws. This freedom allowed them to make their own guidelines regarding levels of torture that could be used to extract information. While the private intelligence contractor did produce some actionable information, they also conducted vicious interrogations on individuals who turned out to be innocent. Once released, the blameless detainees who had been tortured would return to their communities and tell the tales of genital mutilation, sexual assault, being beaten to the point of losing vision and hearing, and being forced to watch family members being raped, tortured, or having their tongues cut out with pliers.

These stories of Muslims being tortured at the hands of Americans became the most valuable tools for radicalizing Muslims who had previously been content to live and let live. It was what the intelligence community referred to as blowback.

As Everett walked to his car, he considered what Jones had told him regarding the blatant mishandling of Iraqi politics by Kissinger's lapdog, Paul Bremer, which had effectively fostered the creation of ISIL. He wondered if CACI had intentionally tortured innocent Iraqis at the behest of the CIA, in order to bolster the Jihadist movement.

Everett chuckled to himself. *If we created Al-Qaeda and ISIL simply because we needed a new boogieman to justify the trillions spent on the military industrial complex after the Cold War, we've got our hands full now. Not only do we have them to worry about, but we've got the Chinese mad at us, and we've managed to reignite the cold war with Russia. That is, if the new cold war doesn't turn into a hot war.*

As Everett started the engine, his phone rang. "Courtney! Wow! She's never called me before."

He answered, "Hello."

"Hey! I was wondering if you want to hang out tonight. I really want to see you."

"I'd love to, but I have to run out to Uncle John's to drop off something. You're welcome to come along. He'd love to meet you." Everett was sure he'd blown the chance to hang out with her, but he was a man of his word.

"Sure, as long as we can hang out. Should I meet you at your apartment?"

Everett was surprised. Courtney had been playing it pretty cool up until now. "That would be great. Can you be there in about an hour?"

"I'll try. Text me your address. See you then."

"Okay, see you in a bit." Everett's mouth was dry, and his heart was beating fast. He was actually falling for this girl. And, it seemed, she was falling for him. Unless she had something important to tell him that she couldn't say over the phone.

An hour later, Everett called in a take-out order to the Thai restaurant around the corner. He put on some comfortable jeans and sneakers.

There was a knock at the door. He opened it to find Courtney standing there, also in comfortable clothes, but still looking very cute. "Right on time."

"Yeah, traffic wasn't too bad, and I left right after we hung up. Are you ready?"

"I am. Listen, there's no reception up at Uncle John's. Would you mind leaving your phone here?"

Courtney put her hands on her hips. "Did you know that's actually a line in a horror movie?"

It struck Everett how creepy that must have sounded. "Oh, yeah. That sounds bad. I'm sorry . . ."

Courtney cut him off. "Just teasing, I left it in my car."

Everett had underestimated Courtney. She was tuned in and evidently didn't trust her bosses either. He closed the door, and they walked to the car.

On the way, Courtney pulled out a different phone. "Just to let you know, I have a burner that I took the battery out of."

Everett was really starting to like this girl. "In case I'm a stalker?"

Courtney laughed. "In case we break down. If you're a stalker, that phone is the least of your worries."

They stopped by the Thai restaurant to pick up dinner and headed out to the cabin.

Courtney looked over at Everett. "Looks like your source was right about America's ability to fend off the assault on the dollar. At least for the short term. If inflation takes off too fast, we still may have a collapse of the US financial system."

Everett kept his eyes on the road. "Whatever happens, it will be at a time of the elites' choosing, and there will be a separate catalyst besides just a financial collapse."

Courtney said, "You know the Chinese have nuclear subs two hundred miles off the coast of California?"

Everett opened his eyes wide. "No! I didn't know that."

"Yep, and they have a carrier taking humanitarian aid to Brazil. The Liaoning and several other ships are in the port of Belem."

Everett snickered. "A carrier hauling humanitarian aid, great cover story. Of course, USAID is completely run by the CIA. I suppose that's no different."

Courtney continued, "The Russians have ships in South Africa, also providing aid, but it looks like three just left for Cuba this morning. Everyone at work is getting nervous. Fifty billion dollars was appropriated to buy off media executives to keep the ship movements out of the news. It could be just saber-rattling, but this is starting to look pretty serious."

Everett said, "No one told us anything. They keep us in the dark about everything except the specific task we're working on."

Courtney furrowed her brow. "I thought you had high-level clearance. Why wouldn't you know about such a serious threat?"

Everett shrugged. "I suppose they figure the less we know, the less potential there is for a leak. My clearance level is DOD collateral clearance."

"Oh, I assumed it was higher." Courtney's voice had a hint of disappointment.

"Yours is higher?" Everett asked.

She flipped her hair. "It doesn't matter. You obviously have a source that's getting stuff from the very top."

"My source isn't active."

"Uncle John?"

Everett had said too much. What was he to do? He really liked Courtney and didn't want to start lying to her, but he also owed his confidence to Agent Jones. "Give me a break." Everett tried to laugh it off.

Courtney didn't fall for it. "Oh, come on. He's the only person in your family that you talk to, and I can't take a phone up there; this isn't a grand mystery."

Everett didn't say anything. Jones was the one who wanted to meet her, after all. If he was mad, it was his own fault.

She patted his leg. "But I won't make you say it, if it makes you feel better."

Everett wasn't about to confirm or deny her accusations. He was happy she wasn't going to push the matter further, but it was obvious that she'd figured it out.

Courtney looked through the takeout bag for a snack. "Anyway, the reason I wanted to talk to you in person was to ask you what you're planning to do if things do go south. Whether it's your conspiracy theory, the meltdown of the financial system due to a cyber attack or decades of bad economic policies, or a hot war with China and Russia, the future is starting to look bleak."

Everett smiled. "I think you're going to like Uncle John's

cabin."

CHAPTER 22

Truth is treason in the empire of lies.

Ron Paul

Noah Parker arrived at the Country Kettle with his family Wednesday evening. Cassie ensured that they were fashionably late by changing her mind about what she would wear not once, but twice. Noah didn't make a fuss about it. As the guests of honor, it made sense for them to arrive after everyone else had been given a chance to get there.

Isaiah met them outside. "There's the happiest family on earth."

Noah held Lacy's hand with one hand and Cassie's with the other. "I feel like the most blessed man on earth. There is nothing like tragedy to remind you of what you have."

Isaiah nodded as he held the door for them.

Inside, Sharon laid out a buffet of fall flavors. She kept the kitchen help at the Kettle and sent the rest of the staff home.

The kitchen staff made a honey ham, macaroni salad, a fruit plate, warm rolls, pecan bars, and a hazelnut cream pumpkin pie. Sharon personally made each guest a hot apple cider topped with whipped cream and caramel. Some people sat at the tables to eat, but most milled around the buffet table as they talked. Most everyone from Isaiah's Bible study was there, and also a few of the Parkers' other friends from church.

Noah shook hands with Jim Taylor. "Thanks for coming out, Sheriff."

Jim smiled. "You can stick to calling me Jim. Besides, this is just temporary."

"Won't you run in the election?" Noah sipped his cider.

Jim nodded. "Sure, but there's no guarantee I'll win. I made some enemies when I cleaned house. In addition to that, by refusing to play ball with DHS, the department has lost all of our federal funding. The sheriff's department is going to have to learn how to do its job with fewer resources. A cutback in services won't be popular with voters.

"We're also losing the MRAP and some of the other equipment that we received through the DOD 1033 program."

Noah shrugged. "Sevier County doesn't really need an armored vehicle, does it?"

"I hope not. I suppose it will depend on the feds. We've lost the carrot for not participating in the federal program, but we've yet to find out what the stick will consist of."

"When you say the stick, you're saying that you expect some type of physical retaliation from DHS for refusing to comply?" Noah tried to understand what Jim was hinting at.

"I hope not. I think DHS has their hands full right now, but if we see the type of economic collapse and heavy-handed government response that Cassie is predicting, our county will be at the top of the list for the feds to demonstrate what happens to dissenters."

"Are you saying that you would instruct your deputies to confront DHS?"

Jim raised his eyebrows. "I'm saying I'll instruct my men to stand their ground and fulfill their oaths. I pray it never comes to that, but I have to run the scenario in my mind in case it does."

"A few deputies wouldn't stand a chance against the federal government." Noah rubbed his chin as he thought about what Jim was implying.

"We'd need the citizens to be on board as well, and prepared."

"You mean, like a militia?"

"Something like that."

Benny Loomis walked up to Noah. "I wanted to congratulate you on winning your custody case. It must have been horrible not having Lacy during that time."

Noah shook Benny's hand. "It was tough, but knowing she was in good hands made it bearable. If we hadn't known the person who had custody of her, I would've gone nuts. You hear so many horror stories about foster homes where children are neglected, physically abused, or sexually abused. That's another arena that the government doesn't belong in."

Benny replied, "I couldn't agree more."

Jim put his finger up to signal that he'd be back in a little while. Noah waved to acknowledge the sign. "Benny, you said you went through something like what I'm going through."

Benny looked from side to side. "I worked for the government for several decades. More specifically, the NSA. I was part of the team that developed the Thinthread Program, which was designed to monitor electronic communications and digital activity of potential terrorists. The team I worked with wanted to be sure that certain restrictions were placed on Thinthread so that it couldn't be used for wholesale surveillance of the American public. But our research was handed over to a government contractor and used in developing a different program, one without the safeguards for US citizens. It was called Trailblazer. Trailblazer was the predecessor to Prism, which actively spied on all phone calls, emails, and social media posts until it was recently decommissioned."

Noah was surprised. "Prism was decommissioned? Does that mean the government isn't spying on us anymore?"

Benny chuckled. "No. There is a vastly more powerful network that handles domestic surveillance now. I still talk with some old friends who keep tabs on things at the Puzzle Palace. From what I gather, the new system is the most advanced artificial intelligence computer ever imagined. It thinks like you and I do, but with much greater capacity. It takes in data from every cell phone, Facebook post, Google search, traffic camera, banking transaction, and credit card purchase. It uses that data to profile every user and store their digital history according to their Social Security number. For people who try to use online aliases, it watches for patterns and tries to associate them to their Social Security numbers. It knows you by name. It knows where you shop, how much money you make, who you call, what videos you watch on YouTube, what temperature you like, how much you weigh . . ."

Noah cut Benny off. "How does it know what temperature I like?"

"Thermal imaging drones and satellites that take readings from inside your home."

"This thing has its own satellites?"

"Oh yes," Benny replied.

"And how does it know my weight?"

"Gas purchases, traffic cams, grocery purchases, cell phone triangulation, that sort of thing. It calculates how much gas you spend, the average mileage for your truck, where you go, tire pressure, and does the math. Those calculations can tell it how much you weigh."

Noah was totally baffled. "How could it come up with tire pressure?"

"Traffic cams on the way to the grocery and on the way home. Through your credit card, it knows what you bought, how much it weighs, and how the weight difference affects your tire pressure. It probably knows you better than you know yourself. It was developed to be omniscient, like God. While it may never know your innermost thoughts or keep count of the hairs on your head, mimicking the omniscience and omnipresence of the Almighty is the goal of its designers."

Noah blinked to try to clear the image from his mind. "How creepy!"

"Yes, but it's necessary to fulfill Bible prophecy. If we're to have a one-world currency, and no one is to be able to buy or sell without the mark of the beast, a very complex monitoring apparatus is necessary."

Noah reluctantly acknowledged what the existence of such a system meant for the future. "I've always believed in Bible prophecy, but I never realized the technology already existed. I suppose I've always thought we'd be out of here by the time something like that came along. Don't you believe in a pretribulation rapture?"

Benny tilted his head from side to side. "Like Isaiah said at the Bible study a while back, one could believe in a pretribulation rapture and still expect things to get very oppressive between now and then. I think we are seeing the beginning of the end. The start of the Tribulation is marked by Revelation 6, which says in verse eight that a quarter of the earth is to be killed by sword, famine, and plague. With the current global population, that's 1.75 billion people, nearly six times the population of the US. In apocalyptic terms, this entire country could die off, and it wouldn't be a drop in the bucket. Which reminds me, China and Russia are both specifically mentioned in prophetic scripture, but nothing that definitively sounds like America is ever mentioned. It could be because we are no longer a going concern."

The concept of America not existing hit Noah like a ton of bricks.

Isaiah walked up and put his hand on Noah's shoulder. "Having fun?"

Noah responded sarcastically, "Yeah, loads."

Isaiah laughed. "What's wrong?"

Noah shook his head. "Benny and I got off on a rabbit trail about the Tribulation and how tough things could get around here."

Isaiah sighed. "Well, it makes sense to be prepared for whatever. Proverbs twenty-two verse three says a prudent man sees danger and takes refuge. So how did that conversation come up?"

Just then, they were interrupted as Cassie came up and took Noah's hand. He was unsure how much of Benny's story he was supposed to share. "Uh, Benny was asking about the trial. What were you saying, Benny?"

Benny looked at Isaiah. "I was telling Noah about my experience with the NSA."

Cassie's eyes lit up. "The NSA?"

Benny brought Cassie up to speed on the story and proceeded to describe his ordeal to the Parkers. "Shortly after 9/11, several of us from the Thinthread team learned about the domestic spying capabilities of Trailblazer, and we filed a formal complaint with the Department of Defense Inspector General. You have to understand, most of us on the Thinthread team had worked at the NSA since the 1970s or early '80s. We'd been taught that spying on the American public was something that you never ever do. We were all shocked at what the agency was willing to do."

Cassie was listening intently. "What happened when you filed the complaint?"

Benny snickered. "The complaint was swept under the rug, so we took it to Congress. We found a sympathetic ear in a top House Intelligence Committee staffer. She drew up a memo and distributed it to the members of the committee. Her boss, who was the chairman of the committee, Congressman Goss, sent her straight to NSA Director Michael Hayden. Hayden basically told her to stop making waves."

Noah asked, "Was it just your team who knew about the program and tried to put a stop to it?"

Benny shook his head. "No. Several Department of Justice

attorneys were also against it, including at least one from the DOJ's Office of Legal Counsel and another, Tom Tamm, who worked with the FISA court."

Cassie interjected, "And FISA is the court that issues warrants for domestic spying?"

Benny nodded. "Yes, they were set up as a watchdog to prevent the abuse of power by the government. Domestic spying without a warrant from FISA is a federal felony. The FISA attorney also got nowhere with his complaints and threatened to inform the press.

"When the concerns were brought to Attorney General John Ashcroft, he informed the administration that he wouldn't sign off to renew the program when it expired. Ashcroft mysteriously had a pancreatitis attack that almost killed him, days after refusing to sign. Since General Ashcroft was incapacitated, Deputy AG James Comey became the acting Attorney General. When he also refused to sign off, Vice President Cheney had the program renewal order redrafted to remove the signature line for the AG and include a line for White House Counsel Alberto Gonzalez, who was on board with the program. If you're the President or Vice President, and what you want to do is illegal, just change the law to make it legal. This sort of thing happens all the time in Washington.

"Long story short, a whole slew of folks, including Acting Attorney General Comey and even FBI Director Mueller, threatened to resign over the renewal. Since it was an election year, Bush rescinded the order and found a sympathetic FISA judge to secretly authorize the renewal under a different legal theory.

"DOJ Attorney Thomas Tamm decided to leak the program to the New York Times, who eventually ran the story. Next, a landslide of leaked stories hit the press. When that happened, the administration came after all the dissenters. Everyone from the Thinthread team who signed the original DOD complaint had their homes raided by the FBI. When I was raided, I felt like I lived in a communist country. My wife looked at me like I'd done something wrong to bring this on the family. Eventually, my family fell apart, and I became a recluse. Some of us were indicted, but the charges were either dropped or reduced to minor charges. It was primarily a scare tactic to let federal employees know that dissent is not tolerated.

"Of course, despite campaign promises about transparency and reining in the surveillance state, Obama increased the unconstitutional powers of the federal government by signing the 2012 NDAA, which contained the indefinite detention clause, which provides for US citizens to be held indefinitely and without being charged with a crime.

"I suspect that Edward Snowden will be the last whistleblower of our kind."

Cassie looked puzzled. "Why? Don't you think there are any true patriots left?"

Benny replied, "There may be some patriots, but after the New York Times article in 2005, the Baltimore Sun article in 2006, and several others outing the federal government for the warrantless surveillance, the public did nothing. There were no massive protests. The Congress who'd sat idly by while the Bush administration pulled this off was never tossed out on their ears, and everyone went back to their day-to-day lives without so much as a shrug. For the people who blew the whistle, it cost us everything: our jobs, our families, the money we spent fighting trumped-up charges, our right to not have our doors kicked in in during the middle of the night, everything. But America didn't care enough to write a letter to their representatives or refuse to vote for anyone who wouldn't vow to restore our freedom.

"Years later, Edward Snowden sacrificed his citizenship to tell the American people about the atrocities that were being committed by the federal government. By then, the public had become rooted in their complacency. I'm convinced nothing will dislodge them at this point, so why would anyone else make such sacrifices to warn them? It's too late anyway. In 2006, an enraged public could have effected a change; when the Snowden leaks came out in 2013, perhaps there was still some hope if Americans would have stood up together. Not today. The infrastructure is established, the Constitution has been nullified, and we're just waiting for the catalyst. When it comes, we're in for a totalitarian regime that will make Hitler, Mao, and Stalin look like Sunday school teachers."

Noah was deeply concerned. He looked at Isaiah, who appeared to be well aware of everything Benny was saying. His eyes then went to his wife, who was drinking in all the information but also seemed unsurprised. "What can we do?"

Benny looked down as he took a deep breath. "Not much we can do. You can make it more difficult for your oppressors to track you. You can quit posting updates on Twitter and Facebook and use encrypted email when you absolutely have to communicate online. Keep the battery out of your phone until you have to make a call, pay with cash, and generally try to reduce your electronic footprint."

Noah said, "Sounds like a hassle."

Benny smiled. "Between convenience, security, and freedom, you can pick two. But you can't have all three."

Noah considered the different combinations of the three attributes Benny offered. "Yeah, I guess convenience should be the lowest priority."

He looked at Isaiah. "And what did you mean by being

prepared? How can you prepare for a totalitarian regime?"

Isaiah winked. "You saw my safe. I suspect you have an idea of what I mean by prepared. Of course, it's more than guns and gold; it's food storage, community, and skills. I'm looking forward to the Homecoming tomorrow. I'm planning to take notes on some of the exhibitors. Especially blacksmithing and sorghum production."

Cassie remarked, "And you'll have a lovely escort, won't you?"

Noah looked away in disbelief that she'd just put Isaiah on the spot like that, but he could still hear the embarrassment in Isaiah's voice.

"Indeed, I will," Isaiah said sheepishly.

David Ray approached the group, and Noah turned toward him, relieved to be distracted from the somewhat awkward conversation. "Did you try the hazelnut pumpkin pie?"

Noah pursed his lips. "Bro, who are you talking to?"

David chuckled. "Oh, yeah. What was I thinking? Did you like the pie better or the pecan bar?"

Noah put his head in his hand and furrowed his brow as if he were in deep thought. Finally, he looked up. "Are you making me pick? I guess I have to go with the pecan bar."

David nodded. "Tough call. Hey, do you guys want to ride out to Clinton with us tomorrow? The girls can keep each other occupied."

Noah replied, "Sounds like a good idea. Lacy and Lynette can keep each other entertained as well."

Cassie slapped Noah on the arm playfully. "Watch it,

mister!"

Noah tried to fight back a smile. As Cassie walked away, Noah winked at David.

David shook his head. "You're a braver man than I am. Why don't you bring that new rifle over on Saturday morning? We can set up a little shoot-and-scoot course over behind the barn."

"That'd be fun. How much ammo should I bring?"

David said, "I'm going in with a couple of buddies to buy a pallet of sixty-two grain mil-spec ammo. You can have 1,000 rounds out of that for $250. Inflation has pushed ammo sky high; that's a real deal."

"Wow. That is a good deal. I think Cassie paid $150 for 200 rounds when she bought the rifle, and that was the cheapest option available at Tim's Guns. I'll take 1,000 rounds."

"Should you check with Cassie before you commit?"

Noah laughed. "No way! She'll be trying to buy a pallet. In fact, I should go ahead and buy 2,000 rounds if you have enough to spare. That will give us a thousand rounds to train with and another thousand to store. Will they keep well?"

"Oh, yeah, we've got plenty, and the ammo is in metal, thirty-cal ammo cans. The cans have a rubber gasket, which creates an airtight seal. That ammo will last longer than we will. Isaiah is coming by on Saturday as well. I think he's planning to pick up a few rounds."

Noah rubbed his brow as he thought about what a valuable commodity ammunition might be after a collapse. "How much is Isaiah buying?"

"At least 5,000 rounds," David replied.

"Really? How much is on the pallet? I mean, how much do you want to get rid of?"

David said, "We'd like to sell as much as possible. The pallet we bought has 80,000 rounds. That was a big nut to come up with, but it was such a good deal that I was sure we could get rid of it."

"Can I take 5,000 rounds?" Noah asked.

"Sure. Are you positive you don't need to ask Cassie?"

Noah curled one side of his mouth. "My only risk is not buying enough. I'm afraid if I give her the option, we'll have ammo cans stacked to the ceiling. Did you tell Jim about the deal? I'm sure he'd buy some."

David nodded. "He's buying a pallet for the sheriff's department. That's part of how we got such a great buy."

"Did he say anything to you about getting ready for hard times ahead?"

David crossed his arms. "Why do you think we're buying a pallet of ammo?"

"Are we doing some type of militia training on Saturday?" Noah asked.

David paused as if he was crafting his response. "Maybe mutual assistance group is a better name for it. But keep a tight lid on it, especially around Henry Whitaker. Benny doesn't trust him."

"Why don't we just kick him out of the group? Wouldn't that be easier than tiptoeing around him?"

David sighed. "That's what I said. Benny seems to think if

Henry is some type of tattletale, he could serve as a conduit to feed misinformation."

Noah looked around to make sure Henry was a good distance away. "What do you think? Is Henry some kind of informant?"

David shrugged. "Benny thinks he is. Isaiah trusts Benny's judgment; I guess I do too. Henry works for code enforcement. It's in his nature to keep an eye on people for the government. That's pretty much his job description."

Noah thought for a moment. "I hate to falsely accuse someone if they're innocent."

David looked at Noah. "Not trusting someone isn't really accusing them. And the consequences of having an informant in our midst could be detrimental if the stuff your wife talks about ever comes true. I'd rather err on the side of caution."

This reasoning seemed sound to Noah. The people from Bible study were putting a lot of stock in what Cassie was saying. It was time for Noah to go all-in as well. "Cassie and I are going to have to share a rifle on Saturday unless one of us can use our shotgun."

David replied, "I can lend one of you an extra rifle. You know you can pick up a good AK-47 for less than $1,000, right?"

Noah said, "That might make a good Christmas present for Cassie. But maybe I should buy another AR so we can use the same ammo."

"That's a valid argument. The good thing about AKs is they're more resilient. They don't need as much maintenance, and they can handle tough battle conditions. Rain, dust, dirt, and mud will ruin an AR if you don't keep that thing super clean and well oiled. An AK will take a lickin' and keep on tickin'.'"

Noah rubbed his chin. "I suppose there is something to be said for diversity."

David added, "But if you're buying it for Cassie, you might want to look around for an AK-74. It's designed the same as the AK-47, but it uses a smaller round and is quite a bit lighter. The smaller round is similar to a 5.56 round. It makes it easier to shoot and easier to carry more ammo into a battle."

"But it looks just like an AK-47?"

"Skinnier barrel and magazine, but otherwise, yes. Most people probably couldn't tell them apart at first glance."

Noah grinned. "Don't say anything to Cassie. That's what she's getting for Christmas."

***

The next morning, Noah and the girls were ready to go as soon as the Rays' minivan pulled into their driveway. Cassie escorted Lacy to the van, and Noah grabbed a small cooler.

Noah sat in front with David, Cassie and Becky sat in the center seats, and the two girls sat in the rear.

"Are you driving through Knoxville?" Noah asked.

David shook his head. "No way. We hear all of the Knoxville EMS calls over the radio. That place is getting to be as bad as all the other major cities. We'll drive out to Emory Road and take that to 441. It's about ten miles out of the way, but it's a scenic drive, especially with the leaves changing. We should get there in about an hour."

Noah snickered. "And it increases our chances of survival."

David nodded. "And then there's that."

Noah sat back in his seat. "Ah, the good old days. Remember when Detroit was the only city in America that looked like a third world country?"

David looked over at Noah and smiled. "I remember when no cities in America looked like a third world country.

"What did you bring in the cooler? You know they'll have all kinds of food out there. Right?"

Noah opened the cooler and handed David a cold bottle of root beer. "Just a few cold drinks and some water."

"Root beer in a glass bottle. Now that's living it up. Good call, Noah."

Noah offered a selection of root beer or cream soda to the girls. Cassie and Becky each took a bottle and passed one back to each of the children.

They soon arrived at the museum, which was spread out over several acres in the form of cabins, barnyards cordoned off by split rail fences and filled with sheep and goats, barns filled with old farming tools and equipment, and a millhouse for grinding corn powered by a nearby stream.

"Animals!" Lacy screamed.

"I want to pet the sheep! Daddy, can we?" Lynette begged.

David slung his daypack over his shoulder as he exited the vehicle. "First stop, petting zoo."

Noah insisted on paying the price of admission for everyone since David had driven.

David took out his wallet. "Noah, come on. That's too much. That's way more than the gas to drive out here."

Noah put his hand up. "Your family has done so much to help us – keeping Lacy while we were fighting for custody, tricking out the AR for us, all those magazines. Please let me do this."

David shook his head and reluctantly put his wallet back in his pocket. "Where did the girls go?"

Noah shrugged. "Petting zoo, I'd imagine. I guess we'd better kick it into high gear if we want to keep up."

The two men headed toward the animal pens in search of the rest of their party.

David nudged Noah in the arm. "Is that Isaiah holding Sharon's hand over there by the quilts?"

Noah smiled. "That's him. He said he was coming out today. He wants to take notes on some of the lost skills. He thinks things are going to get pretty tough."

David's eyes were wide with surprise. "Did you know he and Sharon were an item?"

Noah tipped his head from side to side. "Cassie suspected that they might be. I guess it's out in the open now."

David shook his head. "Or they don't know anyone is watching. Let's go over there and bust them."

Noah tugged David on the arm. "Let's go find the girls and leave the lovebirds in peace for a few more sweet moments."

David pursed his lips. "You're no fun at all."

Noah and David found the girls at the animal pens. Nearby, there was an exhibit of a farmer preparing the shorn wool for spinning.

Lacy pulled Noah's shirt sleeve. "Daddy, does it hurt the sheep when they shave their fur to make wool?"

Noah patted her on the head. "No, honey. They like it. I think they do it in the summer, so the sheep won't be so hot. Are we ready to walk around and see some other exhibits?"

"Okay," Lacy replied. "Can we come back to the animals if we have time?"

"Sure thing, honey." Noah led the way to the next building, which was the blacksmith's shop.

Isaiah and Sharon arrived at the blacksmith's shortly after Noah's party.

Noah acted surprised to see them. "Hey, when did you two get here?"

David looked at Noah. "Yeah, what a shocker."

Isaiah replied, "We've been here for a while. We wanted to get here early, so we wouldn't miss anything."

Lacy and Lynette looked on in amazement as the blacksmith took a simple piece of metal and fashioned it into a horseshoe.

After the demonstration, Isaiah took out his notepad and asked the blacksmith several questions about setting up a forge.

The blacksmith was eager to teach. "Essentially, you need something to hold, heat, and hit your work with. You don't need a super elaborate forge like this. You can build one out of a few cinder blocks as long as you put in a pipe or some other source to get oxygen in from below the fire. For hitting, you could use a ball-peen hammer, but I'd recommend picking up a cross-peen hammer like this one. For holding my work, I made these tongs out of half-inch rebar. Let me see if I have some in the back."

The blacksmith went outside and returned seconds later, holding two lengths of half-inch rebar. He proceeded to hammer out the ends on the anvil to create the surface that would be used to hold a metal object in the intense heat. He heated the next section of the metal rod and hammered out an area where the two bars would meet. "I'll drill this out while it's still hot. It's much harder to drill once the metal cools."

Using an old hand drill, he drilled out a hole in each bar. Then he placed a length of quarter-inch round stock in the holes to connect the two bars and hammered the pin on the anvil so that each side flattened out and secured the two arms of the tongs together. In ten minutes, he'd fashioned the pair of tongs. "These are for you. I hope you'll put them to good use." He handed the tongs to Isaiah.

Isaiah took the tongs. "Thank you very much. What do I owe you?"

"Go home and start blacksmithing. That means more to me than money."

Isaiah nodded. "I will."

The blacksmith drew on Isaiah's notebook to show him how to set up a simple forge at home and gave him some notes on getting the fire up to temperature. Isaiah thanked the man again, and the group headed to the chuck wagon, which was serving fried chicken, biscuits, and gravy. Everyone took their food to one of the many picnic tables set up close by for dining.

After lunch, everyone headed over to watch the sorghum being made. A horse was turning a large pole, which was connected to the cane press. A man fed the sorghum cane into the press, which squeezed out a light green liquid. This liquid was poured into a shallow tub with a fire underneath. The tub created a large surface area, so the water could cook out faster. The woman tending the cook tub kept skimming the greenish foam off as the sorghum cooked. Once the desired thickness and dark brown hue was achieved, the sorghum was ready to be bottled. Isaiah made notes on the production process in his notebook.

"Do we eat sorghum, daddy?" Lacy asked.

Noah tousled her hair. "Yes, sweetie, mom uses it for pecan pies. Sometimes I put it on pancakes or even French toast. Folks used to eat it on a biscuit."

"Can we put some on a biscuit next time we have them?"

"Sure, honey," Noah said.

Next the group all headed over to the main stage to watch the bluegrass band that was playing.

Isaiah said to Noah, "I have an old banjo that I used to pick at in college."

"You should pull it out and dust it off."

Isaiah shook his head. "I could never make it sound like that."

"It just takes practice." Noah leaned in close to whisper, "Besides, I hear chicks like musicians."

Isaiah blushed and looked to make sure Sharon wasn't within earshot. "Maybe I will have to tune it up."

Cassie and Becky took the girls over to an area with special activities for kids, while the rest of the group stayed and watched the musical performance.

Everyone enjoyed themselves immensely. The day was soon over, and they all headed home. Lacy and Lynette were worn out. They fell asleep as soon as they got in the minivan.

David dropped the Parkers off at their house. "We'll see you all on Saturday morning for rifle training, right?"

"We'll be there. Thanks for everything." Noah took his cooler and closed the door of the vehicle.

CHAPTER 23

The LORD is my shepherd, I shall not be in want. He makes me lie down in green pastures, he leads me beside quiet waters, he restores my soul. He guides me in paths of righteousness for his name's sake. Even though I walk through the valley of the shadow of death, I will fear no evil, for you are with me; your rod and your staff, they comfort me. You prepare a table before me in the presence of my enemies. You anoint my head with oil; my cup overflows. Surely goodness and love will follow me all the days of my life, and I will dwell in the house of the LORD forever.

Psalm 23

Soon after Everett Carroll got settled at his desk Monday morning, Tom Doe walked by his cubicle.

"Everett, this is a get-well card for John Jones. He was admitted to the hospital early this morning. Everyone is just jotting down a few words of encouragement. The office is sending him some flowers."

Everett fought to hide the pang of emotion that was coming over him. "Oh, sure."

Everett took a pen and wrote out a short feel-better wish. He handed the card back to Doe and offered a concerned smile.

"Thanks." Tom Doe returned the obligatory smile, took the card and continued to navigate his route through the catacombs of cubicles.

A deep sorrow rushed through Everett's stomach. He knew Jones would likely not recover. Everett continued to perform his tasks almost robotically as he thought about his dying friend. *I need to get out of here and go see him. Time may be short.*

Everett started going over a few fail-safe excuses to get him out of work early. There were no mission-critical events taking place, and he never left early, so he could afford to take a day, from an office politics point of view.

He texted Courtney and had her call the office number that all employees were to give out as their work-emergency contact number. She was to claim to be his apartment manager and leave a message to inform Everett that there was a broken pipe leaking in his apartment.

The message was soon passed to Tom Doe, who called Everett over the speakerphone. "Everett, your apartment manager just called and said you've got water all over your apartment. I'll split up your task list if you want to take a personal day. You have plenty of time saved up. This is a government job; when it comes to paid time off, it's use it or lose it."

Everett picked up the receiver. "No way! Are you sure

you'll be okay without me?"

"Get out of here. We've got you covered."

"Thanks so much, I really appreciate it." Everett followed the protocol for closing out his task box early, and then headed for the door. He knew that Jones had gone to MedStar Hospital in DC when he'd first had trouble breathing, so Everett assumed that would be where Jones had been admitted this time.

Everett thought, I shouldn't show up empty-handed, but I know he won't want flowers. They probably took his chewing tobacco. Maybe I'll bring him some nicotine gum. If he's conscious, he'll probably be wanting a fix.

Everett stopped at the drugstore on his way into DC and picked up two boxes of nicotine gum. He also took a copy of The Weekly Standard for Jones to flip through. He looked at the crossword puzzle books, but decided against it; Jones wasn't likely to have a lot of energy for doing puzzles.

Rush hour traffic had died down, so Everett arrived at the hospital in less than an hour. He wondered what name Jones was admitted under. He asked for John Jones at reception.

The receptionist said, "Room 305. Can I please have a photo ID? And please sign in on this form."

Everett presented his driver's license and signed the form. He handed the pen back to the receptionist and offered a warm smile.

She smiled back. "Follow the hallway to your left, and you'll find an elevator bank at the end. Take that to the ninth floor. The nurses' station will be on your right when you arrive. They'll direct you to the room. Have a nice day."

"Thanks." Everett proceeded down the hall. He wasn't

sure what to expect. He didn't like hospitals or dying or sickness. He steeled himself for whatever the encounter might be like. This wasn't about having an enjoyable experience; it was about being a friend to someone who'd given so much.

He soon reached Jones's room. Jones was lying in the bed with an IV attached to his arm, and the ever-present oxygen tubes were inserted in his nose. His eyes were closed, and he was breathing softly. Wires attached to a heart monitor ran beneath the sheets. His skin was pale, and it looked paper thin, as if the least amount of pressure might break it.

How had he deteriorated so quickly? Everett thought. He took a deep breath and looked for a nurse in the hallway.

"Can I help you?" A slightly overweight woman with a sweet, motherly voice approached Everett.

He looked at her nametag. "Yes, Mrs. Collins? I'm here to see John Jones. He looks like he's sleeping. I don't know if I should disturb him."

She put her hand on Everett's back. "You can talk to him. He's on a high-dosage opioid drip, so he may not be very responsive. He was in a lot of pain when he was admitted."

Everett nodded. "Once the pain is under control, do you think he'll be released?"

Mrs. Collins looked at Everett with compassion and continued to keep her hand on his back. "It's not likely that Mr. Jones will be leaving. The doctor thinks he has less than a week. The cancer has spread all over his chest and is in his liver."

Everett looked at the brightly polished floor, then back up at the nurse. "Does he know?"

She simply nodded.

"Thank you." Everett walked back into Jones's room. He stood near the bed and gently took Jones's hand.

Jones turned his head toward Everett and half opened his eyes. A slight smile came across his face. "Hey there."

"I brought you some nicotine gum and a magazine."

"God bless you. They stole my tobacco." Jones seemed to be coming around. "Push that button on the side of the bed so I can sit up."

Everett complied with the request. "Is that far enough or should I raise it a little more?"

"That's perfect." Jones took the cup from the bedside table and sipped some water through the straw. "Can you open a piece of that nicotine gum for me?"

"Sure." Everett opened the gum and handed a piece to Jones. "So how is the food here? Would you like me to sneak something in for you?"

Jones popped the gum in his mouth. "It isn't too bad. I don't have much of an appetite. Thanks for the offer, but I'm afraid it would be wasted on me. If you have time, though, I'd love a pair of headphones. There's a drugstore down the street. Nothing fancy, just something to plug into my phone."

"No problem. I took the day off work, so I have all day. Is it so you can listen to music on your phone?"

"They're for my phone, but not music. I found a website from some church out in California. The pastor who founded it has passed on, but they still have his sermons available for download. His name was Chuck Smith. Something about the way he speaks. . . it's very soothing. Listening to him read the

Bible really puts me at peace. I'm kind of looking forward to meeting him."

Everett was glad that Jones had found a source of hope, but he didn't want to talk about death, nor the afterlife. "California, huh? Do they still allow churches out there?"

Jones smiled. "For now. So how are things with the little NSA girl?"

"Good. She enjoyed meeting you last week."

Jones looked at Everett. "She seems like a real nice girl. Kind of sassy, but you probably need that. Be sure you tell her I'm sorry that I can't make it to Thanksgiving. That was very nice of both of you to invite me."

Everett felt the lump swelling in his throat, but he was determined not to cry. He shook his head. "You don't know that. You might be around for a while."

Jones sighed. "Don't feel sorry for me. I've made my peace with God. I'm going to a better place. You, on the other hand, you're fixin' to go through the ringer. I couldn't have timed my exit any better. The masses out there, they're the ones I feel sorry for. You kids will be okay. You're smart, so is Courtney, but you'll need to depend on each other. Tough times create a lot of stress. Be nice to one another even when you feel like you're about to snap. People are what matters. Take it from someone standing on the precipice of eternity. I wish I would have invested a lot more in people and relationships and less on all the things that seem so useless from where I sit now."

Everett took in everything Jones was saying. He listened more than he talked. It was difficult for him to come up with conversation at such a time.

Jones picked up the television remote and turned on the

news. Everett sat in the chair by the bed and watched silently.

Several minutes later, Jones said, "I can feel the pain medication in my IV. I might nod out for a while. You're welcome to stay or go. Whatever you decide, I really appreciate you stopping by."

Everett nodded. "I'll hang around for a bit."

Soon, Jones was fast asleep.

Everett pulled the sheet up over Jones's chest. He decided to walk down the street to buy the headphones. He quickly found a nice set of earbuds at the drugstore.

It was well into the afternoon, and Everett was getting hungry. The hospital was part of the Georgetown University campus, which was less than two miles away from George Washington University where Everett had attended college. He quickly found the familiar campus sandwich shop that catered to students on tight budgets. The shop made fantastic sandwiches for a very fair price. Everett went in and ordered the mozzarella caprese sandwich that he'd often treated himself to in college. The look of the place hadn't changed much; of course, it hadn't been that long since he'd been there. The familiar surroundings were comforting. Everett ate his sandwich, but it was hard to enjoy because of his heavy heart. He walked around the campus for a while and took in the cool autumn air. The trees in the green spaces were beautiful hues of gold, orange, and red. Everett thought about how autumn marked the end of the life cycle in nature and how it coincided with the end of his friend's life.

He finished his tour of the campus and made his way back up to Jones's room. Jones was still asleep, but the nurse came in to serve dinner. She nudged Jones gently. He eventually came around. "You still here?"

"You said I could stay. I did step out for a while to buy

your earbuds. Now you can listen to your lectures." Even the word sermon made Everett uncomfortable; he wasn't sure why.

"Thanks. These will be just fine." Jones opened the earbuds and handed the packaging to Everett to throw away. He set the earbuds down and picked at the food on his tray but didn't seem interested in it.

The two men looked at the television screen as Jones scrolled through the channels. They chatted here and there, not talking about much and not really paying attention to what was on TV. Everett could tell that Jones was happy to have him there, even if he wasn't much of a conversationalist at times like this.

Jones eventually fell back asleep. Everett jotted down a short note to tell Jones he would be by the next day after work and headed for the door.

***

The following day Everett pushed himself through his work routine.

At lunch, Everett sat with Ken, as usual, but he let Ken do all the talking. Ken was a wordy fellow, so that required no coaxing on Everett's part.

Tom Doe passed by his desk after lunch. "Did you get that mess cleaned up?"

"Yes, sir. Thanks for being so accommodating."

"Well, these things happen." Doe patted him on the shoulder as he walked away.

Everett tried to stay focused, but the sadness was eating at him. After work, he shot past all of his co-workers to avoid the menial chitchat. Everett thought of hitting a drive-through on the way to the hospital, but couldn't bring himself to do it. Instead, he stopped by a deli on Leesburg Pike on the way into DC. He quickly selected cold cuts for a nice sandwich and was soon back on the road. It was rush hour, but Everett was traveling against traffic. Most commuters lived outside of DC and were on their way home.

Everett arrived in just over an hour, even with the congested roads. He signed in and made his way back toward Jones's room.

He exited the elevator and saw Mrs. Collins at the nurses' station. "Hi, how's he doing today?"

Her eyes were filled with compassion. "Not so good, but I'm sure he'll be glad to see you."

Everett nodded. "Thanks. Is he awake?"

"Probably not. He's been out almost all day. The doctor increased his pain medication. He was really hurting last night. But you go on in there. Hold his hand; see if he comes around."

"Okay." Everett walked into the room. Jones was sleeping and making a deep gurgling sound. Everett quickly went back to the nurses' station.

"Mrs. Collins, it sounds like Mr. Jones is choking," he said frantically.

She stood up. "Calm down. I know it doesn't sound normal, but it is. We gave him a dose of glycopyrronium. I'll give him another dose and see if that helps. What you're hearing is terminal respiratory secretions."

Everett didn't understand, but he was comforted that the nurse seemed to know what she was talking about. "Alright.

Thank you."

He went back in and stood by the bed. He took Jones's hand. "John, it's Everett. I'm here."

Jones was unresponsive.

"Want to watch the news?" Everett turned on the television and watched it as he sat next to his sleeping friend.

The nurse came in and injected the drug into Jones's IV. "That should help. It might not take effect right away. Give it a little bit."

"Thanks for taking such good care of him, Mrs. Collins. Has anyone else been by to visit?"

"Just you. A messenger brought the flowers and a card from his work."

Everett remembered what Jones had once said about the Company. She won't love you back.

"Let me know if you need anything. Anything at all." Mrs. Collins offered a sympathetic smile as she left the room.

Everett pulled the other chair around so he could put his feet up. He sat back and rested comfortably as he watched the news. Shortly thereafter, he drifted into a light sleep.

When he awoke, he checked his phone for the time. "Wow, I was out for almost an hour."

Everett gave Jones's hand a gentle squeeze. "John. Wake up for a little while."

Jones didn't come around. Everett decided to take a short walk around the hospital and the campus to stretch his legs.

He gave Courtney a call as he walked.

"Hey!"

"How're you holding up, soldier?" she asked.

"I'm good."

"Is Uncle John doing any better?"

"No, he's worse. He is completely out. They've got him pretty doped up. He'd be in a lot of pain if he wasn't, though."

"Would you like me to come by for moral support?"

"That's so nice of you to offer, but I'm okay. Uncle John wouldn't even know you were here."

"If you change your mind or you just need to talk, give me a call. I'm here, okay?"

Everett had never really seen this soft side to Courtney, although he'd suspected that it was there. "Thanks, so much. I really appreciate it."

"Anytime. Talk to you soon."

"Okay, bye." Everett hung up and started heading back to the hospital room.

When he arrived, Jones seemed to be coming to. Everett took his hand. "John, hey."

Jones turned his head toward Everett and half opened his eyes. He gave Everett's hand a light squeeze to acknowledge his presence.

A minute later, Jones appeared to be fully awake. It was obvious that even with the high dosage of pain relievers, he was in pain. "Can you pass me my cup?"

Everett did so.

Jones took a small sip from the straw.

Everett asked, "Do you want some nicotine gum?"

"No. I'm fine without it." His voice was weak. His skin looked much worse than it had just the day before.

"Do you want to watch the news, or should I have the nurse bring you something to eat?"

Jones shook his head ever so slightly.

Everett was at a loss for words. He just stood next to his friend's bed.

The minutes passed, and Everett stood patiently.

"Thank you, Everett."

"I'm the one who should be thanking you; what could you possibly be thanking me for?"

"For being my friend. I pray that you'll really dedicate some time to thinking about what you believe. I hope you'll discover that Jesus is real. I hope we'll meet again in glory."

"I'll think about it."

"Good." Jones forced a smile through the pain.

Tears started to flow down Everett's cheeks. He squeezed Jones's hand as he watched the life slowly leave his friend's body. A look of serenity replaced the expression of pain and anguish on John Jones's face, and he breathed his last breath.

***

Everett was straightening his tie in the mirror Tuesday morning when he heard a knock. He walked to the door and opened it. "Wow! You look great."

Courtney walked in and took her coat off. "Thanks. I was worried this dress might be too short for a funeral, but it's the only black dress I have that covers my shoulders. You look nice, too. I've never seen you in a suit."

"Do you want a cup of coffee? We still have a few minutes before we need to leave."

"No thanks. So Lisa and Ken are coming. Was Ken close with John?"

"Not at all. He's coming because I asked him to. I don't want to be the only one from our office at the funeral. I'm sorry I wasn't completely honest about John. He had his reasons for not wanting to tell you his whole history."

Courtney rolled her eyes. "Yeah, I was completely surprised to find out that he wasn't your real uncle. What a shame to have your skill set wasted at an analyst's desk. Clandestine Services is really missing out by not having you on the team."

Everett loved Courtney's playful sarcasm. His only fear was that he was losing control of his feelings for her. He'd never been in a relationship where the thought of losing someone produced so much anxiety. She seemed to be quite interested in Everett as well, but how could he be sure that she wouldn't get bored? Only time would tell.

Everett finished drinking his coffee, brushed his teeth, and put on his jacket. "Okay, let's go."

"Do you have an umbrella? It wasn't raining when I left."

"Sure." Everett retrieved the umbrella and held it for Courtney as they walked to the car.

Once they were on the road, Everett said, "It was very nice of you to come along today. Your boss didn't hassle you too much about taking the day off?"

"No, as long as there's no imminent crisis, we can take personal days. The flipside is that if there is a serious event, we have to drop everything until the threat is evaded. Speaking of events, did you know the US closed over 400 foreign bases and DOD-controlled facilities last night?"

"No, why?"

"They were all reclassified as non-essential."

"If they were non-essential, why were they there in the first place?"

Courtney shook her head. "I suppose they were essential for pilfering the US taxpayer to prop up the military industrial complex. It's big business and bigger politics. They were probably essential for threatening other nations into complying with US fiscal policy as well. But if what Uncle John said is true, that jig is up. Sorry, I meant John."

Everett nodded. "We can still call him Uncle John. He didn't have any family, so I'm sure he'd be honored. He'd mentioned to me that a large-scale repositioning of troops and military assets within the US would be a sign that they're getting ready to pull the trigger."

"And by 'they,' are you referring to the Illuminati?"

Everett curled his mouth. "New World Order, whatever you want to call them. 'They' are whoever have their finger on the button to bring down the political and financial system, so 'they' can replace it with their own global government and global monetary system. Do you know where the military personnel from all of these installations are being sent?"

"No, but I can get into the military's human resources database and track them over the next few days."

Everett nodded. "Fantastic. We should meet up every day or so to keep each other briefed on any new developments."

"Mr. Carroll, you don't have to make up excuses to see me every day. Just come out and ask me."

Everett could feel his face getting red. He tried to will himself to not be embarrassed, but it was to no avail. "Really, I just thought . . ."

"I'm kidding!" Courtney released her seatbelt and leaned over to kiss him on the cheek. She sat back in her seat and put her seatbelt back on. She put her hand on his leg. "I like you too, Everett."

His heart pounded. He suddenly felt somewhat lightheaded and took a deep breath. Everett worried that he might lose consciousness while he was driving. He tried to put his focus on the road and the steering wheel, but he knew the physical symptoms were confirmation of what he already knew: he was in love.

Since Jones had no family, no procession was planned. Everett drove straight to the cemetery. The drizzling rain had stopped, but it was still cloudy. The dampness brought out the familiar smell of the fall leaves decomposing and completing the circle of life. The smell had always evoked a feeling of melancholy for Everett, and it seemed to suit the occasion so well.

The gravesite was a simple headstone. There was no grave, as Jones had been cremated. The urn was secured in a niche within the headstone.

Ken and Lisa arrived minutes later.

"Hey, thanks for coming out," Everett said.

"No problem. There aren't many people here," Ken replied.

"Yeah, well I guess that's what you can expect when your job description is to live your life unnoticed."

Ken asked, "So what's the name on the headstone?"

"It's blank except for the masonic square and compass."

Ken's mouth hung open. "Really? They're going to bury him with no name on the headstone?"

Everett said, "I think the engraver just hasn't gotten to it yet. I'm sure they'll put a name on it."

Ken crossed his arms. "So we'll never know what his real name is."

Lisa said, "I wonder if he'll get a star on the wall at Langley."

Everett shook his head. "That's only if you're killed in action."

Ken stood close to Everett and spoke low. "Did you find out if all the rumors about Jones were true?"

Everett looked around. All of the other six attendees were men who wore sunglasses and long overcoats. While the weather certainly warranted an overcoat, it was odd how everyone looked so uniform. And the sunglasses were certainly not needed on such a dreary day. He whispered to Ken, "Why don't we talk about that later."

One of the men said a short eulogy. He praised Agent Jones for his faithful service, explaining that he had worked with Jones without mentioning any specifics of where, when, in what capacity, or for how long. Everett felt sorry for the man, as he seemed to be sincerely sorrowful over the loss of John Jones. He wondered if the man wished he could more freely express his grief.

After the funeral, one of the other attendees walked over to Everett and Ken. "Mr. Carroll, Mr. Gordon, were you gentlemen close to Mr. Jones?"

"He was a good boss. We felt we should pay our respects. What's your name?" Everett offered his hand to the man.

The man shook Everett's hand. "I worked with Mr. Jones on a project for some time. It was nice to meet you. Perhaps I'll see you gentlemen around." The man walked away without giving his name.

Ken looked at Everett. "On that note, I'm out of here."

Everett caught him by the arm. "Why don't we all meet for lunch at the old diner right before you get to Ashburn?"

"Right before Town Center?"

"That's the one."

"See you there in a bit." Ken took Lisa's hand and headed for his car.

At the diner, Everett laid out the information that Jones had shared with him to Ken and Lisa while they ate. He focused on the fundamental problems that would create the collapse and tried to gloss over most of the conspiracy information. He explained what the world would look like in a very short time, delicately laying out the predictions made by Agent Jones that had already come to pass.

Lisa seemed to accept that the information was true more quickly than Ken. She kept looking at him for answers, but he appeared to have trouble digesting what he was being told.

Ken had finished less than half of his plate when he set down his fork in frustration. "So what are you saying? The whole country is going to look like Mad Max by Christmas."

Courtney said, "More like Hunger Games than Mad Max. Big Brother type of totalitarian dystopia, you know?" She had a way with words.

"So what are we supposed to do?" Ken was clearly in a huff.

Everett calmly explained the course of action that he had begun. "If you and Lisa want to follow suit, we have a place where we can all lay low until this blows over. But everyone has to be all-in."

Ken put his hand in the air. "Whoa, whoa, whoa. Do you know where we work? If this is a government-controlled thing, we'll be taken care of. They need us. Whatever they have to do to make sure we're okay, they'll do it."

Courtney stepped in. "If it's like Jones said, it's not the American government. Besides, you don't even work at Langley; you're probably considered non-essential personnel. Don't think anyone gives two cents about your tail at the Company. Look at Jones. That man gave his life to the Company, and if we hadn't attended his funeral, there would have been six people there. Six! And one of them was probably just a spook assigned to see who came."

Lisa grabbed Ken's arm. "Honey, we have to do something."

Ken put his arms on the table and sighed. "I don't know. I don't know what to do."

Everett reached across the table and patted him on the

hand. "Take tonight and think about it. You and Lisa talk it over tomorrow after work. Thursday night, we'll all go out and discuss it as a group. If you decide, the four of us will develop a plan. Friday after work, we'll start acquiring some supplies. Saturday, we'll take you two out to the place I mentioned."

"Thanks. I believe you. I appreciate what you're trying to do." Ken looked over at Lisa. "We'll talk it over, but we're probably on board."

Lisa looked at Ken and nodded in agreement, and then looked at Courtney with worried eyes.

Courtney reached across the table and took Lisa's hand. "We can get through anything together, as long as we have a plan."

CHAPTER 24

Therefore rejoice, you heavens and you who dwell in them!
But woe to the earth and the sea, because the devil has gone
down to you! He is filled with fury, because he knows that
his time is short.

Revelation 12:12

The day of Noah's trial finally came. The anxiety had kept
him up most of the night, and there was no going to sleep at
that point. He got out of bed at 4:45 AM, well before the
alarm clock was set to go off. Noah closed the door so Cassie
could sleep a little longer. He went to the kitchen and debated
whether to have regular coffee of decaf. "I'm already nervous
enough; the caffeine won't help. But my body is so tired, it
could use a little pick-me-up." Noah decided on mixing the
two and having half-caff. He stuck two pieces of bread in the
toaster. "I'll let this get nice and dark. Maybe it will help with
the acid in my stomach."

Sox wandered into the kitchen. Noah bent down to stroke
the cat. "I bet you're trying to figure out why I'm up so
early." Noah put a scoop of cat food in the bowl for Sox,
then retrieved a jar of strawberry jelly for his toast. Once the

coffee and toast were ready, he sat down at the table with his Bible. He opened it to Isaiah chapter twenty-six. When he came to verse three, he read it aloud. "You will keep in perfect peace him whose mind is steadfast, because he trusts in you."

Noah sat quietly and thought about that verse for a while. Gradually, a sense of peace came over him. He considered how temporal it all was. The trial would soon be over. He hoped he wouldn't get any jail time, even if he was found guilty. But even if he did, it would pass. In comparison to the grand scheme of eternity, his entire life seemed short. Noah muttered to himself, "This ain't heaven. I guess it's not supposed to be."

Noah finished his coffee and kept reading. Soon, he was feeling much better. *Maybe I'll make another pot of coffee. Cassie will be up soon. She'll want a cup*, he thought.

Hours later, they were ready to leave. The first stop was to drop Lacy off at the Rays' house; next they were scheduled to meet Leo at the café across the street from the courthouse at 8:30 AM.

They parked a few blocks away so they could avoid the commotion. As he approached the scene, Noah saw the news trucks and reporters from the local stations in the adjacent parking lot. A handful of supporters, as well as some protestors, were out in front of the courthouse with various signs. The gathering wasn't quite the circus that the Scopes Monkey Trial had been in 1925, but Noah's trial was still the main event in Sevierville on this particular day. Many of the supporters were from his church or folks in the community. As he looked over the crowd from the other side of the street, he recognized none of the protestors.

Cassie asked, "Do you think they had to ship in some atheists from New York to call for your head on a platter?"

Noah chuckled. "No, I'm sure those people are from Knoxville. Probably from UT."

Leo walked into the café. "You ready to go?"

Noah nodded. "Ready as I'll ever be. I've got God on my side, and the best lawyer in Tennessee."

Cassie added, "And a supportive wife."

Noah kissed her cheek. "That, too."

They left the café and made their way toward the courthouse. Leo stopped to give a short comment to the press. "Through today's proceedings, we think the jury will gain vivid insight into what's happening to our God-given rights that are no longer being defended but rather assaulted by a rogue government. We trust that they'll find these charges to be unconstitutional and, therefore, nullify them. Thank you."

Noah smiled at the cameras, but he let Leo do the talking. He and Cassie gave a brief wave as they followed Leo into court.

The court was brought to order, and the trial began with the bailiff's announcement. "All rise for the Honorable Judge Harriet Flynn."

Everyone stood while the judge made her way to the bench. The prosecution and the defense took turns delivering their opening statements. Afterwards, the lead prosecutor, Nathan Williams, called his first witness, Katie Snyder.

He opened with a short question. "Ms. Snyder, were you a student in Mr. Parker's biology class?"

"Yes."

"And have you heard Mr. Parker mention creation or intelligent design during class hours and in the context of the materials you were studying?"

"Yes, but . . ."

Williams cut her off. "A simple yes answer is sufficient. Mr. Cobb, your witness."

Leo took the floor. "Katie, did Mr. Parker ever try to convert you to his religion or tell you that the theory of evolution is unfounded?"

"No, sir."

Leo continued. "He never told you that you'd go to hell for believing that we descended from monkeys? He never marked your tests wrong for answers that reflected what you'd been taught about the origins of life?"

Katie Snyder snickered. "No. All he said was that there are some scientists who think the universe and life were made by a higher being, like God. We never knew what his religion was. He never told us what he thought. I don't see what the big deal is."

Leo smiled at the young girl. "Thank you, Ms. Snyder. That will be all for today."

Next, Williams called another one of Noah's students, Allen Kramer. His line of questioning was the same as for Katie. Leo's cross-examination was also similar.

Williams continued to call student after student with the same questions.

After the fourteenth of these, the judge said, "Mr. Williams, I think you've established what Mr. Parker said to his students. Unless diminishing the patience of the court is part of your overall strategy, might I recommend that we move along?"

Williams stood confidently with his hands behind his back. "Absolutely, Your Honor. Since the jury is well aware of the Community Core criminal code, I trust that it's been established that Noah Parker is in violation of those statues. I have no further witnesses."

Leo took the floor. "The defense calls Doctor Robert Carlton."

Bob Carlton made his way to the stand.

Leo asked, "Professor Carlton, can you tell us what degree you hold and where you're employed?"

"I hold a PhD in Anthropology, which I teach at the University of Tennessee."

Leo nodded. "Does Anthropology fall under social sciences or biology?"

Carlton crossed his legs. "It looks to both biological and social sciences. It's a sort of melting pot for humanities and natural science."

Leo looked at the jury. "So it would be fair to say that you are an expert in both physical and social science, particularly when it comes to the human condition."

Carlton crossed his hands and placed them on his knee. "The University of Tennessee would seem to agree with that statement, at least for the past twenty-three years."

Leo looked at the jury again as he asked the next question. "Professor, is it your opinion that man descended from apes, monkeys, or some other form of primate?"

Williams stood up. "Objection, Your Honor. While the

press has been diligent in reminding us of the similarities between this case and the famous Scopes Monkey Trial, this is not 1925, and evolution is not on trial. We have a law on the books that clearly states that it is a criminal violation to mention creationism or intelligent design in a public classroom."

Judge Flynn thought for a moment. "I'll allow the questioning, but please keep your questioning on topic, Mr. Cobb. Professor, you may answer the question."

Carlton sat back in his chair. "I hope this doesn't come as a shock to the defense, but while I don't think we have sufficient proof for evolution, neither do we have conclusive scientific evidence to prove intelligent design. So to answer your question, no, I don't think we descended from apes, but I'm also not a creationist."

Leo faked a look of surprise. "Oh? Then how do you suppose we came to be?"

Carlton sat smugly. "One can't be sure, but evolution is riddled with holes. Charles Darwin himself said that if his theory was true, we should find a multitude of transitional forms in the fossil layer. These transitional forms simply do not exist. If Mr. Darwin was alive today, I'm not so sure he would be nearly so married to his theory as the rest of the scientific community.

"Another very obvious problem we encounter with the fossil record is that the deeper we dig, the more species we encounter. We find the fossils of all of the existing creatures we have now: cats, dogs, fish, birds, as well as those that have gone extinct – Megalodon, T-rex, the dodo bird. If everything evolved from a single cell organism, we should have a fossil record that resembles an inverted pyramid. As we dig deeper, we should find fewer and fewer species. What we have in actuality is an upright pyramid that becomes narrower as we approach the surface.

"A major hurdle in proving the theory of evolution is the concept of irreducible complexity."

Leo asked, "Could you briefly explain that for us?"

"Think about a car. If such a machine were to evolve from nothing, why would the engine evolve unless there was a transmission? How would any of it come into being unless there was first a gas tank? Without the sum of its parts, the entire thing is useless. We've all had car trouble. Take away one tiny wire in the ignition system, and you're left with a thirty-thousand-dollar CD player. Biological systems are much more complex than an automobile. Translate what I said about the car into any number of systems in the human body. Did we develop our mouth first or our stomach? If it was the mouth, what good would it have done without the stomach? If the stomach was first, why did it evolve when there was no way of getting food into it?

"Mr. Cobb, the scientific community doesn't have a logical answer for your question at this time. There is no way to know where we came from. Millennia ago, people thought the sun was eaten by a great dragon each time they saw an eclipse. It's part of what we do: whatever we don't understand, we create an explanation for. I think science pushes us to look for answers, but when there is no answer, it is best to acknowledge that we don't know. There is nothing more detrimental to the pursuit of truth than this wild goose chase of evolution that has consumed a great amount of valuable resources."

Leo said, "You mentioned the complexity of the automobile. Is complexity evidence of a designer, in your opinion?"

Carlton made an exaggerated nod. "This is certainly one of

the arguments from the intelligent design camp. Complexity does imply that there was a designer, but, unlike the automobile, I can't book a flight and schedule a tour of the factory where humans were made. As a scientist, I don't recognize the theory of intelligent design any more than the theory of evolution. Last week, when the University of Tennessee Volunteers won their football game against the Kentucky Wildcats, many accredited the win to divine intervention. That may very well be, but scientifically, it's impossible to prove."

Leo asked, "Professor, what are your personal religious beliefs? Would you consider yourself to be an atheist?"

Williams stood again. "Your Honor, I object. This line of questioning has nothing to do with the legal merits of the case. Whether there is a God or whether evolution is rock-solid fact or a complete fairytale has no bearing on the law, which Mr. Parker violated."

Judge Flynn nodded. "Mr. Cobb, you need to explain how your witness's testimony applies to this case, or I will instruct the jury to disregard it in its entirety."

Leo turned to face her. "Your Honor, I'm establishing reasoning that the Community Core criminal code that my client violated is unconstitutional and, therefore, invalid."

The judge responded. "Then make your point, Mr. Cobb."

"Thank you, Your Honor." Leo turned back to Carlton. "Professor, you said earlier that you're not a creationist. What would be the opposite of a creationist?"

Carlton furrowed his brow as he thought. "I suppose it would be a Darwinist. And to answer your last question, I'm agnostic. I don't believe one can prove that there either is or isn't a God."

Leo smiled at the jury. "And a Darwinist would be someone who subscribes to the theory of Charles Darwin, much like someone who follows the teachings of Buddha might be called a Buddhist, or someone who follows the teachings of Christ might be termed a Christian.

"As an anthropologist, you're an authority on the social aspects of man. An atheist is someone who believes there is no God, a monotheist describes someone who believes in only one God, a polytheist believes in many gods, and an agnostic, like yourself, is someone who believes that the answer cannot be known. Aren't these all religious beliefs? I mean, we all believe something, even if we don't know what we believe. Isn't each person's perception of the spiritual realm and the afterlife, or lack thereof, a religious belief of some sort?"

Carlton smiled. "That is very well put, Mr. Cobb."

Leo turned back to Carlton. "Are there those in the scientific community who cling to evolution despite the scientific questions about its validity that you described a few moments ago?"

Carlton chuckled. "Yes, they are quite dogmatic about the whole thing."

"So it is almost like a religion to them."

Carlton raised his eyebrows. "Oh, very much so. If you've ever read the Amazon reviews of books on intelligent design, the Darwinists and atheists are downright militant in their attacks. They are religious zealots in the highest form of the word.

"On the other hand, if you scan through the reviews of books on Darwinism and evolution, you'll rarely see a comment from the opposing side. I'm not sure if the creationists are less passionate or if they simply don't feel the need to push their views down the other side's throat."

"Thank you, Mr. Carlton. Mr. Williams, your witness," Leo said.

Williams sat like a deer in the headlights. It was obvious that he'd never anticipated this course of action from the defense. "The prosecution has no questions for the witness."

No other witnesses were called. Williams stumbled through his closing argument, which seemed ridiculous after Leo's final stab.

Leo turned to the jury to make his closing arguments. "Under the 1987 Supreme Court ruling of Edwards versus Aguillard, the establishment clause was interpreted to not allow one religion to advance over another in the public school system. The opinion written on the case cites the Lemon test, which states that the government's action must not have the primary effect of either advancing or inhibiting religion. It is clear that Community Core advances the religion of atheism and Darwinism, while simultaneously inhibiting creationism, Christianity, and all other monotheistic and polytheistic religions. My client simply sought to avoid the gross violation of this particular Supreme Court ruling. Ladies and gentlemen of the jury, thank you for your careful consideration."

As it was late in the day, the judge adjourned the court and instructed the jury to return the following morning to deliberate.

On the way out of the courtroom, Noah was beaming. "Great work, Leo."

Leo shook his head. "I can't believe the judge didn't let the jury meet. They would have given us a verdict in five minutes. She's trying to give them time to think past the truth we just laid out, but their minds are made up. I can see it on their faces."

Noah thanked Leo again, and then he and Cassie left to pick up Lacy. That night, Noah slept like a log.

***

The next morning, the Parkers met Leo Cobb back at the courthouse.

"What time do you expect us to be called back in front of the judge?" Noah asked.

"It depends what the judge is doing when the jury notifies her that they've reached a verdict. I'm hoping we'll be back in by ten o'clock. You two can hang out in the coffee shop if you like, and I'll text you when it's time. You'll have at least a half an hour from the time I shoot you the text."

"You've got a deal," Cassie said.

The Parkers walked across the street to the coffee shop to wait for the notification. Noah ordered a coffee for Cassie and a decaf for himself.

"Decaf?" Cassie commented.

"I don't want anything to make me more anxious."

"Are you nervous? I thought you were confident that you're going to win the case."

Noah took his coffee to a table near one of the television screens and sat down. "I was, until now. Why haven't they delivered a verdict? If it was a slam dunk, we should've been called back into court first thing this morning."

Cassie followed him. "I don't think there's any reason to be concerned. You'll get a verdict by the end of the day."

Noah turned his attention to the news. The reporter was in the studio and "NEWS ALERT!" was scrolling across the top and bottom of the screen. Noah didn't think too much of it, as the notification was always scrolling across the screen. However, the text was much larger than the normal alert, and it was in all caps today, which caused Noah to take notice. Noah manually turned the volume up so they could hear the report.

". . . largest one-day spike in the gold price on record. After the reports of the massive gold purchase made by China, several other countries followed suit. While the overall purchase was only a fraction of the gold buy made by China, Russia made the second largest purchase of the yellow metal this morning. The purchases made by those two countries soaked up all available inventory in the Shanghai Gold Exchange. The Commodities Exchange, or Comex, based in New York also sold out of all physical inventory, as did the London Gold Market.

"Next up after the break, we'll be covering the ongoing riots in Brazil and South Africa."

Cassie grabbed Noah's hand. "And that's how US dollars held outside of the country can trigger massive inflation. Quick, turn it to CNBC."

As it was after nine o'clock and well before lunch, the coffee shop was relatively slow. Noah looked around to see if any of the other patrons were watching the channel; none were. He stood and manually changed the channel to the financial news.

A three-month price chart for gold was displayed onscreen, and an analyst was talking about the recent action.

". . . volatility that's never been seen before. The most important factor that triggered the jump this morning is the paper market. The amount of derivative trading on the precious metals dwarfs that of the physical market. We've seen a massive amount of traders who were short that are now having to cover. And there is no gold, or silver for that matter, to be bought. Although physical delivery is almost never taken, the futures and option contracts are written for delivery. The LBMA and Comex both issued emergency rule changes this morning, which state that gold and silver contracts may be settled for cash instead of the actual metals, but panic buying is still running the price to new all-time highs. If it hadn't been for the emergency rule change declaring cash settlement, we could have easily seen gold quadruple in price. I mean, look at the ticker; it's up three hundred dollars since we started this segment. I don't even want to speculate where the price will close today. And silver, it could potentially triple in price today."

Noah watched the gold and silver tickers, which were on permanent display at the bottom of the screen. Gold had just pushed past its previous all-time high and was rising astronomically. The present price was $3423. Silver was likewise hitting a new high at $120 per ounce.

Noah looked at Cassie. "I'm glad we got in when we did."

"Me too, but this isn't good."

"Why not? We just made a ton of money."

"The value of gold and silver isn't going up; the dollar is crashing. This is signaling a complete collapse of confidence in the US dollar; this is the beginning of the end. We should get rid of all of our cash when we get out of court and buy everything we can think of that we'll need: flour, sugar, coffee, whatever we can store. I'm glad you bought all that ammo from David. We probably should have bought more, but you did good."

315

They turned their attention back to the television. The reporter was questioning the analyst.

"Do you expect the SEC to close the markets today?"

"Gold and silver markets are global. If the SEC closed US markets, it might be akin to throwing a bucket of water on a bonfire, but it wouldn't have a lasting effect. This is what traders call a classic parabolic melt-up. People who bought their physical gold and silver are sitting pretty right now. Those who didn't aren't getting any. It simply isn't there."

"Oil jumped fifteen percent this morning. Is it connected to the metals market?"

"I think so. The lack of physical inventory may have highlighted to investors how important the commodities sector is. We're seeing a big jump in the price of corn, soybeans, pork, basically across the board. At the same time, the equities markets are taking a dive. Stocks aren't selling off at the same pace as commodities are rising, but it's still early in the day."

The reporter then said, "Do you think China made this huge buy today to deliberately push up the price, or did they legitimately see value in the price of gold?"

The analyst answered, "The buy was made by exercising several large option contracts on the Shanghai exchange. The Chinese central bank has been positioning itself for this move for several weeks."

Leo walked in and sat next to the Parkers. "The jury has a verdict. We go before the judge right after lunch, one o'clock."

Noah looked at Cassie and then back at Leo. "So that's good news, right?"

Leo smiled and patted Noah on the shoulder. "Real good news. I think we have this in the bag."

Cassie directed Leo's attention to the screen. "What do you think about the gold market?"

Leo looked at the television. "Wow! That's a big jump. I always get skittish when I see gold move up too fast. I've never seen anything like this before. What triggered it?"

Cassie said, "Big purchase by the Chinese. They cleared all the physical markets. A bunch of speculators got caught short and can't cover."

Leo looked back at the Parkers. "Strange times. I spoke with Robert Carlton after the trial yesterday to thank him. He lives near the UT campus, right by the stadium. He said it was full of military personnel and equipment yesterday morning. He asked campus security why they were there, and he was told it was a training exercise. I'm sure it's nothing, but we've had no media coverage of the exercise. It's quite bizarre."

Cassie sat up attentively. "Did he say how many vehicles or personnel were present?"

Leo shook his head. "Didn't say. He just said the stadium was nearly full of soldiers and equipment."

Cassie took out her phone. "Sounds more like a staging area than a training exercise. These two events might not be unrelated. I'm going to call my friend Linda over at Channel 10."

Noah and Leo walked to the counter for a refill while Cassie called her friend. Feeling more confident about the verdict, Noah treated himself to a cup of regular coffee. The two men returned to the table, and Noah asked, "What did she say?"

Cassie pursed her lips. "Nothing. She clammed up like she was afraid to even talk about it."

The three of them talked about the implications of what all this could mean until it was time to head back into court.

At one o'clock, the bailiff announced the judge's entrance, and the courtroom all stood. The jury entered the room, and the time came for the verdict to be read.

Noah regretted having drunk caffeinated coffee as his heart raced in anticipation. He held Cassie's hand firmly.

"It's going to be okay," she whispered.

The jury foreman read the verdict. "In the case of the State of Tennessee v. Noah Parker, we find the defendant . . ."

Noah held his breath. He prayed silently. "God, please let me win this."

". . . not guilty."

Noah released his breath with a big sigh of relief. "Thank you, Jesus!"

Cassie hugged Noah tightly. "It's all over, baby!"

Leo patted Noah on the back. "Congratulations!"

Noah looked over Cassie's shoulder. "Thank you, Leo. We owe you."

Leo smiled. "You don't owe me a thing."

"At least let us take you and your wife to dinner," Noah pleaded.

Leo nodded. "Okay. We can't do it tonight, but I'll take a rain check."

"Thanks again." Noah finally broke free from Cassie's embrace to shake hands with Leo before he left.

Noah and Cassie headed for the car and then toward the Rays' house to pick up Lacy.

Noah's elation over this victory was buffered by the sobering reality of the new battle on the horizon. "David probably already knows about the gold price spike, but I bet he'll be surprised to hear about the troops in the UT stadium."

Cassie took out her phone. "I bet Isaiah will be too. I'm going to ask him to meet us at the Rays'. I think we need to have a group powwow. Something is stirring in the wind, and we'd better get ready for it."

Thank you for reading
The Days of Noah, Book One: Conspiracy.

Amazon reviews are the most important method of getting The Days of Noah noticed. If you enjoyed the book, please take a moment to leave a five star review on Amazon.com. If you don't feel the book quite measured up to five stars, drop me an e-mail at prepperrecon@gmail.com and let me know how I can make future books better.

Keep watch for
The Days of Noah, Book Two: Persecution.

You may also like my first fiction series, **The Economic Collapse Chronicles**, available on Amazon.com. In the first book, **American Exit Strategy**, America is on the cusp of financial annihilation. Matt and Karen Bair face the challenges of Main Street during a full-scale financial meltdown. Government borrowing and monetary creation have reached their limits. When funds are no longer available for government programs, widespread civil unrest erupts across the country. Matt and Karen are forced to move to a more remote location, and their level of preparedness is revealed as being much less adequate than they believed prior to the crisis.

Stay tuned to PrepperRecon.com for the latest news about my upcoming books and preparedness related subjects. While on the website, you can download or listen to the Prepper Recon Podcast, or subscribe to the show on Stitcher, iTunes and YouTube.

Made in the USA
Columbia, SC
13 June 2020